Seven-Year Seduction
HEIDI BETTS

Their Million-Dollar Night
KATHERINE GARBERA

MILLS & BOON®

Desire™

All the characters in this book have no existence outside the imagination of the author, and have no relation whatsoever to anyone bearing the same name or names. They are not even distantly inspired by any individual known or unknown to the author, and all the incidents are pure invention.

First published in Great Britain 2007
Harlequin Mills & Boon Limited,
Eton House, 18-24 Paradise Road, Richmond, Surrey TW9 1SR

The publisher acknowledges the copyright holders of the individual works as follows:

Seven-Year Seduction © Heidi Betts 2006
Their Million-Dollar Night © Katherine Garbera 2006

ISBN: 978 0 263 85012 3

51-0307

Printed and bound in Spain
by Litografia Rosés S.A., Barcelona

SEVEN-YEAR SEDUCTION

by
Heidi Betts

Seven-Year Seduction
by Heidi Betts

ཀྐ ༄༅ ༀ

"Would you like to dance?" Connor asked.

With him? Definitely not. Beth opened her mouth to politely refuse, but he already had his hand curled around her upper arm, steering her into his embrace.

Because she didn't have a choice, she slid her free hand up to rest on his shoulder. The heat of his body pulsed through the fine wool of his dinner jacket, setting her palm to tingling.

Beth muttered a colourful oath under her breath, annoyed that Connor could still have any sort of impact on her, even a purely physical one.

And that's all it was – the physiological response of her female body to the nearness of such an attractive, obviously male body. Their shared history added to her body's response, but it didn't mean anything. Nothing at all.

Their Million-Dollar Night
by Katherine Garbera

ᔕᔕᔕ

"You are a beautiful woman."

Max's words hurt in a way he couldn't understand – and she dared not explain. At one time, she'd have tossed her hair and given him a smile that would have brought him to his knees. But now…

"Not any more." She couldn't believe those words had escaped. "How long will you be in Vegas?"

"Long enough to convince you that you *are* beautiful." He took her hand in his, his thumb stroking over her knuckle.

"That's not why you came," she said, telling herself he was here for the Vegas allure. The mindless flirting, the hours of gambling.

"My plans have changed."

Available in March 2007 from Mills & Boon Desire

Expecting Lonergan's Baby
by Maureen Child
(Summer of Secrets)
&
The Sins of His Past
by Roxanne St Claire

ဒႢჃႧ

The Elliotts
Cause for Scandal
by Anna DePalo
&
The Forbidden Twin
by Susan Crosby

ဒႢჃႧ

Seven-Year Seduction
by Heidi Betts
&
Their Million-Dollar Night
by Katherine Garbera
(What Happens in Vegas…)

HEIDI BETTS

An avid romance reader since junior school, Heidi knew early on that she wanted to write these wonderful stories of love and adventure. It wasn't until her freshman year of college, however, when she spent the entire night reading a romance novel instead of studying for finals, that she decided to take the road less travelled and follow her dream. In addition to reading, writing and romance, she is the founder of her local Romance Writers of America chapter and has a tendency to take injured and homeless animals of every species into her central Pennsylvania home.

Heidi loves to hear from readers. You can write to her at PO Box 99, Kylertown, PA, 16847, USA (an SAE with return postage is appreciated but not necessary) or e-mail heidi@heidibetts.com. And be sure to visit www.heidibetts.com for news and information about forthcoming books.

To my extremely talented web designer, Shelley Kay, who does such a wonderful job of keeping my tiny corner of cyberspace neat, beautiful and up-to-date. Thank you for always coming up with solutions to my problems and for never losing patience with me, even after a million-and-one silly little questions.

And to Su Kopil of Earthly Charms, for being so helpful with my promotional needs and desires, and who also never seems to lose patience after a million-and-one silly little questions.

And always, for Daddy.

ACKNOWLEDGEMENTS

With extra thanks to the PASIC Loop for helping me with some of the research for this book – especially Lori Handeland, Sharon DeVita and Shelley Galloway. You made my job *so* much easier, thank you!

One

"**Y**es! Go, go, go!"

Fans went wild as the running back for the Crystal Springs Panthers raced across the field, making a touchdown and scoring extra points just as the buzzer sounded, winning the game for his team. Everyone on the home team's side of the bleachers jumped to their feet and began to cheer.

Beth Curtis joined them, yelling and bouncing up and down in celebration of her former high school's football team winning against their greatest rivals. Grinning from ear to ear, she turned and threw herself into the arms of the person on her immediate right—who just happened to be Connor Riordan.

Connor was five years her senior—the same age as

her brother, Nicholas—but from the time she'd turned thirteen, she'd used any excuse to be closer to him, to be the focus of his attention and that coffee-brown gaze that made her weak in the knees.

She pressed her face to his cheek and rubbed against its sandpaper roughness. Even though it was practically freezing, and they were both wrapped up in heavy coats, hats, scarves and mittens, she could smell the musky scent of his evergreen cologne.

God, she loved that smell. Sometimes, when she and her girlfriends took a break from studying the law and all its many intricacies at the University of Cincinnati Law School, they'd take a trip to the mall. Beth almost always found herself standing in the men's fragrance department, sniffing at the colorful bottles until she found one that smelled the most like Connor.

She suspected he wore Aspen, but couldn't be positive without seeing the actual bottle he likely kept on his bedroom dresser. But she was working hard at finding out for sure.

Along with acing her next exam, one of her objectives was to seduce Connor and make her way not only into his bedroom but into his bed. She'd had this aspiration since somewhere around her senior year of high school, but now she was an adult and there was no reason why she and Connor couldn't become lovers. She had been saving herself for him, after all.

He set her back on her feet, still grinning with the thrill of victory as he brushed an errant strand of hair away from her face.

As willing as the crowd had been to sit in the stands

for more than two hours to cheer on their favorite team, they were just as eager to leave now that they knew who'd won. People began collecting their seat warmers and empty cocoa cups and filing out of the stands.

"Hey, Curtis," Connor called over her head to her brother, who had his arm around his longtime girlfriend, Karen Morelli. "We going over to Yancy's for burgers?"

"Nah. Karen and I thought we'd head home. She wants to go shopping in the morning and we need to get an early start." Nick rolled his eyes, letting his friend know just how much he was looking forward to that.

"I could go for a burger," Beth put in quickly, seizing the opportunity to be alone with Connor.

It took him a minute, but finally he agreed. "Okay." He tossed a look at Nicholas. "I'll drop her off after we get a bite to eat."

"Sounds good." Karen and Nick shuffled single file to the end of their row, leaving Beth and Connor to follow.

When they reached the jam-packed parking lot, Nick and Karen headed for his car while Beth stuck with Connor as he ambled toward his truck. The cold night air chilled her fingers, even inside their gloves, and caused her cheeks to tingle.

"*Brr.* It sure is cold tonight."

"Yeah." Connor unlocked the driver's side, then leaned across the seat to push open the passenger-side door. "Get in and I'll crank up the heat."

Beth eagerly climbed in and fastened her seat belt,

holding her hands up to the vents as warm air began pouring out. They crawled like ants toward the exit of the school parking lot, vehicles each taking turns as everyone tried to squeeze out at the same time. Connor turned on the radio and tuned it to a Martina McBride song in an attempt to fill the silence in the pickup's cab and drown out some of the shouts and horn blasts from surrounding cars.

"Yancy's is going to be crowded," Beth pointed out, knowing that just about everyone went there after a game, whether it was to cheer another win for the Panthers' season, or to commiserate over a well-played loss.

Connor slanted her a glance as the car ahead of them eased forward. "I thought you were hungry."

She shrugged a shoulder, leaning back against the seat now that she was no longer chilled.

"Want to go someplace else?"

Taking a deep breath and swallowing down any remaining nerves bouncing around in her stomach, she said, "How about Makeout Point?"

He responded with a bark of laughter, followed by a dark, wide-eyed stare that clearly told her he thought she'd lost her marbles. "You can't be serious."

"Why not? I know why people usually go up there, but it really is a beautiful spot, and there aren't likely to be any teenagers up there tonight, getting themselves into trouble. They'll be too busy celebrating at Yancy's."

"What would your brother say if he found out I took his baby sister up to Makeout Point?"

Her teeth ground together at the mention of being

"the baby sister." That was something she heard way too often for her peace of mind.

She wanted to tell Connor she didn't much care what her brother might say—she was an adult now and it was her life. But she knew how Connor felt about Nick and her parents, and that he would never do anything he thought they'd find unacceptable, especially where she was concerned.

"It's not like we're going up there for some illicit purpose," she told him instead. "I just thought it might be nice to visit the Point on a night we're likely to see more than rocking backseats."

To her surprise, he chuckled. "I suppose you're right. Do you want to pick up some burgers to take with us?"

"Sure."

They followed the cavalcade of taillights through town to Yancy's, but hit the drive-thru instead of going inside with most of the other post-game customers. Even so, they sat in line for quite a while, joining in with the arm waves and honking horns as friends and neighbors passed by in the black and gold colors of the Panthers team.

Once their order was ready, Connor passed the bags and drinks to her while he paid, then rolled up his window and pulled back onto the road, in the opposite direction of most of the town's population. The scents of French fries and grilled hamburgers permeated the cab, and Beth couldn't resist opening one of the bags and sneaking a potato.

Connor tipped his head in her direction, catching

her in the act. "No fair," he grumbled. "I'm hungry, too, you know."

With a laugh, Beth reached into the bag a second time, then lifted a French fry to Connor's lips. He opened his mouth and bit down, nipping the tips of her fingers to catch the entire fry.

A jolt of awareness shot through her hand and straight to her center, where desire and sharp arousal pooled. She wondered if he felt even a fraction the same as she did.

If she was lucky, by the end of the night, she would find out.

They bumped along the dirt road that climbed up to the Point and Connor angled his truck to look out over the pine-dappled ridge that gave this spot its name. The drinks and bags of food sat on the bench seat between them as they divvied up the order. They ate quietly for a while, watching the clouds slip across the moon and over the tree line.

When they'd finished, Connor stuffed their garbage back into the white paper bag and shoved it behind the seat, presumably to be retrieved and thrown away later.

Beth folded one leg beneath the other, vinyl squeaking beneath her jean-clad bottom as she shifted slightly more in his direction. His legs were stretched out in front of him, as much as the truck's console would allow, and he had an arm slung over the steering wheel.

"So how's school going for you?" he asked after several minutes of awkward silence had ticked by.

"Good," she replied. "Some of the classes are kind of hard, but I think I'm doing okay."

"If I know you, you're doing better than just okay. And wait until you're finished. You'll be a big-time lawyer, ready to sue the pants off of anybody who crosses you."

"I'm not going to sue anyone. I'm going to defend them."

"Nah," he put in idly. "You can't make money that way, unless you defend the rich and famous. And they're usually guilty as sin."

"I don't care about money. I want to help people."

He grinned at her then, and she got the distinct feeling he was seeing her as a child again, instead of as a full-grown woman or potential love interest.

"I'm not a kid, you know, Connor," she told him, pulling her shoulders back and thrusting out her breasts. They might not be as impressive as her roommate's 32Cs, but they weren't too shabby.

"I know. You grew up real nice, Beth Ann."

She might have taken his comment as another insult, another reminder that he thought of her as nothing more than his best friend's baby sister, except for his tone. The words came out in a near whisper, and the look in his eyes stroked her straight down to her soul.

It was as vulnerable as she'd ever seen him. As close to being open to seeing her as a woman he might be able to have a relationship with.

Before he could come to his senses or she lost her nerve, Beth leaned in and pressed her lips to his. For a moment, he held perfectly still, not kissing her in return, but not moving away, either.

When she pulled back, he blinked, the expression on his face a cross between shock and curiosity.

"Beth…"

"Don't say it," she murmured softly, staying where she was, pressed close to him on the wide truck seat. The heat from his body seeped past his unzipped winter coat and permeated every inch of her exposed skin.

"I know how you feel about me," she hurried on. "I know you think of me as Nick's little sister, nothing more than a tagalong. But I'm all grown up now, and I want us to be together. To at least explore what there might be between us."

She waited a beat, expecting him to respond. Surprised he hadn't interrupted her midspeech already.

"Haven't you ever thought about it, Connor? Haven't you wondered what it might be like between us?"

Her heart was pounding in her chest like the high school's half-time marching band, and the tension in the air threatened to send the burger she'd eaten into revolt.

But the fact that Connor hadn't immediately begun to argue with her, hadn't physically returned her to the other side of the bench seat and started to drive her home, gave her a modicum of hope. Maybe her infatuation wasn't entirely one-sided. Maybe there was a chance he was interested in her, too.

"Connor," she breathed, struggling to draw oxygen into her lungs even as she moved in to once again align her lips with his. "Please."

A second ticked by, then another while he stared at her, the intensity of his gaze flashing over her hair, her cheeks, her lips, her eyes. And then he was kissing her. Willingly, passionately, without reservation.

His hands snaked under her jacket, molding to her waist and the undersides of her breasts even as she raised herself up on her knees. She hovered above him, trying to get closer, wanting to slide inside and become one with him.

She'd waited so long for this moment, imagined dozens of times being with him this way. It was almost too much to believe, and a part of her thought she might be dreaming.

But then he pinched her nipple through her sweater, through the lace of her bra, and she knew it was blessed reality. Every fantasy she'd ever had about her brother's best friend was going to come true.

He tasted of cola and Yancy's special sauce from the burgers they'd eaten earlier, and smelled like the outdoors. He always smelled like the outdoors, and Beth thought it must be a combination of his own personal, masculine scent and his cologne preference.

She curled her fingers into the soft flannel of his plaid work shirt, skimming his coat off over his shoulders while he fought with the zipper on her own. Once he had it undone, he wasted no time getting her out of the fleece-lined jacket, tossing it to the floor of the cab.

His hands immediately returned to her hips, where they rested for a moment before slipping under the hem of her sweater and gliding upward. The touch of his callused fingertips on the smooth expanse of her torso set off forest fires just beneath the surface of her skin.

It was cold outside, and should have been cold inside the truck by now, without the engine running. Instead, she felt hothouse warm, their mingled breaths fogging up the windows.

They were acting like a couple of randy teenagers, and she didn't even care. Given half a chance, she'd have driven up to Makeout Point with Connor while she'd been in high school, too.

With a moan, his lips parted, leaving her mouth to trail over her chin, down the line of her throat. She arched her neck, granting him better access.

While his tongue flicked and teased, she worked the tail of his soft cotton T-shirt out from the waistband of his jeans. His abdomen tightened as she stroked it, exploring the rock-hard muscles and dancing her fingers over the light dusting of hair that ran from navel to chest and back down. She followed the trail to the edge of his jeans, deftly undoing the metal button at the top.

At the same time, his hands cupped her breasts, pushing the fabric of her bra up to delve beneath. Her beaded nipples pressed into his palms and when he rubbed, tiny shock waves of desire shot straight to her center.

His mouth moved back up, his lips brushing hers as he spoke. "We shouldn't be doing this. It's wrong."

"It's not wrong," she told him, catching his ears and kissing him deeply. "It's right. So very, very right."

He groaned, seeming to give in, regardless of any other arguments that might be crashing through his mind. He wrapped his arms around her and lowered her to the truck seat, following her down.

Her knee bumped the steering wheel as they tried

to find a comfortable position. His foot cracked into the door, his elbow hit the dash, she bumped her head on the opposite door handle. If they hadn't been so turned on, they might have given up altogether.

As it was, they laughed at their awkward positions, shifting until they each found a modicum of comfort. Then they were kissing again, lips meshing, tongues flicking, breaths mingling.

Connor curled his fingers on either side of her jeans closure and pulled the snap free. The *snick snick snick* of the zipper as he released it echoed through the cab. He shoved the pants down her legs, leaving them bunched somewhere around her calves rather than fight to get them off over her shoes. Her panties were next, followed by his trousers and underwear.

As much as Beth wanted this, had been wanting it for so long, the cool air on her lower extremities sent a thread of hesitation through her.

This was Connor. Her brother's best friend. The man she'd been dreaming of being with ever since she'd hit puberty.

She wasn't sorry she'd gotten herself into this situation…if anything, she was relieved she'd *finally* managed to snag Connor's undivided and romantic attention. But she did know that sleeping with him would change things. Forever.

The way they looked at each other, the way they acted around each other. The way he acted around her family.

Of course, she hoped things would change for the better. That she and Connor would become an item after tonight, date for a while, get engaged, then marry and start a family.

A picture of them ten years down the road shimmered in her mind's eye and she smiled, even as Connor's fingers skimmed her inner thigh, making rational thought nearly impossible.

Whatever happened, they could handle it, and everything would be fine. He was already as close to Nicholas as a brother, as close to her parents as another son. Her entire family would be more than accepting of their relationship, and she knew that once Connor recovered from the shock of having slept with his best friend's little sister—if indeed he suffered any shock at all—he would realize they belonged together.

She'd finish law school, of course, then move back home to be close to him, and one day they'd be man and wife. One day they'd be living happily ever after.

Beth smiled for a brief moment, then whimpered when he grazed the curls between her legs with the back of his hand. He nudged her knees open as far as they would go with her jeans still wrapped around her ankles, then settled himself the best he could in the cradle of her thighs.

His palms stroked up and down her bare torso, her sweater pushed up around her breasts. She felt the tip of his hardened length probing intimately while his mouth continued to devour her own.

He was gentle but demanding, considerate but firm. One hand skated along her waist and hip, then cupped around her bare derriere and lifted her.

He slid inside more easily than she'd expected,

given her state of virginity. But he was still big, and filled her until she had to tip her hips to find a more comfortable position.

Her legs were pressed against the steering wheel and back of the truck seat, and she could hear the rubber soles of Connor's work boots as they came in contact with the driver's-side door. His chest rose and fell with the heavy force of his breaths, in synch with her own.

When he thrust even deeper, she gasped, a slight burning assaulting her tender, innocent passage. He stopped moving and lifted his head, giving her time to adjust to his invasion.

"You okay?" he asked, looking down at her with eyes the color of melted chocolate, tiny beads of perspiration dotting his brow.

Her teeth sawed delicately on her bottom lip, more out of habit than any real pain. "I'm fine."

He didn't look as if he believed her, so she reached up to brush a loose lock of hair out of his eyes, a comforting smile lifting her lips.

"I'm fine, really." And then she wrapped her arms around his back and pulled him down. "But I don't think we're finished yet."

Seconds passed while strain continued to etch his face. Then suddenly, the lines tipping down his mouth lifted as he grinned back at her. "No, ma'am. We're just getting started."

His kiss was soft and tender as he took her lips and began moving his hips in a slow, steady rhythm. Friction built, like a length of silk being dragged over sandstone. The faster he moved, the tighter the coil of sweet tension grew, winding low in her belly until she wanted to scream.

And then she did, as the dam seemed to break and a keen, clawing pleasure unlike any she'd ever experienced before washed over her. She continued to shudder with tiny aftershocks while Connor rocked into her once, twice, three times more before going rigid with his own overwhelming completion.

They lay there for long minutes, struggling to regain their equilibrium. Connor's rough jaw tickled her cheek, his uneven breathing whispering in her ear.

Her arms and legs were still wound around him like strands of ivy, and the corners of her mouth lifted slightly at how right it felt to be with him this way. Even in the cramped confines of his truck cab, half dressed, half undressed, the evening was perfect. And there would be plenty of times in the future when they could strip off each other's clothes, take it slow, explore every inch of flesh before climbing under satin sheets and making long, languorous love all night long.

This was just the beginning.

Connor lifted his head, meeting her gaze briefly before pushing himself up and helping her to get untangled from his lithe form. He pulled her sweater down and waited until he was sure she could get her panties and jeans up by herself before righting his own clothing.

Neither of them said anything until they were each back on their own sides of the truck seat.

"Are you all right?" he asked in a low tone. He was looking straight out through the windshield, his fingers wrapped tight around the steering wheel.

"Yes. Are you?"

He didn't answer, just continued to face forward.

With a sigh, he leaned forward and twisted the key in the ignition. The engine turned over, and heat and music began to fill the cab.

"I'd better get you home," he told her. "Before your family starts to worry."

She nodded, knowing they would if she was gone too much longer. Then again, Nick knew she was with Connor, and they trusted him implicitly.

But she didn't blame him for feeling a bit uncomfortable; it might take time for him to get used to the idea of them being an item.

Which was fine. She'd let him take her home tonight, and they could sit down in the morning to discuss the future.

She studied him from the corner of her eye as they drove down the rutted road and away from Makeout Point. His strong jaw, dark blond hair, slightly crooked nose. The strong line of his shoulders and wide, muscled biceps.

This was the man she loved, had *been* in love with since her thirteenth birthday. And now he would be the man she married and spent the rest of her life with.

She couldn't wait.

Two

Seven years later...

Beth Curtis sat at the family table on the dais, sipping from her glass of champagne, watching as the bride, groom and dozens of guests filled the dance floor.

She hated weddings.

She was happy for Nick and Karen, really she was. They had been dating since high school, and she—and everyone else in town—knew they'd marry eventually. Of course, her brother had put off proposing right up until the stick turned blue. Regardless of their reasons for finally tying the knot, though, Beth had no doubt they would make it work. They belonged together.

But she still hated weddings. Especially this one.

Bad enough she'd been roped into being the maid of honor, with all the duties that position entailed. Bad enough she'd had to fly over two thousand miles each way to come back to Crystal Springs for the bridal shower, wedding and reception planning, and now the actual event. Bad enough that Karen's favorite colors were green and pink, and that Beth was therefore decked out in a formfitting satin sheath made up of lime and watermelon shades of each.

Oh, no, all that was bad enough. The worst, the very worst, was that she had to smile and laugh and pretend that seeing Connor Riordan again wasn't a dagger through her heart.

She'd done a pretty good job of avoiding him since he'd taken her virginity all those years ago. Moving to Los Angeles had helped, as had not coming home to visit her parents and brother nearly as often as she might have liked.

And then Nick had decided he just *had* to do the right thing by marrying Karen because he'd gotten her pregnant, and Connor just *had* to be his best man. Which meant Beth and Connor had to see each other more than she'd have preferred. He even walked her down the aisle during the ceremony.

She took another swig of bubbling wine. It was warm and starting to lose its fizz, but she didn't care. The alcohol content would remain the same, and right now she wanted nothing more than to go numb.

Standing in the church's vestibule with Connor, his arm linked with hers while the soft notes of the wedding march played had been like a red-hot brand on her soul. He couldn't have known she was in actual physical pain, of course, and he had no idea that being around him was so hard for her…or why. But that didn't lessen the ache in the pit of her stomach or the harsh memories that ran through her head at the very mention of his name.

And now she was lucky enough to have a bird's-eye view of him dancing cheek to cheek with his live-in girlfriend. Laura, Lori, Lisa…something like that. She was blond and perky and had boobs that bounced when she walked. Beth would bet next month's salary that she'd been a cheerleader in high school. And that the bounce was saline- or silicone-induced.

Not that there was anything wrong with that. Beth was a California girl now; plastic surgery came with the territory. Heck, as an entertainment attorney who worked with some of Hollywood's most beautiful stars, the majority of her clients had been nipped or tucked in one way or another.

So why was she being so judgmental of Lisa-Lori-Laura?

Simple. She was with Connor and Beth wasn't.

Connor had apparently felt strongly enough about the L-woman to ask her to move in with him, when he hadn't felt enough for Beth to even pick up the phone and call her after their one night together in the cab of his truck.

Jealous? Yes, she supposed she was. But more than that, she was hurt and angry. No amount of time or number of miles between them would change that.

Seven years certainly hadn't.

Beth paused with the champagne flute halfway to her mouth. No, that wasn't quite true. She was over him. Absolutely, positively, one hundred percent over him.

The only feelings she still harbored toward Connor were ones of resentment. Just hearing his name raised her blood pressure. Not because she missed him or wished she could be his girlfriend, but because the thought of him made her want to strangle somebody when she didn't typically suffer from homicidal tendencies.

To some, those emotions might be welcome in relation to an ex-lover, but to her, they only served to remind her that he had had an impact on her at all. She hated that. Loathing was better than longing, but she'd prefer to be indifferent toward him.

"What are you doing hiding over here all by yourself? You should be dancing."

Her brother's voice came to her from over her left shoulder and she tipped her head back to look at him. Clear as a bell, steady as a surgeon… Damn, she was still sober.

"It's not my wedding day. I'm not required to make a fool of myself."

"Gee, thanks." He crossed his eyes and stuck his tongue out, mugging for her the way he'd done all her life. "Look, Karen's shoes are pinching her, but I'm still in the mood to dance, so I need a new partner."

Beth scanned the crowd and pointed toward an attractive brunette with the rim of her glass. "Ask her."

"Are you kidding me? If I danced with anyone but

my sister, my new bride would divorce me before the honeymoon." He waggled his eyebrows. "And I'm really looking forward to that honeymoon."

It was Beth's turn to roll her eyes. "Please. It's nothing new to you two, and we both know it. So will everyone else in six or seven months."

"Shh. We're keeping that a secret as long as we can. Now get up and dance with me, or I'll think you aren't happy for your big brother's recent state of wedded bliss."

With a sigh, she set down her empty glass and pushed to her feet. "Well, we can't have that."

Nick grinned as he took her hand and led her onto the crowded dance floor. Rod Stewart's throaty version of "The Way You Look Tonight" was playing, but Beth refused to give the song's lyrics too much thought as Nick's arm wrapped around her and they began to sway.

"I really am happy for you, you know."

The corners of his mouth lifted in a grin. "I know. It took me a while to get here, but I'm awfully glad I did."

She chuckled. "If you didn't put a ring on Karen's finger soon, I think she was about ready to string you up. You have been dating since high school, after all."

"Yeah, but I wanted to make sure she loved me for me and not my millions."

Beth threw back her head and laughed. Nick was lucky he had two nickels to rub together. He and Connor owned a contracting company together and did a lot of the work themselves, but they weren't exactly raking in the dough. Early on in their partnership, there had been months when they barely broke even; more when they were clearly in the hole.

Things were better now, but neither of them was rich by any stretch of the imagination. If Karen had truly been looking for a man with money to spare, she'd have run screaming from Nicholas years ago.

Beth, on the other hand, was doing pretty well for herself. Things had been tight when she'd first moved to L.A. The exorbitant cost of living on the West Coast, in addition to school loans that still had to be paid off, hadn't been easy to swing for a girl who didn't even have a job yet. She'd made ends meet at first by waitressing and temping at a few law firms.

Then she'd lucked out in finding a friend and fellow attorney who did have some cash to spare and was willing to form a partnership with her. Danny Vincent was a great guy. He came from money, so he'd been the one to foot all the start-up costs of Vincent and Curtis, but she'd done her best to pay him back by scouting out the talent, wooing new clients, and even stealing a few from other, more well-established firms.

The first few years had been backbreaking. She'd worked nonstop not only to prove herself, but to build the business so Danny never had a chance to think he'd made a mistake.

And now, they were pretty much set. They had high-profile celebrities and sports figures on their clientele list, with others waiting in line for their expertise, and the firm was operating well into the black on an annual basis.

She wore designer clothes, designer shoes, designer jewelry. A single trip to the salon cost her more than Karen probably spent on her hair in a year.

Which only served to make Beth feel even more removed from the small Ohio town where she'd been raised. She missed it sometimes…the friendly faces, the slow pace, her family. But that's what telephones and e-mail were for. She'd grown up and moved on. She was happy with her life.

The song ended and Nick started to let her go. One of the caterers had just placed a fresh bottle of champagne on the bridal table, and she wanted to get back to refill her glass.

"You're not running off already, are you?"

It wasn't her brother's voice that made her heart drop to her knees. Mentally, she closed her eyes and banged her head a couple of times against the nearest wall. But she'd been working with Hollywood big-wigs too long to let anyone see that she wasn't calm and one hundred percent in control of her emotions.

Licking her lips to buy an extra second, she forced herself to smile and turn in the direction of the loaded question.

"Hello, Connor."

He looked as handsome as ever. Better even, in his best-man tuxedo, when his usual uniform was well-worn blue jeans and soft flannel shirts. His hair was still barbershop short, no signs of gray in the brownish-blond strands. And his brown eyes twinkled as though he carried a secret no one else knew.

He did, of course. He knew what they'd done after

the football game all those years ago, up at Makeout Point. She doubted he'd ever told anyone, though. She certainly hadn't.

"Hey, Beth. I meant to tell you earlier that you're looking good. L.A. must be treating you right."

She nodded. He didn't need to know about the small ulcer she'd developed from eighteen-hour workdays and a demanding clientele, or the antacids she kept in her purse for the occasional flare-up.

As far as the residents of Crystal Springs were concerned, she'd gone off to California and become a huge success. There was no sense in telling them things weren't always as silver lined as they seemed.

"Would you like to dance?" Connor asked when another slow song began to fill the reception hall.

With him? Definitely not. She opened her mouth to politely refuse, but he already had his hand curled around her upper arm, steering her into his embrace, and her brother seemed more than willing to pass her off.

"Great," Nick said. "You dance with Connor, and I'll get back to Karen."

"She's got you on a tight leash already, huh?" Connor joked, throwing her brother a guy-to-guy grin.

"You should try it sometime," Nick replied, tossing his friend an equally teasing smile before sauntering off.

It would have caused a scene if she'd pulled away and returned to the table at that point, even though that's exactly what she wanted to do. Instead, she continued smiling and allowed Connor to put an arm at her waist, entwine his fingers with hers.

Because she didn't have a choice, she slid her free hand up to rest on his shoulder. The heat of his body pulsed through the fine wool of his tuxedo jacket, setting her palm to tingling.

She muttered a colorful oath under her breath, annoyed that he could still have any sort of impact on her, even a purely physical one.

And that's all it was—the physiological response of her female body to the nearness of such an attractive, obviously male body. Their shared history added to her body's response, but it didn't mean anything. Nothing at all.

"How have you been, Beth? I hear you've done well for yourself out there in la-la land."

"I'm doing all right," she said shortly. "And you?"

"Couldn't be better. Nick probably told you the company's doing well, keeping us both busy. Things slow down in the winter, of course, which is the only reason I'm letting him take off on this two-week honeymoon of his."

He shot her a wide, sparkling grin. She didn't respond.

"So what do you think about your big brother finally tying the knot?"

"It's about time, I say. They've only been dating since they were in diapers."

"Yeah. Makes you wonder, though, how much longer he'd have put it off if Karen hadn't surprised him with her little announcement."

"I don't know," Beth told him, trying not to get too drawn in to the conversation...or the warmth of his hold on her...or the lulling sensation of the music and moving around the dance floor with him. "I think Nick just needed an excuse to jump in with both feet. He's been wanting to marry Karen since they were teenagers, but he had all those typical male fears and insecurities. They fell into a comfortable pattern after high school that kept him from having to put his heart on the line until now."

Connor was still smiling, that stupid boy-next-door smile that reminded her of exactly why she'd moved as far across the country as possible after her graduation from law school.

"That's awfully philosophical for a gal who spends her days reading contracts and suing production companies," he remarked.

"Lawyers can be philosophical," she volleyed back. "We just prefer not to show that side of ourselves during billable hours."

Connor threw back his head and laughed at that, and Beth couldn't help but laugh with him. She'd forgotten how infectious his sense of humor was. How his low chuckle or full-belly laugh washed over her like a warm sea breeze.

When the moment passed, she found herself dancing even more closely to him. He'd somehow tightened his grip and brought her flush with his tall, muscular frame without her noticing. He took the lead as they swayed to an old Air Supply ballad, keeping a firm grasp on her so she couldn't slip away or even put space between them again.

Her breasts were pressed against his chest, and her

damn, traitorous nipples began to pucker beneath the satin bodice of her lime green and hot-pink maid-of-honor gown. She only hoped he wouldn't notice through the thick material of his own formal attire.

"Remember that dance back in junior high," he said, "when your folks wouldn't let you go unless Nick and Karen and I went along?"

How could she forget? She'd convinced herself it was a real date, while to Connor, it was nothing more than a favor for his best friend's sister and her parents.

"We danced half the night just like this," he continued.

Not exactly like this, she thought as his pelvis brushed against hers, making her stomach muscles tighten and heat pool thick in her veins.

"I even think they played this same song," he said with a chuckle.

She didn't remember the music from that night so many years ago, only the feel of Connor holding her as they shuffled back and forth in the middle of the darkened gymnasium. Her complete adoration for the boy of her dreams had been embarrassingly clear on her face, she was sure.

Thank God she'd grown up and moved on. She was beyond the starry eyes and stupid, love-struck glances of adolescence. She was strong, independent, and over him.

As soon as the thought passed through her mind, she knew she had to exert a bit of that independence and get away from him. She didn't want to talk about junior high or high school. Or anything from their past, for that matter. Better to let those memories—not a one of them good for her—remain dead and buried.

Before the song even ended, she stopped cold and took a step back. He still held her hand, his other arm extended from her waist.

"What's wrong?" he wanted to know, but he didn't release her.

"Nothing. I just don't want to dance anymore."

"Then let's take a walk." His fingers clenched around hers for a moment before relaxing. "I'll get us something to drink and we can go outside for a breath of fresh air."

"Thank you, but no."

"Come on. Just for a few minutes."

She stopped trying to pull away from him then and simply stared him straight in the eye.

"Why?" she wanted to know, studying him closely. "Why won't you let me go back to the table and leave me alone?"

For a second, he didn't say anything. Then he gave a heartfelt sigh, letting one arm drop to his side, but keeping a grip on her other hand.

"Look, I know things have been weird between us the past few years. It doesn't take a genius to figure out that you do your best to avoid me every time you come home to visit your family, and I just thought that maybe we could talk. Clear the air a bit."

Clear the air. As soon as the words sank in, her hackles went up.

If only life were that simple. If only a breath of fresh air and a few interesting stories about the good old days could wipe away all the pain, misery and anguish from that time in her life.

But they couldn't, and she had no desire to dredge up the past. Coming home for her brother's wedding had been difficult enough. Having a heart-to-heart with Connor was more than she could handle, more than she was *willing* to handle tonight.

She had been telling herself for years that she'd put him and everything that had passed between them behind her. Now seemed like the perfect time to prove it.

She yanked her hand from his, giving him no choice but to finally let go.

"There's nothing to talk about," she told him, leaving no room in her tone for argument. "Consider the air perfectly clear. Now, I'm going back to the bridal table to finish my champagne. And you should go back to your girlfriend."

She cast a glance over his broad shoulder, toward the well-built blonde in a stylish burgundy sheath who'd been glaring at them for the past several minutes. "She doesn't look too happy that you've been dancing with another woman."

With that, Beth turned on her heel and walked away. She grabbed her empty glass and the fresh bottle of champagne from the table as she passed, deciding to catch that breath of fresh air, after all. Alone.

Three

Connor ran a hand over the top of his head, blowing out a frustrated breath. Well, that had gone just great.

He'd meant to smooth things over with Beth, try to repair their old but battered friendship, not piss her off all over again. Or even more, depending on how one looked at it.

And there had to be something seriously wrong with him to be staring at the tight curve of her bottom as she stormed away while she was so obviously annoyed with him *and* while Lori was watching.

He couldn't seem to help himself, though. Beth had been an adorable kid, an attractive teenager, and now, as an adult, she was drop-dead beautiful.

He cursed himself for thinking it, for noticing her

feminine attributes at all. She was his best friend's sister and he was practically engaged to Lori, for God's sake. Or at least, they'd been living together for the past three years, and he knew that was what she expected.

But he was a man, and as much as he might wish it otherwise, he wasn't made of stone. Beth Curtis had eyes like the Hope Diamond—clear and bright and reflective. With one glance, she could either make him squirm or make him want, freeze him out or set fire to his belly and below.

She used to wear her chestnut hair in a ponytail or braid, but the older she'd gotten, the more she let it hang long and loose down her back. The wavy strands reminded him of the finest silk, and he wanted to run his fingers through them every time she was near.

And her body…man, her body had filled out like nothing he'd ever seen. Yeah, Lori was built. Tiny waist, long legs, big breasts. But her chest had been surgically enhanced, and as much as he'd enjoyed the benefits of that work, there was something about the idea of silicone or saline swishing around in there that turned him off. He would never tell Lori he felt that way, of course, but it was true.

Beth, on the other hand, was just as God had made her. And he'd done a damn fine job. She wasn't model thin or tall, but he liked that. He liked the way her breasts filled that awful pink-and-green gown without looking fake. He liked the curve of her waist, the flare of her hips, the sweet little behind the cut of her dress alluded to. He even liked the slim expanse of her ankle, visible above the strap of her pink, three-inch heels.

And that was why he was going straight to hell.

He pressed a finger and thumb to his eye sockets, thinking—not for the first time—that he was either crazy or the unluckiest bastard around to keep getting into these situations. Beth was practically family, but he couldn't seem to stop lusting after her.

Knowing he couldn't put it off any longer, he dragged his gaze away from Beth's retreating form and turned to face Lori.

Beth had been right, she didn't look happy. Which meant he'd managed to piss off two beautiful women in one night. That was a record, even for him.

She was sitting at the table where he'd left her, arms crossed over her ample chest, legs crossed, top foot tapping angrily in midair. A pulsing, upbeat dance number shook the floor beneath their feet, but the music failed to permeate Lori's sour mood.

Well, this should be fun.

He started toward her, but she leaped to her feet and met him halfway, fire brimming in her eyes.

"Hey," he greeted her, smiling and trying to pretend he didn't realize how upset she was.

"So that was her."

"Who?" Connor cocked his head slightly, hoping he would catch another glimpse of Beth before she disappeared too deeply into the crowd. No such luck.

When he turned back around, Lori's expression was even darker, brows drawn and lips pulled down.

"Her. She's the one."

"The one, who?" he asked, growing more confused by the minute.

"The one who's keeping you from making a commitment to me."

"Lori," he began, scoffing at her accusation.

"No," she cut him off. "I knew there was something going on. I knew there was someone or some incident you couldn't put behind you, but I had no idea it was *her.* Your best friend's sister."

She said the last as though it was the gravest of insults, and Connor once again felt his insides tighten with shame.

She was right. Beth was his best friend's sister—off limits, taboo. What he thought about her those times he couldn't control his raging hormones, and what they'd done all those years ago, was reprehensible.

And even though Lori had hit the nail on the head, he wanted to deny it. *Needed* to deny it.

"You don't know what you're talking about," he told her, sliding his hands into the pockets of his tux jacket. "Beth and I are friends. We grew up together. She isn't keeping me from doing anything."

"I *mean,*" she growled, leaning in to be heard over the music, but not by anyone else, "I saw the way you looked at each other. The way you held her while you danced. I'm not blind, Connor. There was more there than friendship. More than dancing with your best friend's sister."

"That's ridiculous."

"It's not." Her voice grew thick and tears glistened along her lower lashes. "It explains a lot, actually. Like why there's no ring on my finger," she said, holding up her bare left hand as proof. "And why I'm at your best friend's wedding instead of my own. We've been dating for six years, Connor. Living together for three. If that doesn't prove you have commitment issues, I don't know what will."

She turned her head in the direction Beth had earlier escaped. "Now I know why."

"Lori…"

"I don't think this is going to work, Connor. I don't think I can live with you anymore, knowing I'm not the woman you really want to be with."

She walked to the table to gather her purse, then returned to stand in front of him. Without meeting his gaze, she murmured, "I don't think you should come home tonight. Maybe not ever."

It crossed his mind to tell her it was his house… she'd moved in with him, not the other way around. But this was hard enough on her. He'd never meant to hurt her, yet here she was, in obvious pain because of him.

His throat was too tight to speak, so he merely nodded.

He saw the hitch in her breathing before she straightened her shoulders and left the reception hall like a queen leaving a grand ballroom, head held high, regal to the core.

Damn, this night just kept getting better and better.

"Hey, buddy."

Nick came up behind him, slapping him on the back and shoving a bottle of cold beer at him. Connor pulled a hand from his pocket and accepted the much-needed drink.

"Thanks, man." He took several long swallows before lowering the bottle.

"No problem. Trouble in paradise?" his best friend asked.

"Yeah. I think I just got kicked out of my own house."

"Ouch. You and Lori had a fight, then. What about?"

Nothing he could share with Nick.

"It's not important," he mumbled, hoping Nick wouldn't press for details.

He took another swig of beer, then dug into his pants pocket to feel for his wallet. "I hate to take off so early, but I'd better start looking for a hotel vacancy or I'm going to end up sleeping in my truck." Which he'd have to walk home to retrieve, since they'd driven to the wedding and reception in Lori's car.

"Listen," Nick told him. "Why don't you stick around a while longer, enjoy yourself, then you can crash at my place. Karen and I are heading straight for the airport after this and won't be back for two weeks. If you and Lori make up, great. But if you don't, you can stay there as long as you like."

"Are you sure?" Connor asked, touched by his friend's generosity. But then, the Curtises had always treated him better than he deserved.

Even as a rough-and-tumble foster kid from across the street, they'd invited him in and acted as if he was no different than Nick or any other boy their age.

Never mind that he was hell on wheels, with a chip on his shoulder the size of Texas, working on getting kicked out of his eighth or ninth foster home. They'd accepted him, trusted him, even grown to love him as much as he loved them.

His eyes grew damp just thinking about how accepting they'd been of him, despite the asinine things he'd done to test them. They'd changed his life, and if it took him until the day he died, he'd do everything he could to repay them.

"Mi casa es su casa," Nick quipped. "I'd feel better knowing someone was around, anyway."

"Thanks, man, I really appreciate it."

"No problem. Now, why don't you come on over to the table with us, and when we leave, we'll swing past your place so you can pick up your truck."

Connor cast a sideways glance at his friend as they negotiated the crowd and headed toward a smiling Karen, still decked out in her white wedding dress and veil.

"You're going to ride me about this after you get back from your honeymoon, aren't you?"

Nick snorted, not bothering to hide his amusement. "Oh, yeah. Getting dumped at my wedding, kicked out of your own house… It's too good to let go." He slung an arm around Connor's shoulders. "Don't worry, buddy, I'll still remember all the details when I get back."

Connor shook his head, rubbing at the headache that was beginning to form right between his eyes. "That's what I'm afraid of."

The scent of fresh-brewed coffee filled the air and tickled Beth's nose where it was buried in her pillowcase. She rolled to her back with a groan and slowly opened her eyes.

Well, the room wasn't spinning. That had to be a good sign.

She wasn't intoxicated—not anymore—but she was hungover. She could feel it, from the throbbing in her brain to the thick pile of cotton coating her tongue.

What had she been thinking? She'd left her brother's wedding reception with a full magnum of champagne and ended up drinking so much the bottle ached.

She never did that sort of thing, and it galled her to realize she'd let things get to her so much last night that she'd turned to alcohol to numb her emotions.

Thank God it was over, though. Nick and Karen would be on their honeymoon by now, or at least on their way to sunny Honolulu. And all of their guests would have gone home, Connor and his peroxide-blond girlfriend included. She never needed to see him again.

Life couldn't get much better.

She pushed herself out of bed and lurched to the connected bathroom, using the nightstand and dresser to keep from falling over. After brushing her teeth and splashing a little water on her face, she felt more human. She was even walking straighter as she made her way downstairs, following the mesmerizing fragrance of java and the promise of a jolt of caffeine.

Turning the corner into the kitchen, covering a yawn with the back of her hand, she opened her eyes to find a man standing at the counter with his back to her.

A yip of fear and surprise passed her lips before she

could stop it, and the man whirled in her direction. If she hadn't been feeling so sluggish and out of sorts when she woke up, she might have figured out earlier that in order for her to smell fresh-brewed coffee, another body had to be in the house to make it.

And she'd been wrong: Life couldn't get much worse.

Connor watched her with wide eyes, just as stunned by her sudden appearance as she was by his presence. He clutched a cup of steaming coffee in his hands, a splotch of the dark brew staining the front of his shirt where it had sloshed over the lip of the mug when he'd spun around.

Good, she hoped he'd burned himself.

"What are you doing here?" she asked, not kindly, grasping for the edges of a robe that wasn't there. Instead, she was standing in the middle of her family's kitchen, covered only by the paper-thin camisole she'd worn beneath her bridesmaid gown.

Last night, after she'd dug her brother's spare house key out of the flower bed where he kept it hidden in the bottom of a resin lawn ornament and climbed the stairs to her old bedroom, she'd shrugged out of the pink-and-green concoction, but left the camisole on. With spaghetti straps and a hem that hit high on the thigh, it was no more revealing than any of her other satin nighties.

Besides, she'd been alone in the house…just her and Dom Pérignon…and not expecting guests.

"I could ask you the same thing," Connor responded, setting his mug on the countertop and grabbing a paper towel to blot at the stain on his shirt, just above the waistband of his low-slung jeans.

Lord, he wore denims like no one else she'd ever seen. Even out in L.A., where every waiter or valet was an aspiring actor or model, the men didn't have waists and hips and buttocks like Connor Riordan. They would never be able to pull off the open flannel shirts over faded T-shirts the way he did, or the worn blue jeans and work boots.

Not that it had any effect on her whatsoever. She was merely making a mental observation, the same as she might be slightly awed by a famous, high-powered celebrity who waltzed into her office back on Wilshire.

"In case you've forgotten, this is my house."

"Since when?"

She lifted a brow, her annoyance growing in direct proportion to the pounding in her skull. What she wouldn't give for a cup of that coffee and fifty aspirin right about now.

But she couldn't have those things just yet. Not until she'd finished this argument with Connor and kicked him out on his tight-but-aggravating butt.

"Since I grew up here. Remember?"

"That was a long time ago," he remarked, picking up his mug once again and taking a slow sip of the black coffee that was making her mouth water. "Seems to me it's not so much your house anymore. Your parents moved to a smaller place on the other side of town, and you moved all the way to Los Angeles. It's your brother's place now...his and Karen's."

Beth's teeth gritted together and she felt her right

eye begin to twitch, which it only did when she was resisting the urge to clobber somebody.

"I'm still family," she told him, jaw clenched tight
so that her words sounded half growled, even to her
own ears. "This is my family home, and I'm sure Nick
won't mind me staying in my old room for a few nights
while he's on his honeymoon."

Like she owed him any explanation! Honestly, this
was *her* house—her family home, at any rate. *He* was
the interloper. *He* should be the one defending himself
and offering up explanations for why he was here.

"Well, sweetheart," he drawled, "that's where we
might have a problem. Because Nick told me I could
stay here until he gets back."

Scowling, she let his words sink in, all the while
wishing her brother were nearby so she could wring his
neck. Was it too much to ask that she be allowed to stay
in her childhood home while she was in Ohio? Alone.
To rest and recuperate before going back to her mile-
a-minute world and no-rest-for-the-weary occupation.

"Why do you need to stay here?" she wanted to
know. "Don't you have a house of your own to go to?"

She could have sworn he blushed at that. His cheekbones turned a dull red and he refused to meet her
gaze.

"Yeah," he said in a low rumble. "You'd think that
would make a difference."

"Excuse me?"

"I got kicked out, okay?" he grumbled, crossing his
arms over his chest and slouching against the counter
cabinets.

He was pouting. And looking decidedly embarrassed, Beth thought.

Oh, the day was taking a turn for the better, after all.

She perked up, fighting the urge to giggle at his obvious discomfort and reversal of fortune.

"You got kicked out," she repeated, trying not to sound too gleeful. "Of your own house. Why?"

The flush disappeared from his face, then was replaced by the flat, grim line of his mouth.

"Never mind why," was his terse reply. "The point is, I needed a place to stay, and your brother offered the use of his house until he and Karen get back from their honeymoon."

It was her turn to cross her arms. At this point, she didn't even care that the gesture pushed her breasts up and caused the flimsy satin and lace bodice to bunch and reveal a fair amount of cleavage.

If the sight offended him, fine. If it turned him off, so be it. And if it turned him on…good. Maybe he would feel intimidated by his attraction to her and hightail it to the nearest hotel.

Or back into Lori-Lisa-Laura's open arms.

Okay, that didn't sit as well with her as the two previous possibilities, but still…whatever got him out of her brother's house while she was there.

"Well, you can't stay here," she told him again, more firmly this time.

"Oh, no? You want to call Nick in Hawaii, interrupt whatever he and Karen are up to at this particular moment—" he waggled his eyebrows to indicate what he predicted they'd be doing, and probably wasn't far off the mark "—and ask him exactly who his choice is for houseguest while he's gone?"

"Sure," she said, calling his bluff. "I'm pretty sure he'll pick me, considering how I'm his *sister* and all. His blood relative."

"And I'm his best friend since fifth grade," Connor put in. "Not to mention *invited*. Does Nick even know you're here?"

"Of course he knows I'm here," she fired back.

When she'd first been making arrangements to return to Ohio for his wedding, she'd offered to get a hotel room. *Wanted* to, to be honest. But Nick had insisted she stay at the house.

"It's your house, too," he'd cajoled. "And besides, Karen and I will be leaving right after the reception. You'll have the whole place to yourself."

She'd agreed, partly because she didn't want to hurt his feelings, and partly because she'd been looking forward to coming home, sleeping in her old bedroom, and just being *alone* with her thoughts and her memories for a few days.

So much for that, she reflected now. She hadn't even been able to wake up and get a cup of coffee on only her second morning back without coming face-to-face with her greatest nemesis.

Well, part of that may be true, but she'd be damned if he'd keep her from her daily shot of caffeine a second longer.

Marching forward, she grabbed a ceramic mug from the cupboard just above Connor's right shoulder and poured herself a cup of rich, black coffee from the still-hot carafe. She crossed to the refrigerator to add a dollop of milk, then leaned back against the opposite countertop to stir in a spoonful of sugar.

She took a sip, savoring the sweet, creamy brew before Connor's voice interrupted her momentary enjoyment.

"So if Nick knows you're here, and he knows I'm here, I guess that means he thought the two of us could act like mature adults and stay together in the same house for a while without killing each other."

Beth swallowed another great gulp of coffee before spearing him with a saccharine grin. "He'd have been wrong."

"Come on, Beth Ann." He set his coffee on the counter with a clink, sliding his thumbs into the front pockets of his jeans as he shifted to face her more fully.

She cringed at his use of both her first and middle names together, hoping he didn't notice. If he did, he would call her that all the more just to annoy her, the same as he had when they were kids.

"Can't we get along well enough to rattle around this place together for a few days? I'll stay out of your way if you stay out of mine."

I'd rather chew broken glass, she thought, downing the last of her coffee, then moving to refill her cup.

"I sincerely doubt it," she told him bluntly, not bothering to look at him. Pivoting on the ball of her bare foot, she started from the room. "I'll find somewhere else to stay."

Four

Connor watched her saunter out of the room, unable to decide whether he'd won or lost that round. Lost, would be his guess.

He should have taken the opportunity to talk to her like he'd wanted to last night. To sit down with her and discuss their relationship. That night seven years ago, when they'd done something they shouldn't have, and how it had affected them to this day.

Instead, he'd been so surprised by her sudden appearance in the kitchen doorway that he'd let her goad him into arguing with her.

Truth be told, it had been kind of fun. She'd stood there in that frilly little excuse for a nightgown...

shoulders bare, breasts heaving, bottom hem barely covering the area where he prayed panties had been.

It was too much for him to imagine her naked under there. He was already hard and throbbing just from her mere presence. Knowing she wasn't wearing underwear would have caused smoke to pour out of his ears for sure.

As it was, a cold shower and a quick dip into a sub-zero freezer weren't out of the question.

Her nose had been pointing up in the air, her glacial gaze implying he was no better than a piece of chewing gum she might scrape off the bottom of her steel-heeled stilettos.

She was a snob, but she hadn't always been like that. Hadn't been anything like that before college. And then he'd seduced her, taken advantage of her, and he was very much afraid he was responsible for the woman she was today.

A successful entertainment attorney, with her own firm, making more money in a year than he'd probably earn in a lifetime? Sure. But also a cold, calculating professional who put her career ahead of her family and personal happiness.

The old Beth would never have let anything come between her and her parents or brother. The new Beth had purposely moved over two thousand miles away and didn't come home unless it was absolutely unavoidable.

It was his fault she'd grown so distant from her family, but damned if he knew what to do to fix the problem.

* * *

"You've got to be kidding me."

Beth flicked mascara over her lashes while balancing the cordless phone between her ear and shoulder. The minute she'd left the kitchen and turned her back on Connor, she'd gone about trying to figure out exactly what she should do to get away from him permanently. She thought about going back downstairs and forcibly removing him from the house, but doubted she could budge his hulking, overbearing frame.

Now, she was on the phone with the airline, trying to change her flight back to L.A. So far, she was having about as much luck as she'd had trying to get a decent, quiet breakfast this morning.

Her stomach growled, sending her an uncomfortable reminder that she still hadn't eaten and was *hungry,* darn it. Which only put her more on edge.

The way she was feeling, she might just stand a decent chance of muscling Connor out of the house, after all.

"All right, if I can't get a flight out today, I'll take one for tomorrow," she told the woman on the other end of the line.

She heard the *clickety-clack* of fingers tapping a keyboard for a second, and then the woman said, "I'm not showing anything for tomorrow, either."

"What about another airline? I don't care if it costs more. I'll even buy another ticket, I just *really* need to fly out of here as soon as possible."

Click-click-clack. "No, ma'am, I'm sorry. And I feel it's only fair to warn you that the storm front moving in has forced us to delay and cancel many of our flights. You may not even be able to get out of town with your current reservation."

Beth muttered a curse, resisting the urge to rub her eyes and smear the makeup she'd just spent the last quarter of an hour applying. She wanted to ask the woman to check the schedule again. She even thought about putting on her dragon-lady act and insisting the airline do whatever it took to get her home. But her current predicament wasn't the woman's fault, and neither was the weather.

"All right, thank you," she forced herself to say in a polite, moderate tone before hanging up.

No flights. Not today, tomorrow…maybe not for the rest of the week. This definitely put a crimp in her plans, but she hadn't gotten where she was in this world by taking no for an answer.

The bathroom door opened with a creak of hinges, and she crossed the hall to her childhood bedroom, where her suitcase lay open on top of the unmade bed. She slipped her stockinged feet into the basic black sling-backs she'd brought to go along with most of the outfits she'd packed and headed downstairs to find a phone book.

She didn't know where Connor was, and told herself she didn't care. It was too much to hope that he might have abandoned the house of his own free will, but maybe if she could avoid him for another few minutes, things would work out okay.

Keeping her ears open for signs that he was moving around the house, she crept into the room her brother used as an office-slash-den and started rooting around. She found the phone book in a drawer beneath the phone. So sensible, it had to be Karen's doing. Nick didn't have an organized bone in his body and was as likely to leave the phone book in the dishwasher as the office.

She dropped into the chair behind the desk and flipped to the lodgings section at the back of the directory. There were any number of two- and three-star motels listed, as well as a couple of decent hotels. She would have to drive an hour or more to find a really nice place to stay, but at this point she would be happy with just a bed and private bathroom.

The telephone receiver was in her hand, her fingers tapping out the first of the hotel numbers, when she suddenly froze.

What was she doing? Why was she the one calling the airline and trying to find another place to stay when this was *her* house?

Well, her brother's house now, but she'd lived here with him and their parents for the first twenty years of her life. That certainly had to count for more than Connor's close friendship with Nick and the fact that he'd lived across the street from them for almost the same amount of time.

Dropping the phone back in its cradle, she slapped the directory closed and stood, sending the chair scuttling back several inches.

No, she wasn't going to do this. She was going to stay in her own house, in her own room, until she flew back to Los Angeles.

Hopefully that would be Thursday, on her original ticket. But if the weather grounded that flight, she would stay until the next one available to the West Coast.

It wouldn't be the most comfortable few days she'd ever spent, she knew. Being in the same town with Connor was difficult enough…staying in the same house with him was bound to give her a migraine of epic proportions.

No problem; she'd brought her Imitrex. Along with plain ibuprofen, antacids and all the other over-the-counter medications she kept on hand for when her body began to protest the long hours and high stress levels she forced it to endure.

The point was, she'd been telling herself for years that she was well and truly over Connor. No more childhood crush, no more unrealistic, adolescent fantasies that he couldn't fulfill. Now was the time to step up and prove it.

She was debating her plan of action where Connor was concerned when he poked his head around the doorway, startling her. For a nanosecond, her heart stopped beating as it jumped into her throat.

"You're still here," he said unnecessarily.

"Yes." She drew herself up, smoothing the front of her white silk blouse, though she doubted she'd picked up any wrinkles in the short amount of time she'd been dressed. "And I'm staying, so you might want to look into finding other accommodations."

"What's the matter? Couldn't get an earlier flight?"

His eyes twinkled devilishly and her jaw snapped

closed. He was so aggravating, the way he seemed to know what she was thinking and find it amusing.

"No, actually. There's a storm front moving in, and they're not sure I'll even be able to leave at the scheduled time."

"You could always go to a hotel," he offered, moving to fill the doorway and leaning a shoulder against the carved-wood jamb.

"So could you."

"Stalemate, then. Since we've been down this road before, and neither of us is willing to leave, I guess that means we're stuck together."

She hated to admit it, but he was right. They were well and truly stuck with each other.

"Come on." Connor pushed away from the wall and motioned toward the kitchen with a hitch of his head. "If we're going to be roommates for a while, we might as well make nice. I fixed breakfast. Come get some."

With that, he turned and walked away, leaving her to follow or not. She stood behind the desk for another minute, debating whether to let down her guard and eat with him or hold tight to her pride and avoid him as much as possible.

A whiff of toast and other unidentifiable scents floated into the room, causing her stomach to rumble and making up her mind for her. She was starving, he'd cooked, and she'd be darned if he'd keep her from eating when she was hungry in her own home.

She crossed the office and strolled down the hall, her high heels clicking in cadence with her steps. When she reached the kitchen, she found Connor at the stove, stirring something in a frying pan and scooping portions onto plates.

As though sensing her presence, he glanced in her direction, then carried the two heaping plates to the table.

"Have a seat," he told her. "I'll get the toast and some napkins."

Waiting until he was back at the counter, she skirted him and settled in the chair nearest the wall. That way, she could see every move he made and map out her escape route, if one became necessary.

He piled four slices of buttered toast on another plate and grabbed a handful of paper napkins from a drawer by the sink before returning to the table.

"Don't wait for me. Go ahead and eat."

She lifted the fork at her place setting, but merely toyed with the omelet fixings in front of her while he continued to move around the room. He opened a cupboard and retrieved two glasses, taking them with him to the refrigerator.

"Milk or juice?" he asked.

Juice would go better with breakfast, but her ulcer wouldn't thank her for it. "Milk. Thank you," she added grudgingly.

After filling the glasses—one with milk for her, the other with orange juice for himself—he sauntered back to the table with that confident, loose-limbed stride of his, kicked his chair out and took a seat.

"How's your omelet?"

She looked down, realizing she hadn't yet tasted a bite.

"Oh." Quickly, she scooped up a forkful of ham,

cheese, onion, mushroom and pepper, mixed in with scrambled egg. Her personal trainer would kill her if he ever found out she'd eaten like this, but she had to admit it was delicious.

Of course, she wasn't going to tell Connor that.

"It's very good," she told him, dabbing the corners of her mouth with her napkin.

"Glad you like it." He dug into his own breakfast like a man who hadn't eaten in a week.

She picked at hers more slowly, feeling the silence growing between them like a weight on her chest.

"I didn't know you cooked," she murmured, when she couldn't stand it any longer.

After taking a swig of orange juice, he shook his head. "I don't much. Just enough to get by."

"I suppose Lori-Laura-Lisa does most of the cooking for you these days." The words sounded bitter, even to her own ears, and Beth regretted voicing them as soon as they passed her lips.

"Lori-Laura-Lisa?" he asked, one brow quirking upward.

She shrugged, refusing to be embarrassed by either her comment or the grouping of names she used for his overly processed girlfriend. "I know it starts with an *L*."

"Lori," he emphasized. "Her name is Lori. And she cooks some, but mostly we go out or order in. How about you? What do you eat out there in L.A.?"

"Not eggs and ham, that's for sure," she said, stabbing at those very ingredients on her plate and relaxing into the conversation. "Tofu, protein shakes, salads. A lot of raw meals."

"Raw?" he wanted to know, wiggling his eyebrows suggestively.

Against her better judgment, Beth found herself smiling at his lighthearted teasing. "Not that kind of raw. Get your mind out of the gutter, pervert," she fired back.

He only grinned and shoveled another pile of omelet into his mouth.

"Raw is a big thing out on the coast. Uncooked, unpreserved, organic foods, like chickpea burgers with shredded coconut or carrots on top."

"Uh-huh. And this keeps you alive?"

"I'm here, aren't I?"

"Yeah, but it wouldn't hurt you to wolf down a real burger or two before you head back. You could stand to put on a couple pounds."

Something warm and pleasant burst low in her solar plexus. She spent so much time working out and watching what she ate, trying hard to fit in with the "the skinnier the better" California mentality. It was an ideal she'd embraced when she'd first moved out there, but now it seemed to be a constant struggle just to maintain her current weight and figure.

Hearing Connor say she was too thin flattered her, even if it shouldn't. He didn't get an opinion about her physical appearance—no man did—and he didn't have a clue what life in L.A. was like.

But after seeing his dress-up-doll girlfriend, knowing that he didn't think she had to maintain a perfect image made her feel somehow normal and accepted. A far cry from her recent frame of mind.

"Red meat is strictly *verboten,*" she said. "And I work out two hours, three days a week to stay just this size, thank you very much."

"I hate to break it to you, sweetheart, but you're eating meat right now."

She looked down at the specks of pink cooked into fluffy clouds of yellow egg. "Yes, well, technically ham isn't red meat, and while I wouldn't normally eat it, I thought it would be rude to turn down your offer of breakfast. Besides, it's not much and there are other, healthier things in here, like onions and peppers."

"Excellent job of justifying."

She shot him a cheeky twist of her lips. "Thank you." He didn't need to know just how well versed she was at the justification game.

"You're welcome to go running after you eat, if you want. Burn off all those nasty calories."

"I just might." But a sidelong glance out the kitchen window told her she wouldn't want to. The day was looking decidedly overcast, and the wind was whipping the leaves around on the trees.

"Actually…" Connor stopped to clear his throat.

He stared down at the table rather than meet her gaze, and a slick, uncomfortable sensation snaked over Beth's skin.

"I was kind of hoping we could talk after breakfast."

Her heart kicked up its pace, sending the blood racing through her veins, and the slick feeling turned to a cool clamminess.

Honestly, she had no idea why Connor was so determined to speak with her. He'd tried to drag her off last night at the reception so they could talk, and now he was making a second attempt to get her to listen to whatever he had to say.

The queasiness in her stomach, though, told her she didn't want to hear it. Or maybe she was just afraid that he'd bring up the past, tearing open a wound long ago healed over.

After all, what else did they have to discuss? They hadn't seen each other, except briefly, in the last seven years.

She swallowed hard, taking a minute to get her thoughts and jumbled emotions in order before forcing herself to respond. "What do we have to talk about?"

He tossed his crumpled-up napkin on top of his now-empty plate and pushed them away from him. Crossing his arms in front of him on the table, he lifted his head and met her eyes with his own, which looked like two chips of brittle brown ice.

His voice rang low but clear as he drawled, "That night."

The words drove into her like bullets and for a moment, she couldn't breathe, even though she'd known exactly what was coming.

Why did he have to bring it up? Why now, after all these years? Why at all?

It had been a mistake, but it had happened. She'd gotten on with her life, and so, obviously, had he.

"What night?" she asked, playing dumb while her brain struggled to regain its equilibrium.

"You know what night, Beth. We both do. That night after the football game, in my truck."

She laughed lightly, doing her best to act nonchalant while her insides continued to quake. "Goodness, why would you bring that up after all these years? It was aeons ago. I would have thought you'd forgotten all about it. I certainly had."

A beat passed while he seemed to absorb her comment, and then his gaze grew shuttered, his mouth thinning into a flat, pale line.

"I'm sorry to hear that. It's something I think about all the time."

She didn't know what to do with that piece of information. Be flattered, angry, curious?

At the moment, she mostly felt cold. He thought about that night all the time, but he hadn't thought enough of her, or of what had passed between them, to pick up the phone and call her afterward. The next day, the next week…she'd have taken anything, any small sign that he was still interested in her.

Even a face-to-face meeting where he sat her down and told her he wasn't interested and didn't want to see her again would have been better than nothing. But he hadn't even had the courtesy to do that, so instead they'd spent nearly a decade flitting around each other, avoiding, pretending, denying anything had ever happened between them.

And now…well, she had no interest in allowing him to bring all those stinging memories and emotions bubbling to the surface again. He'd had his chance to make peace seven years ago; she wasn't willing to give him a fresh opportunity now.

Falling back on her day-to-day, all-business persona, she pushed her chair away from the table and stood, her posture yardstick straight, her movements quick and precise.

"Why are you bringing this up after so long?" she asked, carrying her empty plate and glass to the sink. Then she backtracked and did the same with his dishes.

He turned in his seat to face her, the wood creaking beneath his weight, and propped one arm on the table. "Because we never discussed it before, and it's obviously putting a strain on our relationship."

"We don't have a relationship," she said with a sharp bark of laughter.

For once, she was almost finding this situation amusing. It was the height of irony that Connor suddenly seemed so determined to discuss the state of affairs between them when she'd spent every single one of her teenage years praying for Connor to play a larger part in her life.

"Sure we do, Beth."

She was leaning back against the counter by the sink, her arms up, the heels of her hands propped along the sharp edge at her waistline. When he rose to his feet and stalked toward her, her fingers tightened reflexively on the cool Formica, but she refused to move, refused to flinch or in any other way reveal her discomfort.

Her entire stay in this house with him was going to be an exercise in discomfort, so she might as well get used to it right now and learn to school her features, reactions and body language.

"Everyone in this world has a relationship with everyone else, from married couples to the cashiers and customers down at the Qwik Fill. You're my best friend's sister, practically family—of course we have a relationship. I wasn't implying we were any more intimately involved than that."

"Good," was the best response she could come up with. Her lungs refused to expand and deflate normally, his nearness sucking all the oxygen out of the air around them.

"But we were once, weren't we?" he murmured in a low voice.

The metal edge of the countertop dug into the soft cushion of her palms and she concentrated on that sharp throb of sensation to block the flood of memories threatening to spill into her brain. She would not go back to that time. She wouldn't open herself up to that again, especially with him.

He was standing less than a foot away, his tall form towering over her. A faded forest-green T-shirt clung to the smooth, firm expanse of his chest, partially covered by an open blue-and-white-plaid flannel work shirt.

So informal, so blue collar... Considering the well-dressed businessmen and celebrities she worked with on a daily basis, it amazed her that she could still find his taste in clothing attractive.

After catching her breath and feeling steady enough to answer, she told him, "Once, Connor, a very long time ago. Don't make more of it than it was."

"I won't, if you won't, but that doesn't explain why you've been avoiding me all these years."

Five

"**I** haven't been avoiding you."

Her voice was firm, but the slight flicker in her gaze told him she was lying. Not that he needed the added assurance. It didn't take a rocket scientist to figure out that when one person entered a room and another either made an excuse to leave or simply slipped away unnoticed, something was going on.

Not that he blamed her. He'd acted like an ass all those years ago. Yes, he'd been twenty-six and thought he was grown-up and mature, but he'd handled the entire situation badly.

To start, he'd taken advantage of a twenty-one-year-old Beth. His hormones had gotten the better of him and he'd given in to raging, long-repressed desires that would have been better off remaining repressed. He wasn't sure he could ever forgive himself for that. It ate at him like a wasting disease.

Then what had he done? He'd dropped her off at her house and never spoken to her again. Well, not never, but barely. He hadn't phoned her the next day to see if she was okay, or swung by to talk to her about how their having sex might have changed things between them.

No, he'd taken the coward's way out and stayed away until he knew she was back at school. And then he'd continued skulking around with his tail tucked under, content to keep his mouth shut on the topic for as long as she was.

But that plan had backfired on him, hadn't it? Not discussing it hadn't made the situation go away or allowed their relationship to settle back to normal. Instead, it had turned the incident into a boil that festered and grew not only ugly, but painful.

They'd drifted apart when they used to be so close. They avoided each other, when they used to seek one another out. They couldn't even make eye contact without one or the other of them quickly looking away. And there were no more smiles, no more teasing, no more inside childhood jokes.

He hated that. He hated that his overactive libido and lack of control had caused Beth to throw up a barrier between them as thick and tall as the Great Wall of China.

And once again, he wasn't making great strides at setting things right.

What was it about Beth that put all of his senses on high alert and made him want to push, prod, draw her out?

For better or worse, he wanted to get her to react. Yell at him, scream at him, slap him silly. Cry, laugh, or throw herself into his arms. At this point, he'd take just about anything. Any sign that she wasn't as indifferent toward him as she claimed.

"No?" he put in, in response to her assertion. "What would you call seven years of circling each other like opposing magnets?"

"I don't know what you're talking about."

"Sure you do. It used to be that I'd come over and you'd race downstairs to see me. You'd beg me to stay and watch a movie or drive you to the store for the latest teen magazine. And then there was that night in my truck. After that, any time I came over while you were home, you made yourself scarce. You even moved all the way out to California so you'd have an excuse not to visit very often."

She gave a small huff of laughter that never reached her eyes. "That's ridiculous. I moved to California because I wanted to be an entertainment lawyer, and that's the entertainment capital of the world."

"Did you?" He took a single step closer with the question. "Or did you decide to become an entertainment attorney because it was the one type of law you couldn't practice here at home?"

This time, she didn't laugh. She didn't even scoff at his accusation.

Her arms fell from where they'd been propped against the edge of the counter and took up stiff residence across her chest. Little did she know the gesture lifted her breasts and caused the airy silk of her white blouse to separate just above her cleavage, allowing him a clear view of full, fleshy hills and the deep, shadowed valley between.

The sight made his mouth go dry, but he didn't look for long, for fear she'd catch him staring.

"I'm good at what I do, Connor, and I like living in L.A. Not that I have to justify anything to you."

She was right, of course, but that didn't keep him from being curious.

"Now, if you're finished bringing up incidents from the past that have no relevance to the present and giving me the third degree, I think it's about time we establish some ground rules for however long we'll be forced to stay here together."

"Ground rules, huh?" He crossed his arms, mimicking her defensive stance, even though he was fighting back amusement. "What do you have in mind?"

"For one thing, I get first dibs on the bathroom in the morning."

"How do you figure?"

"It's my brother's house, and I'm the girl," she remarked, deadpan.

He had to bite the inside of his mouth to keep from hooting with laughter.

"You're the girl? Is that a defense that would stand up in court?"

"I don't spend a lot of time in court, so I wouldn't know, but the fact remains that women need more time in the bathroom in the mornings."

Having lived with Lori for the past three years, that was something he knew quite well. "I agree, but there's one small problem with your plan."

"What?"

"I was up a good hour earlier than you were this morning. Do you expect me to wait to use the john just because you're supposed to get first dibs?"

Her lips turned down in a frown, her nose wrinkling only slightly at his frank terminology.

"Fine. If you're up before I am, then you can use the bathroom. But as soon as I'm awake, my needs take precedence."

"Deal. Anything else?"

"Meals. You cooked breakfast this morning, and I appreciate it. It was very good, thank you. But don't feel that you have to do the same every morning, or for any other meals. And don't expect me to cook, either. I say it's every man for himself. If one of us cooks and wants to invite the other to share the meal, fine. But neither of us should expect the other to feed them."

"Fine. How about takeout? Do we confer with each other before calling for pizza or Chinese, or do we treat it like a covert mission?"

"Very funny," she smirked. "That's your call. It might be polite to let each other know if we're calling out for food, but it isn't required."

"Got it. Anything else?"

Several seconds ticked by while she considered, and then she shook her head. "I can't think of anything more at the moment, but we can tack on new rules as they come up."

"Fine by me." He let his arms slip down and planted his hands halfway inside his front jeans pockets.

"So who does the dishes?" he wanted to know, tilting his head toward the dirty ones in the sink behind her.

"You do," she said without batting an eyelash, then turned on her heel and sashayed out of the kitchen.

Connor watched her go, enjoying the sassy, well-dressed view. As soon as she disappeared around the corner, he chuckled, turning to the sink and running water for the dishes he was apparently expected to clean for as long as they were staying in the same house together.

Since she was going to be stuck in Crystal Springs for a few days, anyway, Beth decided to call some of her old friends and touch base. Most of her high-school girlfriends had drifted away, but there were still a few she kept in touch with, a few still living in town.

She was embarrassed to admit it, but she'd nearly let them slip away, too. The occasional phone call when she wasn't working late, or a quickly scrawled note that she then asked her assistant to mail was about the extent of her contact with Jackie and Gail these past few years. And more often than not, those instances were prompted only by a friendly, if nosy, reminder from her mother.

Thankfully, neither of her friends seemed to hold it against her. Both were as giddy and upbeat as ever when she called, and wasted no time in talking her into going out with them to the Longneck, Crystal Springs's local watering hole, on Wednesday night.

She hadn't been out just for fun in years, probably since she'd moved to L.A. There were bars and clubs aplenty out there, of course, but it seemed that any time she got the chance to frequent them, it was for business purposes. Wooing prospective, high-profile clients or meeting with current, equally high-profile ones at a place of their choosing.

The only problem was that she needed a ride. Jackie worked part-time as a receptionist at a local medical clinic and was the mother of four, two still in diapers. Beth knew from previous conversations with her friend that their family's only car was a mess of toys, fast-food containers and diaper-bag supplies. So even if Jackie's husband hadn't needed the car that evening, she was in no hurry to ride around in a vehicle that smelled like sour milk and old French fries.

And Gail, who was married with no children, worked until seven in the evening. She'd insisted it was no problem to swing by and pick up both Jackie and Beth after she'd run home for a shower and change of clothes, but that would have meant not meeting at the Longneck until nine, which would keep them there probably well past midnight, which was too late for Jackie to be away from her kids.

All in all, it would just be easier for Beth to find her own ride.

She thought about renting a car, since it wasn't a bad idea to have transportation of her own while she was home. But the nearest car-rental agency was in the next big town over, forty-five minutes away. So whatever she decided, she'd still need a ride.

It pained her to do it, but she would have to ask Connor to drive her into town Wednesday night. After the way they'd parted company this morning, that would be about as much fun as hanging cinder blocks from her eyelids.

Leaving the office, she headed for the kitchen, thinking she might find him there. But the kitchen was empty, clean breakfast dishes propped and drying in the drainer beside the sink.

She smiled at that, remembering how she'd left them for him. It had been a truly beautiful moment... the flash of stunned disbelief that crossed his face and the fact that she'd been able to get in the last word of their highly charged exchange.

Too bad she was about to lose the upper hand by groveling for a ride into town.

She checked the living room next, and then the dining room, but the whole downstairs was empty. Maybe he was in Nick's room, which he was using as his own.

He'd better not be asleep or in any form of undress. She'd wait to ask him about the ride, if that was the case.

Climbing the stairs, she walked down the short hallway and tapped on her brother's open bedroom door. From what she could see, the bed was made, the blinds on the single window were open, and the only sign of Connor's residence was an open duffel on the floor by the dresser. He'd apparently gone home to his own house at some point to collect a few personal items and changes of clothes.

"Connor?" she called out when he didn't respond to her knock.

She was turning, planning to go back downstairs and see if his truck was even in the driveway, when she heard his muffled voice.

"Connor?"

"Yeah, in here," he repeated more loudly.

It sounded as if he was in Nick's old room—the one he'd occupied all through childhood, until their parents had moved to an apartment in a residential village across town. Karen had moved in with him then, and they'd taken over the master bedroom.

She turned the knob and pushed open the door, not knowing what to expect.

Connor stood on the far side of the room, holding a large cardboard box with Nick's Trophies written on the side in black Magic Marker. He dropped the box on a pile of others and turned to face her as she stepped into the room.

"Hi," he said, wiping his hands on the side of his pants.

"Hi. What are you doing in here?"

"Do you know if Nick and Karen have any plans for this room?" he asked, neatly avoiding her question.

She glanced around, taking in the plain, fawn-colored walls, complete with pinpricks from where Nick had tacked up dozens of posters, and the threadbare gray carpeting that had been there when her parents moved in more than thirty-five years before.

"No, I have no idea. Why?"

"Because it would make a great nursery, don't you think?"

His comment caught her off guard. The room had

been used for storage for so long, and had belonged to a teenage boy for a decade before that. It might be smarter to burn it down and start from scratch.

"I don't know, it looks a little grimy in here." She wrinkled her nose. "And it smells."

Connor chuckled. "Nick's sweaty old gym socks, no doubt. But that should be easy enough to take care of. Seriously," he said, shifting to stand by her side, shoulder to shoulder, facing the room. "Pull up the carpeting, slap on a fresh coat of paint, stick some pastel curtains on the windows, and fill the room with baby furniture... I'd say they'd have themselves a nursery."

He turned his head, meeting her gaze. "Wouldn't it be a great welcome-home present for them?"

"And who's going to do all this marvelous redecorating?" she wanted to know.

His mouth curved upward in a cocky grin. "You forget who you're talking to, sweetheart. Your brother and I are partners in our own contracting company, and we work the jobs ourselves ninety-five percent of the time, right along with our crews. I can have the floor stripped and refinished in no time. And how long could it take to paint four small walls?"

He nudged her in the ribs with his elbow. "Come on, have some faith. What do you say?"

Her brother and new sister-in-law would be delighted, she had no doubt about that. They would need a nursery eventually, anyway, and this way they wouldn't have to do any of the work.

With a small shrug, she said, "Do whatever you want. I'm sure Nick and Karen will appreciate it."

She started to turn, only to have Connor grab her arm, holding her in place. The warmth of his wide, full fingertips soaked straight through the silk of her blouse, heating her skin and thinning her blood.

"Wait." When she returned her attention to his face, he continued. "I thought maybe you could help."

Oh, no. That was too much to ask, too much to bear.

If he wanted to rip the room apart and rebuild, re-paint, remodel, it was his business. His carpentry skills were excellent, so she felt confident he wouldn't leave the room in shambles.

But she wanted nothing to do with it. Truth be told, she didn't even particularly want to know a nursery was being designed anywhere near her.

"I'd rather not," she said, lacing her arms across her chest in a protective gesture. Already she felt chilled, goose bumps rising along her arms and neck.

"Why not? You'd be great. You could help me pick out paint colors, curtains, border paper. Not to mention the crib, changing table, that sort of thing. I'm clueless about baby stuff."

And she was supposed to be so much more knowl-edgeable?

A stab of pain hit her low in the belly. She bit her lip to keep a moan from climbing its way up her throat and blinked her suddenly damp eyes.

"Don't you have to work this week?" she asked in-stead, hoping to divert his attention from how pale she knew her face must be.

"On and off, yeah, but this is a slow time of year for us. Nick wouldn't have agreed to take a two-week honeymoon if it weren't. Most of the deals we have going now are inside jobs, and our men can handle the work in my place for a few days. That's the beauty of owning your own company," he added with a self-assured smile.

Seconds ticked by so slowly, they felt like hours. Her head ached. Her ears buzzed. If he hadn't been holding her arm, she feared she might have fallen over.

"I really need your help, Beth. I'm not sure I can do this without you, and I want to have it done before Nick and Karen come home."

Something in his eyes seeped past her resistance. She didn't want to be involved. *Oh,* how she didn't want to be involved. But it would mean the world to Nick and Karen, Connor was right about that. And she was going to be an aunt soon. It was time to start getting used to the idea of being around a baby, whether she liked it or not.

Swallowing hard, she nodded. Her voice sounded rusty, but she forced the words past her dry lips. "All right. I guess I don't have anything better to do while I'm in town, anyway."

He didn't seem to take offense at her answer, even though she'd been half hoping he would. A nice ugly argument was exactly what she needed to drive away cold and painful memories.

Instead, his expression brightened and he gave her a quick hug. Not enough to get her hackles up, but a light, friendly embrace to say thanks.

"The hardware store is closed on Sundays, and everywhere else will be closing soon, too, so we might as well wait until tomorrow to go shopping for supplies. I'll start making a list right now. Wanna help?"

She shook her head. At the moment, she needed to be alone. She needed a drink and a hot bath and an hour or two to get her mind back on the present rather than wallowing in the past.

"You go ahead. I can add to it tomorrow if I think of anything you've missed."

"Sounds good." He gave her arm one last squeeze before heading out of the room.

"Oh, Connor," she said, stopping him before he could disappear down the hall.

"Yeah?"

She cleared her throat before saying more, not wanting him to hear the emotion in her voice. "Some friends of mine want to get together at the Longneck Wednesday night. Since I don't have a car, while I'm in town, I was wondering if you'd mind driving me. If it's too much trouble," she hurried on, "don't worry about it. I can always bum a ride from someone else, or rent a car between now and then."

She'd already thought through both of those ideas and knew they weren't going to be the least convenient, but if he had other plans, she could do it.

"No problem," he said with a shake of his head. Hitching his thumb into his front jeans pocket, he shot her a brief smile. "I haven't been to the Longneck in a while myself. It might be nice to go in to have a drink and catch up. Just let me know what time you want to leave, okay?"

She made her head move up and down in agreement, and after a moment, he left.

Beth stood where she was for several minutes, fighting back tears.

That hadn't been as hard as she'd expected, not after the punch to the gut he'd given her by asking her to help fix up and decorate a nursery.

She never should have come home. She *knew* it would be this way, *knew* bad memories and old wounds would be brought to the surface.

If only she'd gotten out of town right after the reception instead of agreeing to stay a few extra days to please her parents. If only she'd left the house as soon as she realized Connor would be staying here, too. Sleeping on the street would have been preferable to dealing with this deep, throbbing ache that seemed to take over her entire body.

And she had only herself to blame.

Beth waited until Connor was stretched out on the couch, feet propped on the coffee table, list of supplies on his lap while he sipped a beer and watched something on the sports channel, to sneak into the kitchen for a bottle of wine.

Tiptoeing back upstairs, she shut herself into the bathroom and started drawing a bath. She poured a generous amount of bubble bath into the stream of roaring water and then started to undress as the small room filled with the scent of lavender.

Once she was nude, she poured a glass of the rich red claret, set it on the rim of the tub, leaving the bottle within reach, and stepped inside the foaming, steaming water.

Ah, heaven, she thought as she turned off the water and slipped beneath its heady spell. A good bubble bath went a long way toward curing life's ills.

Unfortunately, it didn't go quite far enough tonight. She would need a lot more bubbles and a lot more wine to block out the memories her latest encounter with Connor had stirred up.

No. She wasn't going to think about that. Not anymore, not right now. This time was for healing, forgetting.

Taking another drink of wine, she leaned her head back against the edge of the tub, closed her eyes and tried to think of anything other than what weighed heaviest on her heart.

She thought about her brother's wedding, and how happy he and Karen had both looked while saying their vows. She thought about her parents' excited faces each time she stepped off the plane after being away for so long, often more than a year.

She thought about all the work that awaited when she got back to Los Angeles. Contracts to go over, phone calls to return, and likely a few high-strung celebrities to calm down.

The more her mind wandered to work issues, the sleepier she got, until her muscles began to relax and she could feel herself starting to fall asleep.

And then the funniest thing happened. Just before she drifted off completely, Connor's face played across her subconscious and pulled the lid right off of everything she'd been fighting so hard to keep under wraps.

Six

She was twenty-one again and a senior in college—old enough to drink but young enough to still feel carefree and invincible.

Most importantly, though, she was in love. And finally, after so many years of wishing and dreaming, she was pretty sure he was in love with her, too.

She'd gone home to Crystal Springs for the weekend, to visit her parents, and ended up going to a hometown football game with them, her brother and Connor. Afterward, she and Connor had gone off by themselves and ended up making love. Her first time and in the cab of his pickup, but as far as she was concerned, it had been absolutely perfect.

She'd been smiling ever since. Even her friends at

school had noticed and asked her about it, pressuring her for details.

But she wouldn't tell them, at least not yet. The entire experience was too new to her. Too special. Too private. It was something that only she and Connor shared, and she wanted to keep it that way a while longer.

A few days after she'd returned to school from her weekend home, though, her happiness began to fade. She'd expected Connor to call, but he hadn't.

The next time she phoned her parents, she'd even asked to talk to her brother and tried to subtly feel him out about his best friend. Had they seen each other or talked since she'd been home? Had Connor mentioned her at all? But her brother didn't seem to know anything and she hadn't wanted him to grow suspicious.

Connor would call; she was just too giddy and anxious to hear from him. In another day or two, he would call.

But the days passed, turning into weeks, and she never heard from him. Not a phone call, not an e-mail, not a short message passed to her through her family. Nothing.

And then she started getting sick. She didn't think much of it at first. A flu bug was going around campus and everyone seemed to be catching it, so she wasn't surprised when she started feeling ill like many of her friends.

Until her virus wouldn't seem to go away. Everyone else got better, but she still felt terrible. She also noticed that she was sick every morning, but started to feel better by the afternoon. By the time she realized she'd missed a period, she was already pretty sure she knew what was wrong.

She was pregnant.

With Connor's baby.

At first she was petrified. She was in her last year of law school…how was she ever going to reach graduation and be able to practice law when she was hugely pregnant or caring for a newborn? How would she tell Connor? What would her parents say when they found out?

So many thoughts and fears raced through her head, jumbling together until her nausea grew.

But what if motherhood was wonderful? What if Connor was delighted that he was going to be a father and proposed on the spot?

They could marry and move into a small house in Crystal Springs. She could do her best to finish school before the baby was born and worry about finding a job at a local law firm later.

The situation might not be ideal, but it could work. And her greatest ambition had always been to marry Connor and have a family with him…so what if they were starting a little early and doing things out of order?

Yes, everything would work out just fine. She would make plans to get home again soon and tell Connor in person.

Then, too, he could explain to her why he hadn't called since the night they spent together up at Make-out Point. She was sure he had a logical explanation and hadn't simply been ignoring her.

That thought kept her spirits up for the next two weeks while she struggled through the first month of pregnancy without letting anyone know what was really going on. It wasn't easy to keep her condition a secret, especially from her roommate, but she managed.

She was getting dressed for class one morning when the cramping began. The sensation was so dull and passed so quickly that she didn't think much of it. An hour later, though, after she'd returned from class, the cramping was much worse, and she knew something was seriously wrong. She went to the bathroom, only to find blood spotting her panties.

At that point, she didn't care who knew about her pregnancy. In tears, she'd gone to her roommate and begged her to help her get to the hospital.

But it was too late. She'd lost the baby.

She cried for weeks afterward. Her grades started to slip because of so many missed classes and exams, but no matter what her friends said or did to try to help her snap out of her depression, she remained inconsolable.

Not only that, but she began to harbor a deep resentment toward Connor, who she blamed for everything she'd been through.

He'd taken her virginity without a backward glance and left her to deal with the repercussions on her own. They'd known each other nearly all their lives, but she hadn't even warranted a phone call after they'd slept together.

Had he even once considered that she might get

pregnant and need his support? Of course not. Typical man—out for his own pleasure and to hell with the consequences.

And even though she hadn't gotten the chance to tell him about the baby, she blamed him for the miscarriage, too. If he'd called or driven up to the university to visit even once after they'd had sex, he would have known and they could have begun making plans together.

She might have moved back home with him and not had to keep to a hectic class schedule that wore her out and increased her stress level. Or he might have been with her when the first cramp hit and driven her to the doctor in time for the baby to be saved. Either way, she felt certain that the situation would have turned out differently if he had made any effort to contact her after their night together.

Even if she had still lost the baby, they could have grieved together, healed together, made plans to have another baby somewhere down the road.

Instead, she was alone and hurting, and it was all Connor's fault.

A sharp rap on the door jarred her awake. She sat up with a jerk, sending now-cool, bubbleless water sloshing over the edge of the tub.

Her face, she realized, was streaked with tears. Even in her sleep, she'd grieved for the child she'd lost all those years ago.

"Beth, you okay in there?"

Connor's voice permeated her still-sluggish brain,

adding the residual emotions causing her heart to ache. A wounded moan trembled from her lips and she covered her mouth to keep from being heard.

Pushing to her feet, she grabbed a towel from the rack on the wall and wrapped it around her naked torso. Rivulets of water sluiced down her skin, dripping onto the mat on the floor as she quickly patted herself dry.

"Beth?"

"Yes, I'm fine," she called out, embarrassed to be caught sleeping, dreaming, sobbing in the tub.

"You've been in there for quite a while, and I heard you cry out. Are you sure you're all right?"

Making sure to dry her face and remove any sign that she'd been weeping, she tucked the ends of the towel above her breasts and opened the bathroom door a crack. She made herself give him a small smile as their gazes met.

"I'm fine, Connor, really. I must have dozed off in the tub."

"You look a little pale," he pointed out, studying her from head to toe as much as he could through the narrow opening.

"I've been sitting in cold water too long, I guess," she said with forced cheerfulness. "I'm all pruny."

His eyes went dark at that, his lips thinning slightly.

"If you're sure you're okay…"

"I am, thank you. I'll be out in just a minute, in case you need to use the bathroom."

"No, I'm good," he said in a low tone. "I was just worried about you."

She didn't know what to say to that, and was afraid

she wouldn't be able to speak past the lump growing in her throat, so she merely nodded with downcast eyes and closed the bathroom door with a click.

Ten minutes later, she emerged with her hair freshly combed, wearing a short satin nightgown with matching sunflower yellow robe. Her feet were bare as she padded down the hardwood hallway and stairs, wineglass and bottle in hand.

Surprisingly, she was feeling better than when she'd first been startled awake from her dream…or maybe it had been more of a series of relived memories. Lord knew it was all true and had happened to her seven years before.

She tried not to think about those times any more than she had to, but being home and so near Connor muddied the waters and made it almost impossible to deny the past.

Still, it had been nice of Connor to check on her, to be worried about her. And for once, she hadn't snapped at him or thrown up her ice-princess veneer.

Being in Crystal Springs again reminded her of the kind, innocent girl she used to be. She hadn't had much of a chance to be either kind or innocent lately. Polite, civil, professional…but not naturally, sincerely, down-home pleasant.

Detouring through the kitchen, she retrieved a second wineglass, then headed for the living room, where Connor was once again propped on the couch watching television.

She wasn't sure why she felt compelled to talk with him. She could just as easily have gone to her room and avoided him until morning. But for once, her dreams or memories or whatever they were about the pregnancy and miscarriage didn't make her hate him more. For the first time, it occurred to her that she'd piled an awful lot of blame at his feet.

Yes, he'd gotten her pregnant. Yes, he'd failed to call afterward, which she still thought he should have done. But in the same vein, she could have just as easily called him—and should have after she realized that their night together had resulted in a baby.

And because he hadn't known, he really didn't bear any responsibility for the loss of that baby or for the roller-coaster ride her emotions took because of it.

She wasn't ready to tell him about the pregnancy and miscarriage…not now, maybe not ever…but it wouldn't hurt to sit and talk with him a bit. She hadn't exactly been Sister Mary Sunshine since they'd gotten stuck together in her brother's house.

He watched her cross the carpeted floor with hooded eyes, but to his credit, his gaze never wandered to her legs, bare from a little above midthigh down. As she took a seat on the sofa beside him, setting the long-stemmed glasses on the low coffee table, he sat up and cleared his throat.

"So what do you think—pizza for supper? I was just going to call one in."

She nodded, pouring them each a healthy portion of wine. "Sounds good to me."

Pushing himself up from the couch, he set his beer aside and sauntered to the phone. Her mood was just generous enough that she watched him walking away and appreciated the view. My, he really did fill out a pair of jeans nicely.

He dialed the local pizza place and ordered a large pie, then covered the mouthpiece and asked, "I'm getting the works on my half, what do you want on yours?"

She shouldn't, but she said, "The same." She'd make up for it later…maybe get up early in the morning and go running, regardless of the weather.

"Make that one large with everything," he told the person on the other end, then gave his name and directions to the house.

Once that was done, he moved back to the sofa and reached for his beer, but she handed him a glass of wine instead.

He eyed her warily for a moment before accepting the dark claret. No doubt he was wondering if she'd slipped some sort of poison into his drink. Considering her attitude so far this week, she couldn't blame him.

"What's the occasion?" he asked, taking a small sip.

She leaned back against the overstuffed cushions, balancing her painted toes on the edge of the coffee table, mimicking Connor's relaxed pose.

"Nothing special. I just thought it was awfully nice of you to worry about me when I disappeared into the bathroom for so long, and I wanted to thank you."

"It wouldn't do for my best friend to come home from his honeymoon and discover I'd let his little sister drown," he quipped.

She grinned. "No, I guess it wouldn't. Although, after the way I've treated you since discovering we'd both be staying here for a few days, I'm surprised you didn't come in and try to hold me under."

One side of his mouth quirked up at that. "Thought about it. Didn't want a criminal record."

"Gee, thanks."

Time passed while they enjoyed their wine, the only sound in the room coming from the low volume of the television, playing a family sitcom.

The calm serenity of the moment washed over her. She hadn't felt this way in far too long…weightless, almost light-headed, without a care in the world. It was a far cry from her life back in L.A., where she had to keep on her toes and almost every waking moment was filled with tension.

She never got to sit and just unwind. Or if she did, it was alone, not in the company of a handsome, average, everyday guy who preferred beer to martinis and pizza to nouveau cuisine. It was comforting to know Connor didn't care what she was wearing, whether her makeup was flawless, or every strand of hair was in place.

As desperately as she'd been avoiding him for nearly a decade, she had to admit she could be herself around him. He'd seen her with scraped knees and gum in her hair. Sobbing her heart out when her pet cat had been killed by a car. While her eyes were red and swollen, her nose running, he'd helped her bury Zoey in the backyard. He'd even seen her throw up macaroni and cheese in the school cafeteria when she was nine, and had been the only student other than her brother not laughing, pointing or making gross gagging noises. Instead, he'd put his arm around her shoulders and walked her to the nurse's office, waiting with her until her mom came to pick her up.

Growing up, he'd been her hero. If she were being honest with herself, she'd have to admit he still was. An imperfect one, true, but still her hero.

Everybody was entitled to a few mistakes in their lifetime, weren't they?

Hmm. Taking another slow sip of wine, she let her head fall back against the couch, balancing the glass on her upper thigh. She must really be feeling relaxed if she was thinking about forgiving him.

But she didn't know if she was ready to be *that* charitable just yet. It was enough that she was even allowing it as an option. She considered that growth— and quite enough growth for one night. After all, Rome wasn't built in a day, and seven-year-old emotional wounds couldn't be healed that quickly, either.

"Do you ever wonder," Connor said in a low murmur, breaking into her thoughts, "what might have happened if we hadn't grown up together? If we'd met each other back then as complete strangers?"

She didn't need him to identify what he meant by "back then." He was talking about that night again.

Surprisingly, her stomach didn't clutch and her temperature didn't begin to rise. Her muscles did tense, but she took another small drink of wine and mentally forced herself to relax.

He obviously needed to talk about it—he'd certainly

cornered her often enough—but she had never been in a frame of mind to listen before. She wasn't sure how long she could listen now, either, but at least she was willing to give it a shot.

"I'm not sure I know what you mean," she said softly, rolling her head on the sofa cushion to look at him.

"I've always thought of you as my sister, Beth. You were Nick's sister by blood, but we grew up together, your family practically adopted me, so it felt like you were my sister, too."

His brandy brown eyes darkened, the corners crinkling slightly as he offered a tight smile. "But we both know I didn't treat you like a sister that night after the football game, in the cab of my truck. I've been wanting to apologize for that for years."

Her heart squeezed for a moment and the old anger and pain tried to break through. She tamped it down, determined not to backslide into her previous attitude and mind-set.

"Why would you apologize? You weren't in the truck by yourself."

"I took advantage of you," he pushed on, glossing over any responsibility she might take for her own actions. "You were young and confused…and a virgin. I was older and more experienced, I should have stopped things before they got out of hand."

With a harsh laugh, she said, "You can get down off the cross now, Connor, no one's blaming you for taking my virginity. I wouldn't have been in your truck if I hadn't wanted to be, and I wouldn't have had sex with you if I hadn't wanted to, either."

From the corner of her eyes, she saw his thumb rubbing absently up and down the stem of his wineglass.

"That still doesn't make it right," he told her. "Your parents have always treated me like one of their own. They trusted me to take care of you, protect you...not to take advantage of you."

"For the last time, you didn't take advantage of me."

With all the negative thoughts she'd had toward him over the years, that had never been one of them.

"Connor," she said in a near whisper, "from the time I turned thirteen, I had a huge crush on you."

It cost her to admit it, but if he'd been living with this guilt for seven years, he deserved to know the truth. Granted, a part of her wanted him to feel guilty, but about other things. About not calling her after their night together. About not making a point of finding out if there were repercussions—such as an unplanned pregnancy—involved.

But this conversation, this delicate peace they seemed to have developed, wasn't about that, it was about setting him straight on what he *was* feeling guilty over.

"I don't know how you could have missed it," she continued with a light laugh. "I was positively cow-eyed over you. I followed you and Nick around like a puppy, wrote 'Mrs. Connor Riordan' in my notebooks a thousand times and did everything I could think of to catch your attention. I *wanted* to be with you that night. If anything, I orchestrated it so that the situation would play out exactly as it did."

He was sitting up on the sofa now, his arms resting

on his denim-clad thighs, staring at her. She straightened under his intense gaze, resisting the need to squirm with embarrassment at her admission.

At least he wasn't laughing at her. She wasn't sure she'd have been able to bear that.

But Connor looked anything but amused by her confession. His eyes were blazing, warming her from head to toe with something other than the flush of humiliation.

"I never knew," he said finally, his voice rasping like velvet over sandpaper.

Blowing out a breath, he ran the splayed fingers of one hand through his short, dirty-blond hair. "And I wish to hell I had, because I felt the same damn way."

Shock and disbelief slammed into her like a bolt of lightning. For a moment, she felt dizzy, almost as though she were floating outside of her body.

This wasn't happening, not really. She was still asleep in the tub upstairs, and her dream had segued from memories of the past into some sordid mix of her juvenile hopes and her present circumstances with Connor.

But then he started speaking again, and even though the words roared in her ears, she could hear them, make out what he was saying.

"I watched you grow up and kept telling myself that you were as much as my sister. Your family was my family...I had no business being attracted to you." He paused to take a deep breath. "But I was. God knows I fought it, and I never would have admitted to it, not even under penalty of death, but there it was. Every time you walked down the hall at school or into a class-room. Every time I came over to see your brother and you were bopping around in sweatpants and a skimpy little tank top, I just about swallowed my tongue.

"And then that night after the football game, I couldn't seem to help myself. You were so beautiful, and I'd been wanting you for so long."

All these years, she thought she'd thrown herself at him and he'd only slept with her because...well, he was a man and she'd been available. But the whole time she had a crush on him, he'd been interested in her, too? It was too much to absorb all at once.

She shook her head, trying to clear her mind and her vision. "I can't believe this," she murmured.

He shifted closer to her on the sofa. Their legs touched, the denim of his jeans brushing against her bare skin. He reached out with one hand and covered her thigh just below the hem of her nightie, his thumb drawing circles on the smooth, sensitive flesh of her inner knee.

"I know. All this time we've felt the same way about each other without even realizing it."

He paused for a moment, his gaze zeroing in on her lips, which suddenly felt so dry, she darted her tongue out to moisten them.

"You know what else?" he asked in a low tone that slid down her spine like warm honey as he leaned in even closer. "I still do...want you."

Seven

As soon as their mouths touched, the years melted away and every fantasy he'd ever had that revolved around Beth flooded his mind.

Her lips were warm beneath his, closed at first, and then parting until their tongues touched. She tasted of the claret they'd been drinking—and something else, something uniquely Beth.

His fingertips slid beneath the hem of her short, sexy nightgown, caressing the silken smoothness of her legs and traveling higher. She seemed as involved in the kiss as he was, her hands cupping the back of his head, tangling in his hair.

With a groan, he pressed her back against the sofa,

one arm around her waist to keep her flush with his chest and lower body.

She smelled so good. Fresh from her bath, with her hair still damp in places and falling down her back in a loose, carefree tangle. He could feel the budding of her nipples through the layers of fabric separating their bodies, and he wanted them in his mouth, against his palms.

He abandoned her mouth, only to pay homage to her chin, her jawline, the pouty little lobe of her ear. She arched into him, a purr of pleasure rumbling low in her throat. And then she lifted one leg to hug his hips and the desire already pumping through his veins like a drug shot straight to his groin.

He ground against her, wishing they were naked already so he could be inside her at that very moment. His lips dragged down the column of her neck, the tip of his tongue darting out to trace the line of her collarbone.

From there, he kissed his way to her breast, licking the pearled tip through the slinky material covering her. A wet patch began to grow and he fed it, opening his mouth wider, suckling her until she moaned and held his head in place.

Power surged, lust arcing between them so strongly, he felt almost light-headed. He wanted her—more than he could remember ever wanting another woman. Possibly more than he'd wanted her even back in high school.

Reaching down, he tugged at the bottom of her nightie and dragged the yellow fabric to her waist. His knuckles brushed the sides of her high-cut panties and he started to sweat.

He had to have her. Now, before she changed her

mind or he admitted all the reasons they shouldn't be together.

Their hands went for the waistband of his jeans at the same time. Eyes meeting, chests heaving, they both gave a breathless chuckle.

His pants opened with a snap and her hand was on the zipper covering his straining erection when the doorbell rang.

His heart stuttered to a stop and then sank as her fingers stilled at their task. For a split second, he considered grabbing her up and kissing her silly, until she forgot about the door, forgot about being interrupted, forgot even her own name.

But already the passion was clearing from her gaze, replaced by stark reality. She didn't look horrified, exactly, but she also didn't look ready to roll to the floor and finish what they'd started.

The doorbell buzzed again.

"I think that's the pizza," she said finally, her voice husky with unspent desire.

"Yeah." He held her gaze for another minute, concentrating on his breathing and trying to get some of the blood that had taken up residence south of the border back to his brain.

His chin dropped to his chest when the delivery guy switched from leaning on the bell to pounding on the door frame.

"Coming," he barked, pushing to his feet and crossing the living room. He tugged at the front of his jeans, attempting to alleviate the pressure behind his fly and then dug in his hip pocket for his wallet.

As soon as he opened the door, a gangly teenage boy in a Pizza Palace T-shirt shoved the flat white box at him and snapped out the price. Connor threw in an extra five for the kid's trouble before kicking the door closed with the toe of his boot.

When he turned, Beth was off the couch, arranging her short, shimmery robe to cover the wet spots his mouth had made on her bodice. The memory slugged him in the gut and sent the air from his lungs with a whoosh.

If he had his way, he'd toss the pizza on the kitchen table, stalk back across the living room and sweep her off her feet so they could pick up where they'd left off. He wouldn't give her time to think or breathe or protest.

But Beth didn't look as if she was ready or willing to return to that place of passion where they'd just been.

He sighed. Too bad. He'd thought they were making progress.

"Pizza smells good," he said, hoping to break the tension growing between them. "Wanna get some plates?"

"Sure." The arms that had been hugging her waist fell to her sides as she headed for the kitchen from the opposite direction.

He wasn't offended by her decision to avoid brushing past him. He understood her need for distance, even if he didn't particularly like it.

Crossing back to the sofa, he set the box on the long rectangular coffee table and took a seat to pop open the lid. A second later, Beth sat down beside him, two din-ner plates and a stack of napkins in hand.

He served up two slices on each plate, then refilled their wineglasses. Beth accepted the pizza he offered, balancing it on her knees while her eyes remained downcast.

"Maybe I should take mine up to my room," she murmured, brushing a lock of hair behind one ear. "You could finish watching your television show or what-ever."

She wouldn't look at him, and Connor nearly cursed.

Where had the hot, frantic woman from only mo-ments ago gone? Or even the prickly, sharp-tongued one from earlier in the day?

"No, don't do that," he said, brushing his hand down the length of her arm. His touch didn't linger, and he was relieved that she didn't stiffen up on him. "Stay here. We'll stick in a DVD and stuff ourselves silly."

At first, she didn't answer him. Then she raised her head, met his eyes and curled her lips in a small smile. "All right. But I get to pick the film."

He threw himself against the back of the couch, clutching his chest and giving an exaggerated groan. "Oh, no. Not some girlie movie."

Her grin widened. "Maybe."

She took a bite off the tip of her pizza slice, then got up and sauntered to the entertainment center on the other side of the room.

Connor watched her go, admiring the sway of her bottom and the long, pale line of her legs. She looked like a million bucks, and in that sunny-colored nightgown, good enough to eat. Next to her, the pizza he'd been so hungry for only an hour before might as well have been cardboard.

After shuffling around in the cupboard, she placed a disc in the player on top of the television, then made her way back to the sofa. She kept her distance this time, leaving one full cushion between them before retrieving her glass of wine and pressing Play on the remote control.

"Should I be worried?" he asked around a mouthful of cheese and crust and assorted toppings.

Her shoulder lifted and fell, but her eyes never left the television screen. "Depends."

The opening credits began to play, along with music he recognized. He grinned as he realized she'd chosen one of his favorites…Keanu Reeves and Sandra Bullock trying to stay alive on a speeding bus. It was an action/adventure flick, but could probably also be categorized as a romance.

"A woman after my own heart," he told her, taking an even bigger bite of pizza.

"I'm a Curtis," she retorted, "so of course I have exceptional taste."

"Uh-huh. I'm just glad I didn't let you order the pizza. We might have ended up with some horrible tofu-and-pineapple concoction."

"Don't scoff. Tofu is good for you."

"I'll stick with my meat and vegetables, thanks."

"Suit yourself." She picked at a green pepper melted into the cheese of what was left of her first slice. "You know, I'm going to have to run ten miles tomorrow to burn this off."

Even as she said it, she lifted the crust to her lips, so he knew she must not be too concerned.

"Maybe I'll go with you." He blurted it out before he had a chance to rethink the idea, but when she shot him a look of pure disbelief, he almost wished he'd kept his mouth shut.

So he didn't make a habit of jogging. He worked hard on a daily basis, building and renovating houses—carrying lumber, shingles, climbing ladders... And he stopped at the gym once in a while, though probably not as often as he should. No, he didn't tend to put on shorts and sneakers and go running around the neighborhood—but for Beth, he'd be willing to give it a try.

"What?" he asked, feigning insult. "You don't think I can run?"

"Oh, I'm sure you can run. Away from a bear. Toward a cold beer. But for exercise?" She laughed, and then covered her mouth with a napkin when she started to choke. "No, I'm sorry, I can't picture that."

He quirked a brow, staring hard until her gaze faltered. "Fine. I'll just have to prove it to you. What time do you want to go in the morning?"

"Six."

That wasn't even particularly early for him. He was up before that lots of mornings in order to get to job sites on time.

"Six it is."

She eyed him warily over the rim of her wineglass. "You're really going through with this, huh?"

"Just see if you can keep up."

* * *

Beth was trying hard not to laugh. She concentrated on her pace and her breathing, struggling not to burst a lung with the effort to hide her amusement.

He was hanging in there, she'd give him that.

He'd been up bright and early this morning, already dressed in shorts and a T-shirt when she'd come downstairs. The sneakers were Nick's, found in a hall closet, he told her, but they seemed to fit well enough. Connor and Nick had always been about the same size, sharing clothes and shoes and everything else.

They'd grabbed bottles of water before heading out, then started at a slow trot from the curb. It was still dusky outside, with just a hint of sunrise peeking through on the bluish purple horizon.

And it was chilly. That odd time of year when true winter has passed, but spring hadn't quite made its birds-and-flowers appearance yet. The ground was wet, the air chilly, the sky studded with clouds.

At first, Connor did great. He even seemed to be doing better than she was, since she was used to running on a state-of-the-art treadmill at the gym with her headset to keep her company instead of an unswept, leaf- and gravel-strewn sidewalk with the sounds of dogs barking and car doors slamming as neighbors left for work.

Jogging side by side, they chatted about the weather—typical for central Ohio at this time of year, but a far cry from the sunny California she was used to—and some of the items they needed to pick up at the hardware store later that day to start work on the nursery.

Then she'd kicked it up a notch, increasing her pace and working her arms for the added burn. She gave him credit for his effort, but it wasn't long before he fell behind and started heaving for breath.

Not that he was out of shape. Far from it, judging by his firm thighs and calves, and the rippling muscles outlined beneath his sweat-dampened T-shirt. He was simply used to a different kind of exercise—hauling and sawing and hammering.

She pictured him in his usual uniform of faded jeans and open flannel shirt, doing what he did best amidst sawhorses and power tools, and nearly lost her footing.

Righting herself, she glanced at Connor from her peripheral vision and decided he'd had enough. They'd been out for at least an hour, and stubborn as he was, he would probably keep running until it killed him, just to prove a point.

She slowed a bit, waiting for him to catch up as the house came into view. It was lighter now, though still overcast, with a hint of rain in the air. Likely that storm the lady at the airline had warned her about...though she still thought she should have been able to get a flight out before it hit.

"You doing okay?" she asked, knowing full well what his answer would be.

"Oh, yeah," he huffed, beads of sweat rolling down his face. "I could keep running like this all day."

Sure he could. She turned her head so he wouldn't see her grin.

"That's great," she said, "but I think we've had enough for today. With any luck, we've burned off at least one slice of pizza and one glass of wine from last night."

They stopped at the walk to her brother's house. She continued to jog in place until her heart rate slowed while Connor bent at the waist, hands on his knees as he fought to fill his lungs with oxygen.

Her breathing was labored, too, but she was used to it. She loved it, actually, found it exhilarating.

"I say we get cleaned up and go into town."

Part of the reason she'd wanted to go running was to offset some of her anxiety about not only spending the day shopping and working with Connor, but about buying baby things and concentrating on designing a nursery.

She knew it would be difficult, was already bracing herself for the pain. Surprisingly, though, she now felt more prepared for the task. Not exactly looking forward to it, but stronger and better able to handle whatever emotions the day stirred up.

"Sounds good. Do you want first dibs on the shower?"

He straightened, wiping his forehead with the tail of his shirt, giving her a clear glimpse of those tight, well-defined abdominals she'd fantasized about earlier. It was enough to make a girl drool.

She took a long swig of water to wet her parched throat, wiping the corners of her mouth afterward, just in case.

"No, you go ahead."

He looked as if he needed it more. And besides, she could use a few minutes alone before getting undressed and stepping into the shower. If she went upstairs now, she would have to turn the spray to full cold, but if she waited a while, she might be able to go with moderate to lukewarm.

"You sure?"

She nodded, starting up the front steps and fitting the key in the lock.

Brushing past her, he made his way through the house and up the stairs. She listened to his footfalls, followed by the sound of the water coming on in the bathroom.

While he was busy in the shower, she put their half-empty bottles of water in the fridge, then went to her room to lay out an outfit for the rest of the day. She hadn't packed work clothes...wasn't sure she even owned true down-and-dirty work clothes anymore. But she found a pair of navy blue slacks and a lightweight tan knit top that would hopefully be casual enough—as long as Connor didn't put her to work painting or scrubbing.

The water in the bathroom cut off, and she heard him moving around for a few minutes before the door opened. When she glanced up, he was standing in the hall just outside her bedroom.

His close-cropped hair was wet, making it appear more dark brown than dirty blond. A drop of water fell from one of the spiky locks, rolling down his temple, cheek and stubbled jawline before dripping onto his bare chest.

What a fine chest it was, too. Broad and firm. Smooth in places, a sprinkling of light hair in others.

She watched the drop of water slide past one flat, bronze nipple to the plane of his washboard stomach. A few inches below, a stark white towel was wrapped around his hips.

"The bathroom is all yours," he said in a low tone.

Licking her lips, she dragged her gaze back to his face. His eyes smoldered, lips twisted in the hint of a grin.

Great. Not only had she ogled him, but he'd caught her at it.

Way to maintain your distance, Beth, she thought with derision.

Then again, their little makeout session on the couch last night hadn't exactly screamed *disinterest*.

"Thanks," she said, embarrassed when her voice actually squeaked.

She'd moved to L.A. to get away from Connor and had matured by leaps and bounds. But ever since returning to Crystal Springs, she seemed to be regressing to her pathetic, high-school-crush persona.

All the more reason to get out of here and fly back to California as soon as possible. Maybe then she could regain a bit of her equilibrium.

Seconds ticked by while they stood there staring at each other. They didn't speak, didn't move until stars started to burst behind Beth's eyeballs and she realized she'd been holding her breath almost the entire time.

With conscious effort, she exhaled and began to breathe normally. Turning, she gathered the pile of fresh clothes from the bed, then slipped through the doorway and toward the bathroom, careful not to touch Connor's bare arm or chest as she passed.

"I'll only be a few minutes," she told him.

"Take your time."

She cast one last glance over her shoulder before closing the bathroom door, and a shiver raced down her spine at the look of lustful intent on his face.

Worse yet was the echo of that expression strumming low in her belly.

The door clicked shut, and she released a weary sigh.

It looked as if she'd be taking that cold shower, after all.

"Clowns are passé."

"Oh, and teddy bears are all the rage?"

Beth cocked a hip and crossed her arms beneath her breasts. "At least they're cute and cuddly." She pointed to one of the clowns on the border wallpaper he was holding. "Those are downright scary."

He lowered his gaze and studied the colorful artwork for a minute, then stuck the roll back on the rack. "You're right. These clowns would probably give the kid nightmares. But I can't say I love the bears."

The teddy-bear border in her hand was cute—soft and cuddly in an array of pastels. But he had a point; they were kind of boring and probably like every other border in every other nursery in the world.

"All right. No clowns and no teddy bears. What are our other options?"

They started to investigate their choices again, and she thought—not for the first time—how much she was enjoying herself.

She hadn't expected to. If anything, she'd been prepared for the day to be akin to shoving bamboo shoots under her fingernails.

After they were both cleaned up, dressed and had grabbed a quick breakfast of toast and orange juice, they'd headed for the hardware store. Beth pretty much let Connor take the lead there, since he made his living building things. Her knowledge of carpentry didn't extend much beyond the difference between a hammer and measuring tape.

He'd bought supplies to make some new shelving, and to pull up the old carpet and refinish the hardwood floor beneath. If the floor was in too much disrepair to be left bare, he'd told her, they'd go out and buy new carpeting later.

But now they were in Crystal Springs's one and only retail store, and she'd taken over the shopping list. They were holding off buying furniture…partly because there wouldn't be space to store it until the room was finished, and partly because she didn't think they could be completely sure what type of crib, changing table or rocking chair they needed until everything else was done. They were waiting to decide on curtains and area rugs for the same reason.

Unfortunately, they'd made the mistake of buying paint already at the hardware store. In retrospect, they'd have been better off waiting until they picked out a border or other items before settling on a color for the room. It was too late now, though; the soft seafoam, a cross between green and blue that would be perfect for either a boy or a girl, was already mixed and waiting in the back of Connor's truck.

"What about this?" Beth asked, holding up a roll of paper for him to see, along with the paint sample they'd brought along from the hardware store. "The blues and greens will match," she said. "And the little sea creatures are just adorable."

There were playful dolphins and turtles, orcas and jellyfish…even a few sharks and octopi that anyone would find charming.

Connor met her gaze and gave her one of those sexy, lopsided grins that filled her belly with butterfly wings. "I like it. We could even buy a bunch of stuffed animals for the crib and shelves and rocker to match."

"You don't think Nick and Karen will be upset that we're choosing the theme of the nursery for them?" she asked, voicing a concern she'd had since the beginning.

"Nah. They'll love it. And if there's anything they don't like, we just have to make it clear that we won't be hurt or offended if they change it. After all, it is their house and their baby."

"Yeah," she agreed, fighting not to let the moment turn bittersweet. "We should probably keep that in mind."

"We will. Now grab up a bunch of those so we can get moving."

She did as he requested, filling her arms with the number of wallpaper rolls they'd agreed earlier should do the trick and dumping them in the shopping cart.

"Only one thing left on the list." He stood with legs splayed, hands on hips, studying her from head to toe.

"What?" She looked down at herself. Had she spilled orange juice on her sweater earlier?

"Are those the best work clothes you have, or were you going to change when we get back home?"

Biting her bottom lip, she linked her arms self-consciously across her waist. "I'm afraid this is it. I didn't exactly pack for my brother's wedding with the intention of getting sweaty and dirty." And she didn't exactly spend a lot of time getting sweaty and dirty back in L.A., unless it was at her personal trainer's command.

Connor's nostrils flared at that, his eyes wandering back to the area of her breasts. She bit her lip to keep from fidgeting under his concentrated scrutiny.

"Well, that won't do. Sorry. We're going to have to buy you some jeans and T-shirts."

"Are you sure?" She cast another glance at her dark slacks with their nearly razor-sharp creases down the front from where they'd been pressed and folded with almost military precision, and the expensive sweater she really wasn't looking forward to ruining.

"Yep. It's gotta be done." Pressing his palm to the mesh end of the cart, he gave it a little shove, nudging her in the side. "Come on...to women's clothing we go."

She turned obediently and started walking in the direction he pointed.

"Do you really want to take the time for me to try on work clothes?" she asked, half hoping he'd change his mind.

Instead, he speared her with a cocky grin, keeping the cart on course. "Oh, yeah. I'm looking forward to it. If I'm lucky, I figure you might even let me in the dressing room with you to see how everything fits."

She shot him a quelling glare. "Keep dreaming, bub."

But as she slipped between the racks of blue jeans to hunt for a pair in her size, she thought she heard him murmur, "Oh, I will, believe me."

Eight

The sounds of sawing and hammering echoed through the house, along with music from a radio they'd set up in the hall. They'd been working for three days straight, and Beth had to admit the room was looking good.

Connor was in charge, no doubt about it. But he was a good boss, explaining what needed to be done and showing her how to handle certain things without growing short on patience or making her feel stupid.

So far, they'd taken down the plain, dusty white curtains from the windows, pulled up the old, worn carpet from the floor and repolished the golden wood beneath. Now the floor was covered with plastic and drop cloths, and Connor had set up sawhorses and a wide array of tools to use while he worked.

At the moment, he was standing on a ladder on the far side of the room, looking sexier than any man had a right to. His gray cotton shirt molded to his back and biceps like a second skin, and his jeans rode low on his narrow hips, showcasing his truly spectacular rear. And if that wasn't enough to drive every sensible thought from her mind, the tool belt strapped around his waist actually turned her on. She could watch him remove and replace tools from the worn leather all day.

There was just something about a man who was good with his hands…

Shaking her head, she turned back to what she was supposed to be doing. Connor was tacking up beautiful crown molding and she was putting the first coat of seafoam paint on the walls. The artfully carved strips of wood he was handling were bare now, but later they would paint them white to create a bright, clean border along the ceiling.

She dipped her roller in the pan of paint on the floor and took up where she'd left off before Connor's fluid, masculine movements had distracted her.

He'd been right about her needing a set of work clothes, too. As careful as she tried to be, after three days of manual labor, she was covered with specks of paint, streaks of dirt and a layer of sawdust. She'd even managed to snag her bright red Hot Stuff ballerina tee in two different places.

As she transformed the walls from boring eggshell to a green-blue sea fit for the marine life they would eventually add, she hummed along and danced a little to the B-52's song playing in the background.

"You having fun over here?"

Connor's voice, coming from just over her left shoulder, caused her to jump and splash more paint on herself.

"Geez," she yelped, pressing her free hand to her heart. "You scared the life out of me."

"Sorry," he said with a sneaky grin that told her he wasn't sorry at all. His gaze moved back to the wall she'd been working on. "Looks good. You should come to work for Nick and me."

"Thanks."

She grinned with obvious pleasure, the light in her eyes slipping under his skin and twisting his guts.

God, she was beautiful. Over the last seven years, he thought he'd made more of her appearance than there was. Imagined the glossy russet of her hair, the periwinkle blue of her eyes, the sparkle in her smile.

But if anything, she looked better than he remembered. Confident, alluring…she'd really grown into herself.

When he'd finished with the last piece of molding and turned to see how she was doing with the walls, he'd just about fallen off the ladder. She was stroking the paint roller up and down, and doing some kind of little jiggle in time with the music from the radio that had her hips swaying and her bottom rocking, the hem of her top riding up to show an inch of creamy torso.

It was enough to send him into cardiac arrest, which was why he'd slipped his hammer into his tool belt and very carefully climbed down off the ladder before he tripped over his wagging tongue and broke his neck.

He cleared his throat, dragging his attention back to the present. "If you're about finished, I say we wrap things up for today and start getting ready to head over to the Longneck. You're still meeting your friends there, right?"

She looked startled for the space of a heartbeat before lowering the paint roller and sticking her hands in the back pockets of those low-riding jeans.

"Oh, yeah. I didn't realize it was so late already. What time is it?"

With a quick glance at his watch, he said, "Almost six. We probably have time to grab a quick bite after we get cleaned up and dressed, unless you plan to order dinner at the bar."

"We probably will get something to eat there. You're welcome to join us," she added in a low voice.

At first he thought she was only being polite, but he could tell by the look in her eyes that the offer was sincere. And for a minute, he seriously considered taking her up on it, if only as an excuse to stay close to her.

"Thanks, but I think I'll pass," he finally forced himself to respond. "You and your friends probably want a little time alone to bash men and discuss panty lines."

She laughed, wiping the back of her wrist across her nose. The gesture left a small streak of seafoam paint behind.

"Is that what you really think women talk about when they get together?"

He shrugged. "I'm close, aren't I?" he murmured, distracted by that tiny smudge and the energy it took to keep from reaching out and wiping it away.

"Only if one of us has recently been dumped. Then, I admit, we're none too charitable about the opposite sex. But other than that, we don't usually spend much time disparaging the male race."

"So what do you talk about?"

"Our jobs, our families. Once in a while we do discuss the latest fashions, but that's usually after we've had a couple of drinks or run out of other topics of conversation."

"Good to know," he said, and then gave in to temptation by lifting a hand and brushing the paint from the tip of her nose. When she gave him an odd look, he held up his fingers to show the blue-green tint.

"Thanks." She rubbed absently at the spot herself. "Guess we both need a shower."

Connor's blood thickened and pooled low in his belly at her words. Being this close to her, watching her breasts rise and fall as she breathed, smelling her spicy floral perfume was sheer torture.

He wanted to do more than reach out and swipe paint from her nose. He wanted to grab her up and kiss her senseless. Run his fingers through that long, silky mass of chestnut hair. Suggest they conserve water and shower together…or skip bathing altogether and head straight for the bedroom.

Swallowing hard, he made himself stop that train of thought before it got out of hand. Or worse, he acted on it.

That night on the couch had been a fluke. They'd had wine on empty stomachs and gotten a little carried away.

For God's sake, Beth had barely spoken to him during the last seven years, and he was living with another woman. At least, he had been until very recently.

This…whatever it was…must be residual attraction from their teenage and young-adult years. Unresolved issues from their one night together.

As soon as she flew back to California—which would probably be sooner rather than later—whatever was between them would pass. The electricity, the longing, the teeth-rattling, knee-buckling lust.

They would both get over it and go on with their respective lives, so it was better not to start anything now, no matter how much he might wish it could be otherwise. Especially something that would cause them to avoid each other for another seven to ten years.

The same as in high school, he never wanted to do anything to hurt her or her family. Nothing to cause tension or pain between them…between any of them. Beth and him, Nick and him, Beth and her parents, or her parents and him.

It was a tangled, convoluted mess, and he felt like a fly struggling uselessly to free itself from the sticky web of a hungry spider. Except that he was as responsible for spinning this particular web as anyone else.

Unfastening his tool belt, he lowered it carefully to the newly polished hardwood floor. "We should probably start getting ready," he told her, though it was the last thing he wanted to do.

He would much prefer to spend the evening just like this. With Beth, standing close, looking into her eyes, maybe curling up on the couch to watch another

movie. Even if nothing happened between them—
which it wouldn't, *couldn't*—being alone with Beth
still beat hanging out at the Longneck any day of the
week.

"Right."

She glanced away guiltily and turned to clean up her
work area, but not before he saw the tip of her tongue
dart out to wet her lips.

Damn. He had to get out of here before he did something stupid, like pulling her up from where she now
crouched on the floor, pressing her back against the wall,
and taking her the way he'd imagined for over a decade.

Man, he was warped. He'd just finished convincing
himself he needed to walk away, keep his distance, yet
here he was picturing her with her top yanked up and
her legs wrapped around his waist.

Struggling for breath, he asked, "Do you need any
help?"

She cocked her head, fixing him with those soft
blue eyes. "No, that's all right. Thanks, though. I just
want to get the lid on this paint, then I'll stick the roller
and brushes in the sink to soak while I get cleaned up.
How about you?"

"I'm good." Or doomed. He hitched a thumb over his
right shoulder. "I'll start getting ready. It shouldn't take
me more than a few minutes, then I can be out of your
way."

Beth nodded. "Take your time. Gail and Jackie
won't care if I'm a little late."

Inclining his head, he turned and started through the
doorway to the hall.

"Oh, and Connor?" she called after him.

He turned back, giving her his undivided attention. "Yeah?"

"Women don't usually talk about panty lines when they get together because we already know how to avoid them."

"How's that?" he asked, his voice thick with restrained arousal.

"Simple. Don't wear panties."

She shot him a quick, wicked smile, then turned back to what she was doing while he stood there like a deer caught in headlights.

Damn.

The Longneck was already jumping when they walked in a few minutes after eight. Music blared from the jukebox along the far wall, couples two-stepped across the dance floor, and just about every table and seat at the bar was occupied.

"Wow, it's really busy for a Wednesday night." She leaned close to Connor, raising her voice to be heard over the din of the music and crowd. His arm was at her waist, but she let it go, telling herself it was a protective gesture only, to keep her from getting jostled around by the bar's exuberant patrons.

"You should see it on Friday and Saturday nights. This is tame in comparison."

She returned his grin with one of her own. She'd forgotten what it meant to go out and have fun in Crystal Springs. No stiletto heels, skintight sheaths or sparkling diamonds necessary. No fancy mixed drinks in even fancier glasses. In central Ohio, jeans were dressy enough for both men and women, and beer was the beverage of choice, whether it came in a bottle or a frosted glass.

This type of thing hadn't been her scene for a very long time, so she was surprised by how comfortable she felt the minute she walked through the door. Even the loud country music, which normally would have set her on the fast track to a migraine, seemed to seep into her bones instead. She found herself tapping her toe already.

"Are your friends here yet?" he wanted to know.

"One of them is." She pointed across the room at the booth her friend had staked out for them. From the looks of it, Jackie had gotten the ball rolling on their girls' night out with a bottle of light beer and a tray of nachos.

With a slight pressure at the small of her back, Connor accompanied her through the crowd.

"Beth!" As soon as Jackie spotted her, she jumped up and threw her arms around her friend. "It's so good to see you again. I missed you so much!"

Beth laughed with genuine happiness. "I missed you, too. You look great."

"Me?" Jackie glanced down at herself, brushing her hands over the hem of her sweater where it hugged her well-rounded hips. "Honey, I've had four kids...I haven't looked great since high school."

It was obvious her friend was joking and was actually quite comfortable with her robust figure, so Beth felt safe chuckling in response. But she couldn't resist adding a gentle chastisement. "Don't say that. You're still beautiful, your children are adorable, and your husband is hopelessly devoted. You're one of the luckiest women in this town, and you darn well know it."

Jackie's cheeks turned crimson and the corners of her mouth lifted in a goofy grin. "Yeah, I know it. But you…" She stood back, eyeing Beth from head to toe. "L.A. agrees with you. You look like one of those gorgeous runway models, putting everyone here to shame."

Since the only pair of jeans she currently owned was spattered with paint, Beth had opted for a tailored gray pantsuit with a pale blue blouse to add a touch of color, and her black, all-purpose sling-backs. She felt slightly out of place among the sweatshirts and western wear, but not nearly as much as she'd expected. Here, she was simply one of the girls, a Crystal Springs native, no matter how she was dressed.

"Thanks. Jackie, you know Connor Riordan, don't you?" she asked, pulling Connor forward a few steps in hopes of diverting her friend's attention.

"Of course." She reached out to take the hand he offered. "How are you, Connor?"

"Just fine, thanks. And you?"

They chatted for a few brief minutes before Beth spotted Gail at the entrance of the restaurant. She lifted an arm and waved until her friend saw them and started in their direction.

Again, Beth made the introductions, and then Gail and Jackie slipped into the booth and waved for a waitress to bring them more drinks.

"I'll call you when I need a ride home," Beth told Connor. "Or get one of the girls to drop me off."

"No, that's all right," he said. "I think I'll stick around a while. Have a drink, catch up with old friends. I'll let you know when I'm ready to leave, and you can either come with me or make other arrangements."

She nodded, watching him cross the room toward the bar and feeling oddly bereft at the loss of his hand at her waist. Shaking off the bizarre emotion, she pasted a smile on her face and slipped onto the padded bench seat next to her friend.

She'd been looking forward to this evening all week, and would be darned if she'd let her mixed-up, indecisive feelings about Connor ruin it for her.

After laughing and joking and catching up on any number of things that had happened since the last time they saw each other, Jackie and Gail both said they had to get home.

Beth was immediately disappointed. She didn't want to leave; she was having too good a time. Even given the nachos and beer instead of the cosmopolitans and finger sandwiches she was used to, hanging out at the Longneck was just plain *fun*.

She hugged her friends and walked them to the door to say goodbye. It was raining out, she noticed as Jackie and Gail darted across the parking lot, holding their jackets over their heads to keep from getting drenched. Then she turned back around and scanned the still-crowded room for Connor.

He said he'd let her know before he took off, and

since she hadn't seen him since then, she assumed he was still here. Maybe at the bar, or on the dance floor, or in one of the back rooms playing pool.

If the Longneck even still had pool tables. Good Lord, she hadn't been home or to her old haunts in so long, she couldn't be sure what changes had been made. For all she knew, the pool tables that had been so popular when she was in college had been replaced by video or pinball games.

Returning to the table she'd shared with the girls, she grabbed up her half-full bottle of light beer, making her way toward the back rooms. She scanned the crowd as she walked, looking for Connor's short, dirty-blond hair and blue chambray shirt as she passed.

He wasn't at the bar or any of the tables, and she didn't see him on the dance floor. Good thing. She wasn't sure she could handle the sight of him with his arms around another woman.

What a silly notion, she thought, pausing long enough to scan the sea of people and take another sip of beer. She had no claim on him. Didn't want to lay claim to him. If anything, it would be best for them to each go their separate ways.

But even though she'd been telling herself for years that she was over him, she still didn't like the idea of seeing some other woman curled around him like a weed.

It had been that way back in high school, too. Connor hadn't seemed to notice she was alive, but it ate her up inside any time he'd come around with a new girlfriend. Some tall, skinny, blond cheerleader who giggled like an idiot and never sat down unless she could be draped across his lap.

Beth stopped at the wide-open entryway to the dance area, which also led off to back rooms on either side. A slow country ballad was playing, and couples swayed together to the languid beat.

When she didn't spot Connor among the dancers, she headed left, toward the pool room. And it was still a pool room, she noticed with nostalgic pleasure. Six or eight men stood around watching four others play through at two different tables. Biker leather and silver studs mixed with cowboy boots and hats.

Connor was leaning over the edge of one of the tables, lining up his shot. He struck out and the ball he'd been aiming for sailed straight into a corner pocket. Half the audience in the room groaned while the other half high-fived.

Connor grinned, retrieving his beer from the side of the table and taking a celebratory swig. He turned to lean against the wall while his opponent took his shot, and spotted her.

"Hey," he said, pushing away and crossing the space of the room to her side. "You and your friends ready to head home?"

She nodded. "Gail and Jackie already left."

He glanced over his shoulder. It was his turn at the table again, but he looked back at her first. "Do you want to leave? I can get someone else to cover the rest of the game for me."

For a moment, she considered his offer. "How much do you have riding on it?"

A slight flush reddened his cheekbones, and then his mouth lifted up in a grin. "Fifty bucks."

"Go ahead and finish," she told him with a smile of her own, tipping the brown bottle she was holding in his direction. "Win some money and maybe you can buy me another drink."

"How many have you had so far?" he wanted to know.

"Only two or three."

"You coming or not?" the bearded man he had the bet going with called out.

"Yeah," Connor retorted. "Just a minute." Turning his attention back to Beth, he said, "All right. As soon as I finish this game, I'll buy you another drink...on one condition."

"What's that?"

"You dance with me first."

She glanced over her shoulder at the dance floor, taking in all the couples moving in tandem to a style of music that was quickly growing on her. It was probably a mistake to agree, considering her recent train of thought, but she couldn't seem to help herself. She'd never gotten to dance with him all those years ago, and even though it was too late for everything, in every sense of the word, she still wanted what those girls in high school had experienced.

Just one dance. What could it hurt?

Meeting his soft brown gaze, she inclined her head. "Deal."

He flashed her a wide, pearly-white smile. "Back in a minute. This shouldn't take long."

True to his word, the game ended in another ten minutes, with Connor winning and collecting fifty dollars from his defeated but good-natured opponent. He passed his stick off to the next guy in line for a round at the tables and made his way over to Beth.

"Congratulations," she said, watching him add the bills to his wallet.

"Told you it wouldn't take long. Ready for that dance?"

Her chest tightened at his intense expression and a skittering of anxiousness skated along her nerve endings. The current song on the jukebox was coming to an end, putting her even more on the spot. Not that she was actually considering backing out.

Bending her knees, she crouched down just far enough to set her empty beer bottle on the floor beside the open archway to the pool room. Hopefully a waitress would be by to gather them, but if not, they should be out of the way enough not to trip anyone up before closing.

Connor did the same before taking her hand and starting toward the jukebox. There was one song left before new selections would begin to play.

"The next song is a fast one, but I had something slow in mind for our dance," he said, feeding quarters into the machine and punching the button for his choice. "What do you say? Would you be willing to dance with me twice in a row?"

What the heck. Maybe dancing to a fast song, away from him and without touching, would prepare her for the moment when his arms would go around her and their bodies would press together.

"Sure," she answered with more conviction than she felt.

The upward tilt of his lips in response made her stomach flutter, and she drew a deep breath to keep her lungs functioning properly. He wrapped his fingers around her elbow and led her to the center of the dance floor.

He slid his hand from her elbow, down the length of her arm, and over her wrist, raising shivers and gooseflesh everywhere he touched. Linking his fingers with hers, he gave a small tug, causing her to stumble into the solid wall of his chest.

So much for keeping her distance through the first song. Instead of standing by themselves, dancing independently as she'd expected, he kept her hand grasped in his own and curled the other over the curve of her hip as they bounced and jiggled.

If this was how he danced with a woman to a quick, upbeat tune, she could only imagine where his hands would be during a more subdued ballad. And since she'd promised him a slow song, she supposed she'd soon find out.

"So did you have a good time with your friends?" he spoke against her ear.

It wasn't easy to carry on a conversation this close to the source of the loud music, but she nodded. "It was good to catch up with them."

A minute later, the song came to an end and there was a brief pause while the next set up. Connor didn't loosen his hold, and when the slow song began, he pulled her even closer.

"Ah, here we go. This is what I've been waiting for."

He slid the hand at her hip around to her back until his arm completely encircled her waist. The position brought them together like playing cards, her breasts pressed flat, their lower bodies brushing in a sensual, intimate way.

She tried at first to pull away, to put just a modicum of distance between them, but he wouldn't let her go. And then, as the music filled the room and began to seep into her soul, she gave up. Surrendered.

It was only a dance. One she'd agreed to and been looking forward to, at that.

It was also Connor…her brother's best friend, one of *her* best friends through most of her childhood, and one of the people she used to trust most in the world. If she wasn't safe in his arms, she wasn't safe in anyone's.

Nine

He knew the exact moment the tension drained from Beth's body and she began to relax. Her spine—which she'd been holding almost ramrod straight—bent slightly beneath his palm. The muscles in her arms became less rigid, and she settled against him instead of trying so hard to hold herself away.

He wanted to whoop with triumph, sigh with relief. But to avoid spooking her back into skittish-colt mode, he merely continued to dance, enjoying her closeness.

She smelled of that same spicy floral scent he was coming to associate with her, even after hours of hanging out in a smoky bar. Her hair fell around her face and over her shoulders in wavy mahogany curls, perfectly framing her robin's-egg eyes and flawless, heart-shaped face.

They swayed together to the music, letting the slow beat and soulful voice of the singer direct their movements. The thumb of his left hand stroked slowly up and down, caressing her back.

He wished she weren't wearing the jacket that went with her suit so he could feel her skin more easily through the tissue-paper thinness of her blouse. Better yet, she should be nude…they should both be nude so he could feel her petal-soft skin beneath his hands, her pert breasts pressing into his bare chest.

She lifted her head and their gazes met. If he hadn't already been painfully aroused from his fantasies about having her naked in his arms while they danced, then the look in her eyes would have done it. They were warm and tender and vulnerable.

Maybe it was the beer she'd been drinking with her friends, or maybe she was starting to remember what it was like to live in a small town, to be around people you knew and who cared about you. She might even be remembering what things had been like between the two of them before it went so wrong.

The chords of the song strummed to an end and everyone stopped dancing, returning to their tables or waiting for the next song to begin. Beth and Connor had already slowed and now stood still, staring at each other.

Clearing his throat, he said, "Song's over. Wanna dance again?"

She shook her head.

"Want a drink?"

She shook her head again.

"Want to go home?"

She nodded and the gesture sent a jolt of excitement rocking through his system.

He didn't want to assume anything...didn't want to take for granted that just because she was asking him to take her home, she also meant to go to bed with him. Though it *was* numbers one through ten on his wish list at the moment, for all he knew, she wanted to go back to the house to sleep off whatever alcohol she'd consumed this evening.

But he also wasn't going to look a gift horse in the mouth. She might not be suggesting they make love, but it had been a hell of a night already, in his estimation, and he would rather leave now than stick around and risk something happening to tarnish the memory of it.

"Okay," he murmured, still standing in the middle of the dance floor, still gazing down at her face, still holding her tight. "Let's get out of here."

Keeping a grip on her hand, he turned and headed through the crowd, toward the main entrance at the other end of the bar. Beth stayed close on his heels, bumping into him when he stepped back to open the door. A gust of cold air blew in, along with a good amount of the rain that was pouring down in buckets outside.

"Whoa."

"Oh, I forgot. It's raining," she said, as though he couldn't see that for himself. He was getting damp just standing inside the open door.

"No kidding." He glanced at her over his shoulder. "Did you bring a coat?"

"No. I didn't think I'd need one."

Neither had he. It had been cool when they'd left the house, but he hadn't expected to be out this late. He also hadn't expected this much of a deluge.

"Stay here," he told her. "I'll get the truck and bring it around." At least that way she would stay mostly dry.

But she shook her head, sending the long locks of her hair bouncing. "I'm not a sugar cube, I won't melt."

It was a saying he'd heard her father utter a million times…but to his recollection, Beth had always balked at getting too wet and wouldn't go out without a hat or umbrella.

"You sure?" he asked her.

"Yep. Let's get out of here before we flood the place."

He smiled, squeezed her hand and took off at a run across the parking lot. They both held their free hands over their heads to ward off as much of the downpour as possible, but it was a wasted effort. The rain soaked through their clothes and wet their skin long before they reached the truck.

Unlocking the passenger-side door, he helped her into the cab, then ran around the front of the vehicle and jumped behind the wheel.

"Whoo!" He shook himself like a dog after a bath, sending droplets of water spraying everywhere. "Guess this is the storm those meteorologists have been talking about all week."

She chuckled, wiping her face and wringing moisture out of her own hair. When he noticed her rubbing her arms to ward off a chill, he started the engine and turned the heat on high.

They drove home in near silence, wipers working furiously to keep the windshield clear. When they reached the house, he pulled into the driveway and parked as close to the front door as possible.

The neighborhood was dark, but he didn't know if that was due to the late hour, or a possible storm-induced power outage. He also couldn't remember if he'd turned on the porch light before leaving. It was off now, though.

"Ready for this?" he asked after shutting off the engine and separating the house key from the rest.

"I can't get any wetter than I already am," she replied.

And then they were out of the truck and jogging for the porch. He got the front door open, stepping aside for her to precede him.

The warmth of the house enveloped them, a welcome change from the cold of the driving rain. They stood in the entryway for a moment, laughing and dripping.

Connor reached over to flip the switch for the kitchen lights, but nothing happened. He flipped it again for good measure, then tried the others on the same panel.

"Looks like the electricity is out."

"I'm not surprised. That wind is enough to knock over entire power stations."

Shrugging out of her soggy jacket, she tiptoed

across the linoleum kitchen floor, dropping it into the sink. Lifting one leg and then the other, she peeled off her black high heels and left them dangling by the straps from her fingertips.

"I'll run upstairs to change and get some towels," she said. "Do you want me to bring anything down for you?"

"No, thanks," he said. "I'll run up and change myself soon, but first I think I'd better get a fire started in the fireplace. With the power out, the furnace won't be running, and even though it's warm enough in here now, if this storm rages all night, it's bound to get chilly."

"Sounds great."

"Do you need a flashlight?" he asked. His eyes had acclimated enough to the inky blackness that he could see the quick smile she tossed his way.

"Are you kidding? Nick and I used to sneak around the house in the dark all the time to keep from waking Mom and Dad. I could maneuver around this place blindfolded."

With that, she rounded the corner and disappeared. He could hear her footsteps as she moved through the house, and for a minute he just stood there, listening.

Bending down, he untied his boots and left them sitting by the door to dry. Next, he peeled off his shirt and let it drop on top of her jacket in the sink, followed by his heavy, rain-soaked jeans.

She probably wouldn't appreciate him walking around in his boxer shorts, but they were about the only stitch of dry clothing on his body at the moment, and he wanted to get that fire started before going upstairs to find something else to wear. Besides, they were nice boxers. Clean, new, navy blue with tiny white polka dots, and not a hole to be found. Lori had restocked his underwear drawer just last month. He hadn't much appreciated it at the time, but now he supposed he owed her a thank-you.

At the thought of Lori, guilt twisted through his gut. He hadn't even attempted to contact her since the night of Nick's wedding when she'd kicked him out of his own house. Worse yet, he didn't particularly miss her. He'd been perfectly content this week to stay at Nick's house, with Nick's sister.

With Beth.

As hard as he'd fought it all these years, he was attracted to her. Ha! That was the understatement of the century. He wanted her with a burning, seething, all-encompassing passion. And the more he tried to deny it, the more obsessed he became.

Even having her seven years ago hadn't dulled the desire coursing through his veins. Making love to her in the cab of his truck had only sharpened his feelings, turning her into a drug and him into a junkie.

Lori was a great girl, and he'd honestly tried to build a life with her. But now that Beth was back in town, now that this flame he'd held for her was flaring to life again, he realized that he'd only been lying to himself…and using Lori as a Band-Aid to treat a severed limb.

He heard a squeak and turned to see Beth coming down the stairs, a stack of fluffy white towels in her hands. She was wearing that short, sexy yellow nightie again, the equally short matching robe tied at her waist. Her wet hair was caught up at the back of her head with a silver clip.

Forcing himself to look away, he concentrated once again on getting a fire going in the living room hearth. Feeling more than seeing his way around, he un-wrapped one of the pretreated starter bricks and struck a match, chagrined to notice that his hand was shak-ing.

Damn, she affected him. One whiff of her spicy per-fume, one glimpse of her wide blue eyes and he started to sweat.

"Here you go."

She shook out a towel and draped it over his bare shoulders. His half-naked state didn't seem to bother her nearly as much as he'd expected.

The flames caught, filling the fireplace and begin-ning to throw flickering light and heat into the room. He stood, rubbing the towel over his close-cut hair and then drying his still-damp arms and chest. Beth had taken the clip out of her hair and was using her own towel to squeeze and separate the strands.

"I see you decided to go straight to the quick-dry method," she said, tipping her head in the direction of his bare body and boxer shorts.

"I didn't want to drip on your brother's hardwood floor. I can run upstairs and put on something else, if it bothers you."

He wasn't sure why he threw the offer out there and in that particular wording. It's what he'd intended from the start, but for some reason, he suddenly found himself wanting to know what her reaction would be to his remaining in this state of undress.

Would she ask him to go throw some clothes on, or be just as comfortable with him walking around half-nude as she was walking around that way herself? Because that slinky little nightgown she'd been wearing lately sure didn't leave much to the imagination.

"It doesn't bother me," she said breezily, walking to the couch and plopping down on one of the overstuffed cushions. She propped her feet on the coffee table and the seashell pink of her painted toenails winked in the flickering light of the fire.

"I've seen you and Nick both in a lot less." She grinned, looking at him from beneath lowered lashes. "Remember that time out at the lake when the two of you went skinny-dipping? You teased and badgered until I agreed to strip down and jump in with you, then you sneaked out and stole my clothes."

He chuckled at the memory, dropping the towel on the stone hearth to dry before taking a seat beside her on the sofa. He did remember that day, though he hadn't thought of it in years. "You cried so hard, we were afraid you'd drown."

"Which had no impact whatsoever on you two hooligans."

"No, but your screaming and threatening to walk home naked to tell your parents what we'd done certainly did."

"Yeah. So what did you do in response? You threw

my clothes on the bank, then went running home without me."

"We had to get there before you did to make sure you wouldn't rat on us."

"Don't worry, I didn't. I still don't think Mom and Dad know about that incident."

"That's probably for the best. They'd think Nick and I were complete pervs."

She slanted a wicked glance in his direction. "What do you mean *were?*"

It took a second for the gibe to sink in, another for him to realize she was falling back on their old, teasing banter. Something she hadn't done in seven long years.

Before he could question why or tamp down his instinctive response, he narrowed his eyes, lowered his tone and said, "Low blow. Now you'll have to be punished."

Her brows lifted as understanding dawned, and she gave a shriek loud enough to rattle the pictures on the wall before trying to dart away. He grabbed her, snaking an arm around her waist before she got two inches off the couch, pulling her back against him. With his free hand, he dug into the tender flesh of her side and started to tickle.

"No! Aaack, stop! Connor, stop!"

She continued to scream and thrash, laughing uncontrollably. It was like old times. He used to tickle her like this when they were kids, and sometimes he and Nick would gang up on her.

Of course, she always got her revenge. By going to her folks and getting them grounded, but more often by putting garter snakes in their beds or itching powder in their shorts. She was nothing if not cruel and ingenious in her acts of vengeance.

Somehow, with all her wiggling, she got twisted around so they were facing each other. Her breasts were pressed flat between them and he could feel her pebbled nipples digging into his bare chest through the thin fabric of her robe and nightie.

Though her knees nearly emasculated him more than once, the sensation of her smooth, silky legs gliding between his own sent signals to both his brain and nether regions, reminding him that he was definitely a man. And she was definitely a woman.

A woman he craved like a bear craved honey.

He stopped tickling, and her movements abruptly halted. She was panting for breath, the aftershocks of her laughter still rippling through her body.

Her face hovered above his, the damp tendrils of her hair hanging around them in dark spirals. Her eyes, which normally shone like bright, glittering sapphires, were now a deep, fathomless ocean blue. He read passion there, and longing…feelings he was more than willing to reciprocate.

He thought about kissing her, was lifting his head to do just that, when she leaned down and beat him to the punch. And what a punch it was. Right to the solar plexus. Her lips were warm and as soft as rose petals. Her fragrance invaded his senses, filling every pore.

He brought his hands up to frame her face and deepened the kiss, tasting her, absorbing her texture. Their tongues stroked, twined.

His fingers trailed through her hair, massaging her scalp, while she explored the expanse of his chest. She outlined the ridges of each pectoral muscle, his taut abdomen, brushing with her fingertips, clawing with her nails. He sucked in a ragged breath when she traced a path from his navel to the elastic waist of his boxers, stirring through the crisp hair there, sending shocks of electricity to every cell of his being.

She was smiling down at him, her lips puffy, her eyes half-lidded with desire.

"Do you want me to stop?" she asked, even as he felt the manicured tips of her fingernails worm their way between his fever-hot skin and the only piece of clothing that kept him from being indecent.

Beneath that material, though, he throbbed, straining for her touch. He wanted to beg her to keep going, to answer her question with a desperate *No, don't stop. Don't ever stop!*

But he couldn't take advantage of her, not again. If this was going to happen, if they were going to be together again, then he needed to know she wanted him as much as he wanted her. That there was nothing standing between them, nothing impairing her decision-making process.

Tucking a lock of hair behind her ear and keeping his hand on the nape of her neck, he asked, "How much did you have to drink tonight?"

She blinked, her eyes widening slightly as she realized his question wasn't an intimate or suggestive one.

"Why? Do you think I'm drunk?" She spoke slowly and deliberately, but she didn't seem to be offended.

"I just want to be sure," he replied with measured care. So far, she hadn't slapped his face and stormed off, and if he was lucky, he wouldn't say anything to make her do either.

"I had three light beers over a four-hour period. I'm not drunk, Connor. I know exactly what I'm doing."

As soon as the words were out of her mouth, she recognized them as the truth. She might not be kissing him, caressing him for all the right reasons, but she still wanted him.

Heck, she'd wanted him for years. Even during that terrible time when she'd convinced herself she hated him, she'd never really managed to quash her desire for him. These past few days, trapped together in the same house, trying to keep their distance but only managing to strike sparks off one another, had only served to amplify that yearning.

What would it hurt to be with him one more—one last—time? It was obvious they were both charged and ready...willing and more than able. They were both adults, both unattached.

Sadly, she hadn't dated anyone significant in the last three or four years. In the past twelve to eighteen months, she hadn't dated *anyone*.

She was due, a little voice in her head whispered. But more than that, sleeping with Connor would get this low-level hum of longing out of her system and prove, once and for all, that she was over him.

Sleeping with him would not only scratch the itch that had developed by spending so much time together this past week, but also give her the closure she'd been needing ever since the first time they'd made love seven years ago.

Closure, yes. That's exactly what she needed. One night with Connor to extinguish the fire beating in her blood and exorcise any hard feelings still lingering between them. Then she would be able to fly back to L.A. without any of the ugly demons that had plagued her in the past.

She met his gaze, letting the backs of her fingers roam deeper beneath the waistband of his cute little polka-dot boxer shorts until she felt him twitch.

"I know exactly what I'm doing," she told him again, slowly and succinctly so he would have no doubt that she meant what she said. "Is that clear?"

"Yes, ma'am," was his strained but heartfelt response. "I'll never doubt your intentions again."

An amused smile stole across her lips. "See that you don't."

His eyes sparkled with devilish purpose, and then he was lifting himself up on his elbows, covering her mouth with his. He kissed her breathless, kissed her until she was purring with pleasure and leaning into him, wanting to melt, merge, become one with him.

He smelled fresh and clean, like the rain that had drenched them both. And he felt…he felt like heaven. Hard and firm, his muscles bunching beneath her touch. His chest was a work of art, chiseled, well defined, a masterpiece. His legs rubbed against her own, the crisp hairs tickling, sending ripples of sensual awareness along her spine.

But it was his face that intrigued her, his face that

could turn her on from across the room. The strong line of his jaw, sometimes stubbled with a sexy five o'clock shadow. The smooth, powerful brow that furrowed when he was annoyed or deep in thought. The straight, narrow nose with a tiny bump high on the bridge from the time he and Nick had gotten into a fight with some members of the opposing team after an away-from-home football game. And those gentle, brandy brown eyes that made her knees go weak with a single smoldering glance.

Connor's hands dragged through her hair, moving down her back and sides and around to the front of her waist. He untied the sash of her robe, causing the silky material to fall open, and then pushed it over her shoulders and down her arms.

As reluctant as she was to remove her fingers from the cozy nest of his boxers, she wanted to feel him, skin to skin. With a little shake, she let the airy material flutter to the floor.

She was in her nightgown and panties now, her arms, legs and back bare. Instead of being chilled, waves of heat washed over her, and she doubted they were from the fireplace.

Their breaths mingled and heaved as Connor's lips moved to her cheek, her jaw. His hands stroked the backs of her legs, his callused fingers sending shivers and shock waves straight to her core. He traced the lines behind her knees before straying higher, higher. He cupped her bottom, groaning when he discovered she was wearing a thong.

"You're so damn hot," he breathed against the taut

column of her throat. "You make me crazy. You make me want to lick every inch of your luscious body. Suck your toes and fingers, your nipples and your lips. I want to carry you to my bed and never let you leave."

His hands on her buttocks and tongue on her collarbone had her senses reeling, but she struggled to absorb everything he was saying. The words warmed her all the way through and sent her level of arousal ratcheting up several notches.

"Since the bed upstairs is my brother's and it's quite a walk to your place," she asked in a ragged voice, "will the sofa do?"

"Oh, yeah, the sofa will do just fine."

His rough palms moved from her bottom to her hips, his fingers slipping under the thin straps holding her panties in place. With excruciating slowness, he tugged the scrap of fabric down, revealing her private places and leaving her open to the warm air circulating through the room. She lifted her legs, one and then the other, to help him remove the garment altogether.

At the same time, his mouth found and fastened upon one of her breasts, wetting her nipple through the material of her nightgown and causing the already pebbled tip to tighten even further. She arched her back, granting him better access, urging him on.

He played her body like a finely tuned instrument, knowing just where to touch and stroke, just how much pressure to use. Her head was spinning, blood pounding in her ears and pooling low in her belly, between her legs.

But something was missing. Connor was turned on,

but not desperately, sweating and writhing beneath her. She wanted that. She wanted to touch and caress him, drive him to the brink of insanity and make him beg for more.

"Connor."

He continued to suckle and her inner muscles clenched.

"Connor."

"Hmm?"

He hummed in reply and the vibrations rippled straight to her core.

"Stop," she said, and was amazed at the speed in which he halted the motions of his tongue and hands. With this man, it appeared, no meant no.

He fell back on the couch, staring up at her. His hands still cradled her hips, his chest heaving with the pace of his breathing. She admired his control, considering how aroused she knew he was.

Leaning down, she gave him a long, lingering kiss. When she raised up again, his eyes flashed with bewilderment.

"I didn't mean stop-stop," she clarified rather than leave him in a state of confusion.

He moved his hands from beneath the hem of her nightie, lightly tracing the underside of her forearms before linking the fingers of both hands. "What did you mean, then?"

She spread her legs, straddling his thighs to find a better balance as she hovered above him. Bringing their twined hands up, she used her lower body to perform a slow gyration atop his straining erection. Connor inhaled sharply, his lips rolling back to reveal gritted teeth.

"I meant...my turn."

Ten

As if her erotic declaration alone wasn't enough to set off miniature explosions throughout his bloodstream, Beth outdid herself by sitting up, crossing her arms in front of her and whipping her thin little wisp of a nightgown up and over her head in one quick movement. She tossed the garment aside, smiling down at him in all her naked glory.

She was magnificent. Smooth, pale flesh...glorious round breasts with small, plum-colored nipples, drawn tight with her arousal...narrow, sculpted waist leading down to the flare of feminine hips...

More beautiful than a pinup girl, she was the sexiest thing he'd ever seen. And for tonight, at least, she was his.

He reached for her, but she stopped him.

"Ah, ah, ah." Catching his wrists, she pressed his arms above his head, flat to the cushions of the couch. "My turn, my rules. No touching from you—for now."

A short, sharp laugh burst past his lips. "I'm not sure I can abide by that rule. It might kill me."

"If it does," she murmured, sliding her hands back down his arms, into the sensitive dip of his armpits, to his chest, "I'll perform mouth-to-mouth and resuscitate you."

The very thought made his diaphragm constrict. "Only to have your wicked way with me again, no doubt."

She shrugged one slim shoulder. "A girl has to have her fun."

Thankfully, Beth was more than willing to include him in her idea of fun. Her nails raked down his chest, skimming his nipples, leaving twin paths of ecstasy in their wake. And then her hands jumped to her own body, running along the tops of her thighs, over her waist, to the globes of her breasts. She palmed their weight and held them up for his perusal.

Like he needed to be reminded of her mouthwatering assets. He'd already tasted one of those pert nipples—albeit through the material of her nightgown—and felt it bud against his tongue.

"Do you like what you see?"

Rather than answer her question, he rotated his hips, letting her feel his straining length between her legs, tenting the front of his boxers. "What do you think?"

She leaned forward, draping the upper half of her body along the upper half of his. He could feel her heat and wetness even through his shorts, and though he wouldn't have thought it possible a second earlier, he grew harder.

"I think…"

She placed an open-mouthed kiss to his neck. His senses were so heightened that he could hear the sandpaper scrape of her tongue against the underside of his whiskered jaw, like the raspy lick of a kitten.

"…you do."

Her mouth continued downward, leaving behind a path of moisture that all but sizzled on his overheated skin.

"I also think…"

She was at his pectorals now, flicking one tiny nipple before moving on to his rib cage.

"I like what *I* see."

The tip of her tongue swirled into his navel and the air seized in his lungs.

"I'm…glad," he managed in ragged pants.

"Connor?"

He couldn't breathe, which made it somewhat difficult to answer. But what made it absolutely impossible was the sight of her teeth biting into and lifting the waistband of his boxer shorts. When he didn't answer, she released the elastic band with a snap. He barely felt the sting.

"I want you inside me."

Yes. Please. *Finally.*

Rules be damned. Jackknifing into a sitting position, he cupped her bare bottom and pulled her more fully onto his lap.

"Wrap your arms around my neck," he told her.

For once, she didn't argue. With a sensually contented grin, she threw herself onto him, plastering her breasts between them and looping her arms together in a near stranglehold.

Holding tight, he pushed to his feet. "Now wrap your legs around my waist."

"Yes, master."

One corner of his mouth quirked at her cheeky reply. "Behave or you'll have to be punished."

"Ooh, please don't hurt me," she cooed. "I promise I'll be good."

"But not too good."

"No, not too good," she agreed as he started walking.

She was stuck to him like a burr…just the way he liked it.

"Where are we going?"

"Kitchen. I left my pants in the sink."

"I thought we were getting *un*dressed. Why do you need your pants?"

They reached the kitchen and he propped her on the edge of the counter, freeing his hands to dig through his wet jeans. He got his wallet out of the rear pocket and found what he needed.

"Condom," he said, holding up the silver foil packet like it was an Olympic medal.

A look of startled realization flashed in her eyes. He guessed she hadn't given the need for protection much thought. But then, things had moved rather quickly once they'd decided being together this way was inevitable.

"Smart thinking." She ran her fingers from the nape of his neck up through his hair. "You keep one with you in case of sexual emergencies?" she teased.

"Yep. And there's a whole box upstairs, too. You never know when some hot babe is going to jump your bones."

She tipped her head to the side, studying him for a moment. "Men live in a constant state of fantastic optimism, don't they?"

He flashed her a wide grin. "Of course. And sometimes it pays off."

She smiled back at him. "So are you going to use that condom, or stand around talking about it?"

And just like that, his libido was flying full throttle again.

"I'm going to use it." He shucked off his boxers and tore the foil square open with his teeth at the same time. "Do you want to stay here or go back to the couch?"

She glanced around at the countertops and cleared kitchen table before meeting his gaze. "Here." She pulled him closer with both her arms and legs. "Now. Hurry."

"Be careful what you wish for, sweetheart." He was already full to bursting, aching for her. Too much more and it would be over before it began.

Making short work of covering himself with the thin layer of protection, he grabbed her up and kissed her. Her nails raked across his back, her ankles locked over his buttocks.

While their mouths meshed and their breaths mingled, he lifted her from the counter and carried her to the table, laying her on the flat surface like a delectably erotic feast.

She sighed and arched toward him, and he took the opportunity to nuzzle her throat, her chest. He circled one breast, then the other, purposely avoiding the straining peaks and leaving her wanting.

With his lips on the soft, flat plane of her belly, he nudged the tip of his throbbing erection against her warm, wet opening. She writhed, trying to get closer, and he was so wildly aroused that he knew he couldn't tease either of them any longer. He wanted her, needed her, had to have her right that moment or die.

Surging forward, he buried himself inside her to the hilt, meeting her mouth and swallowing her gasp of delight.

She felt like heaven, wet and hot and tight around him. He could have stayed that way forever, nestled in the cradle of her thighs, but she flexed her hips, urging him on, and his desperate libido took over.

They moved together, thrusting, driving, fighting for air as their muscles strained and the blood pounded in their veins.

Beth bit her bottom lip to keep from crying out at the sensations washed over her, but she kept her eyes open, watching Connor move above her. Her stomach quivered, her tender inner muscles clenching and releasing around him as he filled her.

She held him close with her arms and legs wound around him, wanting to bring him as deep as possible, to become one with him. The soft, springy hair on his chest abraded her breasts, sending a Morse code of awareness down to her core.

Moaning her pleasure, she nipped at his earlobe with her teeth. She could feel the pressure building, release just beyond her grasp, and she reached for it, straining, striving, lifting to meet every pounding drive of his hips.

"Faster, Connor. Please."

"Yes."

He hooked his arms under her knees, pushing them even closer to her body to grant him better access as he increased his pace, and within seconds they both came, completion washing over them in wave after wave of the most intense pleasure she'd ever experienced. The tremors wracking her body went on and on as he thrust once, twice more and then fell still above her.

His weight draped across her torso, heavy, but in an intimate, comforting way. Her fingertips drew nonsensical designs on his sweat-slick back and her lips were tipped up in what she knew must be a goofy grin.

Raising his tousled head, he stared down at her, satisfaction glittering in his dark brown eyes.

"You're smiling," he said.

"I know."

His fingers brushed over the hair at her temples. "You look amazing."

"I feel pretty amazing." She clutched at him where he rested inside her and felt him begin to stiffen again. "So do you."

He raised a brow. "Again?"

"I'm ready when you are." She flexed once more, just in case he had any doubts.

"Well, I'll be damned."

He scooped her up from the table, keeping them connected, and swung around, heading out of the kitchen.

"You sure do move around a lot," she told him, hanging on and enjoying the jostling of their lower bodies with each step he took. "Now where are we going?"

"Upstairs for more condoms. We may even make it into a bed this time."

"Mmm, making love in a bed. What a novel idea."

He chuckled, slapping her bare bottom. "Don't be sarcastic. If you hadn't been in such an all-fired hurry, we might have made it there the first time."

"Oh, sure. Blame the poor defenseless naked woman being carted around like a sack of potatoes."

A second later, he cracked his shin into a piece of furniture and swore.

It was Beth's turn to laugh. "Are you okay?"

"I'll live," he replied through gritted teeth, rubbing absently at the bruised spot before continuing.

"Need a flashlight?" she asked sweetly, throwing his earlier words back at him.

"Very funny. Now be quiet while I concentrate on getting upstairs *without* maiming myself."

"I won't say another word," she promised in a hushed whisper.

Instead, she brushed her lips along his cheekbone to his ear, where she sucked the fleshy lobe into her mouth and bit down gently with her teeth. He grunted, stumbling over the next step.

"You're killing me," he grumbled. "I hope you know that."

She grinned, but didn't respond. After all, she'd agreed to be quiet.

At the top of the stairs, he tripped again, letting her fall to the landing and following her down. His body covered hers as he kissed her, releasing every ounce of passion and frustration that had built up in the last few minutes. When he pulled away, they were both breathing heavily.

"Enough is enough," he said, slipping out of her.

She moaned in disappointment, already missing the feel of him inside her. But then he stood, scooping her into his arms, and made a beeline for the master bedroom.

Reaching the bed, he dropped her in its center, and without a word crossed to the dresser. The mattress hadn't stopped bouncing by the time he returned, old condom gone and a box of new condoms in his hand.

He removed a single packet and tore it open, covering himself before he climbed onto the bed beside her.

"Where were we?" he wanted to know.

"Right about here." She lifted her leg to drape over his hip and ran her fingers up and down his bare, bulging bicep. The tip of his masculinity pressed against her slick opening, seeking entrance, and she was more than willing to let him in.

As he sank into her and her arms wrapped around

him, drawing him closer, Beth sighed with content-
ment. She was getting exactly what she wanted: one
night with Connor Riordan.

It would all evaporate like mist in the morning, but
for tonight, he was hers.

Beth's eyes fluttered open what must have been
hours later. The room was still dark, but a hint of early-
morning light filtered through the blinds from outside.
The rain had stopped sometime during the night, and
for long minutes, she lay there, unmoving, listening to
the sounds of birdsong.

She was cuddled up to Connor, her back to his front,
with the blankets pulled up to their chests. Beneath the
sheets, his arm circled her waist and her arm ran along
his, her palm covering the back of his hand so that their
fingers linked.

She felt warm and safe and never wanted to move.
A part of her even wanted to roll over and coax Connor awake with kisses and a gentle caress.

But she knew she couldn't. She'd promised herself
one night to wash him from her system, to prove she
was over him, and that one night was now passed.

It was time to start distancing herself, and the sooner
she did that, the sooner things would get back to normal.

Freeing her fingers, she loosened the sheets on her
side of the bed and slid her feet out, then carefully
slipped out from under his hold. She tiptoed across the
hall to her bedroom, dressing in the first items of clothing she found, the low-riding jeans and cotton top she'd
worn yesterday to paint.

She used the hallway bathroom, planning to go downstairs and start a pot of coffee. But as she passed the open doorway of the nursery, the weak rays of morning sunlight flooding through the curtainless windows, spilling across the newly refinished floor, stopped her in her tracks.

Even without furniture, the room was beautiful. Nick and Karen were going to love it. Any baby would be lucky to grow up here, especially knowing his aunt and "uncle" had put so much time and love into the renovations.

So why did just looking at the fresh paint and unopened rolls of sea-creatures border paper make her sad?

Letting her fingertips trace over the carved wooden doorjamb and new seafoam-colored walls, she stepped inside. She could picture the nursery exactly as it would be when it was finished, complete with a crib, changing table and rocking chair. Maybe even a bassinet for when the baby was still tiny and newborn.

She imagined her brother and his wife bringing their first child home from the hospital…Nick rocking the baby while it slept; Karen sitting there, breast-feeding.

But suddenly, it wasn't Karen rocking Beth's little niece or nephew. It was she, rocking *her* child. Her baby with Connor.

She'd never seen their child, having miscarried so early in her pregnancy, but she had no problem now making out every detail of her baby's features. The tiny little dot of a nose, the puffy baby cheeks, the delicate rosebud lips puckering in sleep.

A sob escaped her and she backed against the wall, feeling the impact of the loss like a musket ball to the stomach. She covered her mouth with her hand and sank to the floor, feeling tears streaming down her face.

Except for a lingering resentment toward Connor, she really thought she'd gotten over the emotional upheaval of the miscarriage years ago. How ironic to discover that while she'd managed to forgive Connor only days before for any part he did or didn't play in the events of seven years ago, it was the actual loss that still hung so heavily on her heart and soul.

It was so easy to envision what her life might have been if she hadn't lost the baby. If she'd remained pregnant and found the courage to tell Connor that they were going to be parents, she knew exactly what would have happened. They'd have gotten married and found somewhere to live right here in Crystal Springs, where they could be near her mom and dad.

And they would have been happy. She'd have finished school eventually and gone on to get her law degree…or maybe she'd have been happy as a stay-at-home mom. She and Connor might have had a couple more kids, her days filled with running carpools, cooking dinners and throwing birthday parties the envy of the neighborhood.

And as successful, as happy as she'd been with her life in L.A., she knew she would have been equally— maybe even more—happy staying in her own hometown as a wife and mother.

But only to Connor and his children.

How had life gone so terribly wrong? She'd had such big hopes and dreams in high school and her first years of college, all of which had come crashing down in a matter of weeks. Whether it was the miscarriage or Connor's failure to call her after the night they were together didn't seem to matter now. None of it did. It was just life, with all its ups and downs, joys and disappointments.

She'd made mistakes along the way, too. Not telling Connor the truth from the very beginning possibly being one of the biggest.

Before she went back to California, she would be sure to rectify that. It wouldn't be easy, she knew, but it had to be done. He deserved to know, and she deserved to spend the rest of her life with a clear conscience.

They could never go back, never reclaim what was already lost, but they could move forward and continue to be friends instead of avoiding each other like the plague.

Of course, after last night, that might not be entirely possible. But getting past secret-sex guilt had to be simpler than getting past secret-pregnancy guilt and seven years of lies.

Taking a deep breath, Beth wiped her eyes and climbed to her feet. To her surprise, she felt relieved and more comfortable in her own skin than she had in ages. It wasn't just the crying jag that cleansed her spirit, she realized, but her decision to come clean with Connor. What a crushing weight that had been to carry around all these years.

She was still sniffing, drying her face with the hem of her shirt when a floorboard squeaked and she lifted her head to find Connor standing on the other side of the doorway. He'd pulled on a clean pair of boxer shorts, but was otherwise gloriously naked. The sun spilling through the windows was brighter now, turning his legs and chest a golden bronze.

"Are you all right?" he asked, brows drawing together in concern. "What's wrong?"

She made one last swipe at her face, even though she knew it was too late to hide the fact that she'd been crying. He'd already noticed her tear-stained cheeks and red, swollen nose.

"Nothing, I'm fine," she said. And then she shook her head. "No, that's not entirely true."

Reaching out, she took his hand and pulled him farther into the room. "Connor, there's something I need to tell you."

His face blanched, his grip on her hand tightening as he sensed it was bad news. "Okay."

She took a deep breath and dived in, knowing if she didn't, she might never get it out. "I never told you this, but seven years ago, when we slept together after that football game, I got pregnant."

His expression didn't change, but she felt his entire body turn to stone. Whether that meant he was furious with her or merely digesting the information, she pressed on.

"I didn't tell you, and I should have. I think I would have, early on, if you had ever called or come to see me."

She held up her free hand, not to ward off any arguments he might make, but to keep herself from traveling down that tired, well-worn path.

"I'm not blaming you or saying you did anything wrong. We both made mistakes seven years ago, and if we had it to do over again, I'm sure we would do things a bit differently. I'm just telling you this because…" She lowered her eyes and licked her dry lips. "You deserve to know. And I'm tired of keeping it a secret, tired of being mad at you for something you weren't even aware of."

"I don't understand." His voice rasped, his Adam's apple bobbing as he swallowed hard, searching for words. "If you were pregnant, where's the baby?"

She blinked, caught off guard by the question. She'd been expecting a barrage of anger, a furious *why didn't you tell me?* Instead, she realized she hadn't shared with him the most important part of what had happened all those years ago.

"I'm sorry, Connor. I should have told you right away," she said, her own throat threatening to close on her. "I lost the baby."

For long minutes, he held her gaze, barely blinking, barely breathing. "I don't know what to say," he finally forced out.

"It's all right, you don't have to say anything. I just…don't want you to hate me. I spent a lot of time carrying this pain around with me, and even though I think you have the right to know everything that happened back then, I don't want you to make the same mistake now."

"I wish you'd told me. As soon as you found out."

She nodded in agreement. "I know. I wish I had, too. But I was young and scared, and I hadn't heard from you since that night."

His fingers clamped around hers. "If I'd known, I would have done the right thing. I never would have let you go through that alone."

One corner of her mouth turned up in a bittersweet half smile. "I know you wouldn't have. And I appreciate it."

They stood there for several more seconds, each at a loss as to what else needed to be said. Beth hoped her confession would ease her conscience, but she also hoped Connor wouldn't dwell too long on the past… the way she had.

"I'm flying back to California tomorrow," she said after the silence had dragged on for a full minute. Running her palm over his stubbled cheek, she added, "Thank you for last night, and thank you for that night seven years ago. Despite everything, I really am glad you were my first."

With that, she pulled her hand from his and stepped around him, out of the room.

Eleven

Connor stood in stunned silence long after Beth walked away. Minutes or even hours might have passed, he wasn't sure which. And he didn't care.

He heard Beth's footsteps as she paced down the hall, heard her moving around in her bedroom, likely packing. And he wanted to chase after her, he really did. But his feet seemed glued to the floor, and his brain refused to function past the bomb she'd just dropped on him.

They'd made a baby together and he'd never known it. She'd lost that baby and he'd never known it. The ramifications of those facts whirled through his head like a tornado.

He thought he'd been an idiot seven years ago for

letting things get out of hand with her in the first place, but now he *knew* he was an idiot for not checking on her afterward. For not calling to see if she was all right, both physically and emotionally. For not driving up to the university to be sure there'd been no consequences from his lapse of judgment.

He'd been young, sure, but old enough to take responsibility for his actions, especially where Beth was concerned. If anything, he owed her more courtesy and respect than other girls because they'd grown up together, practically as family.

A baby. He couldn't believe it. He'd fought his attraction to her for so long, and the one time he'd given in, he'd gotten her pregnant. Worse, she hadn't felt comfortable enough to come to him when she'd found out.

He had no one but himself to blame for that. The signals he'd been sending her since their early teens must have confused her beyond reason. Between treating her like a pesky little sister, then casting longing glances in her direction when he thought she wasn't looking, she probably hadn't known which end was up. And then he hadn't even had the courtesy to contact her the day after taking her virginity.

What a heel! What a dumb, selfish jerk! He'd walked away seven years ago, thinking they could forget, pretend that night hadn't happened.

But she hadn't been able to pretend or forget, had she? She'd been young, alone and unexpectedly pregnant by a man who not only didn't call her after sleeping with her, but did his level best to avoid being alone with her any time she came home for a visit.

To top it all off, she'd also been alone when she miscarried. He couldn't imagine how horrible that must have been for her. The fear, the pain, the sadness. No wonder she'd treated him like a particularly foul species of vermin whenever he was around. He deserved every ounce of her disdain—that and more.

And he didn't have a clue how to make up for any of it…or if he ever could.

His head was still spinning when Beth peeked around the corner and caught his attention. She wore her work clothes, the jeans and top they'd bought during their trip for nursery supplies.

"I called the airline," she said softly. "Now that the storm has passed, flights are back on track. My plane for L.A. leaves tomorrow afternoon. I was wondering if you'd drive me over to say goodbye to Mom and Dad in the morning, then drop me off at the airport."

He nodded, not quite able to manage actual words yet. His throat felt as though someone had their hands around his neck, squeezing, *squeezing* until he couldn't breathe.

A beat passed before she murmured a quiet thank-you and returned to her room.

God, how was he going to resolve this? How could he assimilate everything that had happened, everything she'd told him, and put it right? And if she was leaving tomorrow, did he even have time?

He didn't want her to leave again, fly all the way across the country, with this between them. Possibly forever. They'd spent the last seven years feeling awkward and avoiding each other…he didn't want to slip back into that strained behavior simply because he was fool enough to let her get on a plane before they'd cleared the air.

But how he was going to do that, he hadn't a clue.

Connor sat in his truck at the curb while Beth said goodbye to her parents. He'd driven her over earlier, expecting a quick visit before taking her the rest of the way to the airport, but Helen and Patrick had been so happy to see their daughter again and so sorry to see her go, that they'd insisted Beth and Connor sit down with them for a nice lunch of cold-meat sandwiches and fruit salad.

It had reminded him of old times, but he'd still felt uncomfortable. Helen and Patrick Curtis had always treated him like one of their own, even though he'd been nothing more than the scruffy foster child from across the street. He'd been a troublemaker, but they'd looked beyond that to the boy beneath who was desperate for a family, a place to belong, and for someone to love him. They'd given him all that and more, and continued to into his adulthood.

He would do anything for them, which included *not* betraying their trust by taking advantage of their only daughter.

But it was a little late to avoid that trap, wasn't it? He'd not only slept with Beth the night before last, he'd taken her virginity seven years ago, leaving her pregnant and alone. Thankfully, those particular gems of information hadn't come up during lunch.

He also hadn't thought of a single solution for settling things between them. She was saying her farewells to her mom and dad on the front lawn, then he would drop her off for her flight to California. Never to be seen again.

At least not for a good long while. She didn't come home very often. And she most especially wouldn't come home just to see him.

Dammit. What was he going to do?

The passenger door opened, breaking into his troubled thoughts. She climbed in beside him and he noticed the telltale glimmer in her eyes.

"You okay?"

She turned to look at him, sniffing to hold back tears. "Yeah, I just…never expected it to be so hard to leave." Digging in her purse for a tissue, she dabbed at her nose. "I've been back other times, but it's never felt this bad to take off again."

"Maybe that's because this time felt more like coming home."

The sudden leeching of color from her face told him he'd hit a little too close to the bone. But instead of responding, she glanced out the window, waving to her parents, who still stood in the yard. He took the hint and started the truck, lifting his own hand to Helen and Patrick as they pulled away from the curb.

The ride to the airport passed in silence. Not uncomfortable, just…quiet. He tried a dozen times to broach the subject of their relationship—past and present. The words swirled in his head, forming and then fading away before they reached the tip of his tongue.

He wanted to punch the steering wheel in frustration. Why couldn't he figure out what to say to her?

Pulling into the airport parking area, he shut off the pickup's engine and got out to unload her luggage from the truck bed. They made their way into the terminal. Beth checked her suitcase at the desk, and they walked together toward security.

Before reaching the metal detectors, she stopped, twisting slowly on the sole of her black pumps to lift her head and meet his gaze.

She was wearing a black power suit that made her look every inch the competent lawyer. Black slacks, black jacket, with a burnt-orange blouse underneath to brighten things up. Small gold hoops adorned her ears, a thin gold chain sparkling around her neck beneath the collar of her blouse. If he didn't know better, he'd think she was on her way to a multimillion-dollar contract negotiation. And he had no doubt she'd win every argument she made.

Her blue eyes shone up at him and his gut clenched at her never-ending beauty. Not just on the outside, but on the inside, too. She was everything he'd ever wanted in a woman, yet they were destined to revolve around each other, never stopping long enough to figure out what was really going on. Like asteroids, flying through space, occasionally crashing into one another before shooting off again in the opposite direction.

Tucking a strand of loose hair behind her ear, she said, "You don't have to go the rest of the way with me. I'll be fine, and I know you must have better things to do with your day than sitting around waiting for my plane to board."

He shoved his hands into the front pockets of his jeans, rocking back on the heels of his work boots. "Are you sure?"

She offered him a kind smile. "I'm sure."

Reaching out, she brushed her hand down the length of his arm, her heat warming him even through the light blue material. "Thank you for all you did while I was home this time. We may have started out on the wrong foot, but it was nice of you to drive me around when I needed it."

"No problem." A beat passed while he attempted to bring one of his earlier speeches to the forefront of his mind. Instead, all he could think to say was, "It was good to see you again."

"You, too, Connor."

"I'm sorry about everything, Beth Ann," he blurted out.

He would have said more, but she raised a hand, covering his mouth with two soft, manicured fingers.

"I told you, it's all right." She let her fingertips fall from his lips, landing on his forearm instead. "I'm glad we're friends again. I've missed you."

His mouth went stone dry at that and he could have sworn he felt tears prickling behind his eyes.

"Call me sometime," she added.

And then, before he could clear his throat to respond, she shifted the strap of her purse higher on her shoulder, offered him one final, friendly smile, and turned to leave.

He watched her pass through security, walking off toward her gate without a backward glance. His stomach churned, his palms sweating as he realized it was too late. She was gone. He'd missed his chance.

He stood there for several more minutes, watching after her—wishing she would come back into view, that he could relive their conversation and do it right instead of letting her slip away before he'd cleared his mind and his conscience.

With a heavy sigh, he let his chin drop to his chest dejectedly. That's it, it was over.

He wasn't even sure what he'd hoped to accomplish, other than making sure she knew how sorry he was for not being there for her seven years ago, for not being around to learn about the baby or help her through the miscarriage.

But the single resounding thought looping through his mind as he left the airport and headed for his truck wasn't that he'd failed to call her after they slept together the first time, or that he'd never known he was almost a father.

It was that he'd lost her.

A week later, Connor stood in the doorway of the finished nursery, his shoulder against the jamb as he studied the ocean-blue walls, the sea-creatures wallpaper border, the billowy white curtains. He'd put together a crib for the corner and a changing table for the far wall, and even installed a shelf above the table for powder, wipes, stuffed animals, whatever.

He'd done it all on his own, without Beth's guidance and feminine touch. And he'd missed it, dammit. He'd missed her.

Luckily, a woman at the store had pointed him in the right direction and helped him pick out some of the items. But just in case, he'd kept the receipts so Nick and Karen could return or exchange anything they didn't care for.

They'd gotten back from their honeymoon yesterday, and he'd reluctantly shown them the room. He'd wanted it to be a surprise, wanted to do something special for his best friend and his new wife and child. And he thought he'd accomplished that. Nick had been shocked at the transformation of his old bedroom, and Karen had burst into tears, sniffing and laughing happily as she moved around touching every stuffed animal, admiring each and every detail.

He was glad his friends liked the room, but his own pleasure in their reactions had been dampened by Beth's absence. It had been *their* project, not just his. She should have been there to see her brother's face and receive one of Karen's bone-crushing hugs.

He could picture her standing on a stepladder, affixing the border paper to the top of the wall, glue in her hair, paper unrolling out of control. He could hear her laughter as she struggled to keep her balance, see the gentle curve of her bottom beneath those low-riding jeans she'd worn while they worked, and imagined himself walking up behind her, running his hands over her legs and derriere until she gave up on her task and turned to kiss him instead.

Skipping ahead a few years, his brain decided to take a sharp detour into what their lives would be if they actually got together, if they married and started a family of their own. They would have a nursery just like this someday…or at least similar. Beth would bring her own unique sense of style to the decorating process, so their child could definitely look forward to something more exciting than clowns or teddy bears.

She would rock their babies to sleep while he watched from the doorway, then they would both put the child to bed and stand at the side of the crib, hand in hand, gazing down at the miracle they'd created.

God, he wanted that, he thought, pinching the bridge of his nose where a headache was starting to throb.

So why did he only figure that out now, when it was already too late?

Distracted by his daydreams and self-flagellation, Connor didn't hear Nick come up behind him until his friend slapped a hand on his shoulder and squeezed.

"Admiring your handiwork?"

"Yeah," he said, returning Nick's grin, even though it wasn't close to his true train of thought.

"I still can't believe you and Beth did all this. I wish she'd stuck around long enough for Karen and me to thank her." He gave Connor's shoulder another squeeze. "Thank you, too, man. You can't know what this means to us."

Connor inclined his head. "You deserve it. Both of you. I hope you'll be happy together for a long, long time."

Pushing away from the wall, he dug into his hip pocket and pulled out a small stack of paper slips. "Here. In case you want to return anything."

Nick took the receipts, shoving them into his own

pocket, but said, "Are you kidding me? After a honeymoon in Hawaii, I thought I'd be lucky if Karen didn't start begging me to build a dolphin enclosure in the backyard. Now she's got this to remind her. Good call, buddy."

Taking a deep breath, Connor swallowed hard. "It wasn't my idea, it was your sister's."

Maybe it was the tone of his voice or the tension in every fiber of his body, but Nick shifted to face him, leaning back against the opposite side of the doorway and crossing his arms over his chest.

"Something going on between you and my sister that I should know about?"

Connor's spine snapped carpenter's-level straight. He took a step back, meeting his friend's serious expression, and the denial leaped immediately to his lips. "No, of course not." He paused for a single kettledrum beat of his heart. "Why do you ask?"

"Come on," Nick scoffed with a wry chuckle. "You think I haven't noticed the way you two look at each other? The sparks that go off whenever you're together? It's been going on since we were kids."

"I—" He gave a strangled laugh. "I don't know what you're talking about."

"What's the big deal?" his friend wanted to know. "You like each other. You might as well see where it goes. And if it works out, all the better." He shrugged. "You're practically family already. I'd like nothing more than to be able to call you my brother-in-law, as well as my best friend."

Connor's chest grew tight, a ball of emotion the size

of his fist blocking his airway. He strained for breath, fought to keep the tears from gathering in the corners of his eyes.

"You're sure?" he finally managed, the words scraping like sandpaper past his dry lips while his head spun. "You wouldn't mind if I dated Beth?"

"Hell, no," Nick responded, landing a playful punch to his bicep. "Marry her, for all I care. Just make sure you're good to her," he warned with a pointed finger, "or I'll have to kick your ass."

He might have laughed, if the ground weren't still shifting dangerously beneath his feet.

"What about your parents?" he made himself ask. "Don't you think they'd mind if the foster kid from across the street started messing around with their daughter?"

Nick grew serious, his brows drawing together, twin lines of concern bracketing his mouth. "You're the only one who ever thought of yourself as a foster child. The rest of us just thought of you as Connor…our friend, and another member of the Curtis clan. Mom and Dad would probably love it if you and Beth hooked up. Even if they didn't think much of it at first, they'd be fine as long as Beth was happy. That's all they really want, anyway…and I don't mind telling you they don't think she is right now. Happy, I mean."

"No?"

He shook his head. "California is too far away. We hardly ever hear from her, she works too hard, and she pops antacids like they're candy. We're worried about her. Mom, Dad and I would like nothing better than for her to come to her senses and move back to Crystal Springs."

Connor's hands were clenching and unclenching at his sides, the shock of Nick's admission warring with the need to rush out and track down Beth. "You think she would?"

"I don't know," Nick said carefully. "Depends on what she had to come home to."

He met his friend's compassionate blue eyes, so much like his sister's, and blurted out the secret he'd been keeping for more than ten years. "I'm in love with her. I'm in love with your sister."

A wide grin broke out across Nick's face. "Yeah? She feel the same way?"

"I don't know," he answered honestly. And that suddenly terrified him more than the idea that her parents might not approve.

"Well, what are you standing here for?" Nick challenged, giving Connor a less-than-subtle nudge in the ribs with his elbow. "Go find out."

Taking a deep breath, he squared his shoulders and nodded in agreement. "Yeah, I think I need to go find out."

He started down the hall, determined now.

"Call if you need anything," Nick shouted after him.

He lifted a hand to wave in acknowledgment, but didn't slow his steps. He was on a mission, to hunt down the woman he loved.

And make damn sure she loved him back.

Twelve

Beth finished making notations on one of her clients' latest contracts, pleased to get the review out of the way before her lunch appointment.

She'd been playing catch-up ever since returning from Ohio. The scheduled time away would have been difficult enough to work around, but now she had to go out and schmooze one of Danny's more difficult clients because he was at home with his sick son and she'd promised to cover his appointments until he returned.

Her stomach pitched and she automatically reached for the roll of antacids she kept next to the sticky-note dispenser on her desk. Funny that she hadn't needed the medication even once while she'd been home.

Home. As hard as she'd tried to deny it, she did still think of Crystal Springs as home. Her family was there, and if she was brave enough to admit it, so was her heart.

Tamping down that thought, she bit into another tablet, grinding it between her teeth.

So she hadn't needed ulcer or migraine medicine while she'd been in Ohio. The same could probably be said if she'd spent a week in Jamaica. Being away from work was bound to reduce her stress level, regardless of what occurred during her vacation.

Setting the contract folder aside until she could discuss the proposed changes with her client, she walked to the bathroom to check her hair and makeup. She was unlocking the bottom drawer of her desk to retrieve her purse when the intercom buzzed.

"Yes, Nina?"

"There's a gentleman here to see you, Miss Curtis."

She frowned. Nina usually gave her adequate warning of exactly who was seeking an appointment and why. And she certainly didn't have time today for unexpected visitors or potential new clients.

"Who is it?" she asked.

"He…would rather not say."

With an annoyed sigh, she checked her watch. "Fine," she said shortly. "But please explain to him that I'm on my way out and only have a couple of minutes. If he needs more time than that, he'll have to make an appointment."

"This won't take long."

At the sound of his voice, her heart stuttered to a halt

in her chest, then picked up again at the speed of a racing freight train.

She hadn't heard the door open, but she heard it click quietly closed, and forced herself to lift her head, to meet his gaze.

He looked good. Lord, how could she think he looked better than he had the last time she'd seen him, when that was only a week and a half ago?

But even though it defied logic, he was more handsome than ever, standing across the room in his faded denims, well-worn boots and jean jacket open to reveal a red-plaid button-down shirt. His face was clean-shaven, his short hair combed and neat. His brown eyes burned into her, narrowed with determination.

"Connor," she said breathlessly. "What are you doing here?"

"I forgot to tell you something before you left."

Her eyes went wide in astonishment. "So you climbed on a plane and flew out here? You couldn't just pick up the phone?"

"Nope."

He took a step toward her and her knees threatened to buckle. She held herself upright with her palms pressed flat to the top of the desk, when what she really wanted to do was fall backward into her big, wheeled leather chair. But she was too curious about why he'd traveled cross-country to see her, and she didn't want to be sitting down when the answer came.

"All right." The words came out strangled and she swallowed hard before continuing. "What did you want to tell me?"

He moved forward another dogged pace, his thumbs hooked under the edges of his pant pockets, and her stomach fluttered wildly with anticipation.

"I love you."

She blinked, not sure she'd heard him correctly. But she must have, because the air in her lungs dried up and her ears began to buzz. Surely her body wouldn't have such a strong physical reaction to a more benign statement.

Lifting a hand to cover her pounding heart, she leaned heavily against the side of the desk and licked her parched lips. "Did you just say—"

"I love you."

This time, he came around the desk, grasping her by the tops of her arms and pulling her up to her full height. She craned her neck to meet his potent gaze.

"I'll say it as many times as it takes to make you believe," he told her with a slight shake. "I love you, Beth. I was crazy to let you walk away from me at the airport without telling you. I was crazy to pretend it wasn't true seven years ago…hell, ten years ago when I started to notice you less as my best friend's sister and more as a girl I wanted to go out with."

She wanted to weep, wanted to throw her arms around his neck and kiss him with all the love and passion in her soul. But she'd been hurt before. Gotten her hopes up, only to have them smash back down, lying broken on the ground at her feet. She couldn't go through that again.

"Why…" She cleared her throat and tried again. "Why are you telling me this now?"

"Because I've been a fool long enough. And I finally had a conversation with Nick that I probably should have had a decade ago. I told him I was in love with you, even though I was scared to death he'd bloody my nose for it…or worse, tell me to get lost. Tell me he wasn't my friend anymore, that I wasn't welcome near your family ever again."

His eyes closed for a brief moment, then opened again, myriad emotions visible in their coffee brown depths. "That's always been my biggest fear. That I'd do something stupid to screw up what I had with you guys. I was just this scruffy foster kid who landed across the street from the greatest family in the world. You treated me like one of your own, but I knew that wasn't true. I knew you and Nick belonged, and I was an interloper. One mistake, and you'd realize what a fraud I really was, and it would all come crashing down around my ears."

"Oh, Connor." The protective walls surrounding her crumbled and she lifted a hand to feather through the soft hair at his temple. "We never thought of you that way."

A crooked smile creased the corner of his mouth. "I guess I know that…now. But I didn't when we were teenagers, when I started to have feelings for you that I didn't think your folks would appreciate."

"Is that why you started to avoid me in high school? And why you never called after we slept together the night of the big football game?"

He nodded ruefully. "I was petrified about messing things up with you, that if your parents knew I had the hots for their daughter, they'd run me out of town on a rail."

"They never—"

"Yeah, your brother sort of convinced me of that the other day. After I told him how I really feel about you." His hands slipped down her arms, sliding around her waist. "He and Karen loved the nursery, by the way. I finished it up as best I could. She cried, and he was speechless for a good three minutes…which is the longest I think I've ever seen him go without having something to say."

Pulling her close, he lowered his head and rested his brow against hers. "I wish you had been there with me when I showed them the room, though. I want you with me always, Beth. I've been an idiot for so long…I don't want to go on making the same mistakes with you. If you're willing to give me a chance, I'll do everything in my power to make you happy. And if your family doesn't approve…"

She felt him swallow, felt his fingers flex at her back.

"Well, then, I'm sorry, but I'm not going to love you any less, and I'm not going to waste any more time hiding my feelings. If they reject me, so be it. But they'll have a hard time getting rid of me, considering I'll hopefully be married to their little girl by then."

Beth jerked back, studying him with a rapidly beating pulse and a yearning building in her chest like a tidal wave. "What are you saying?" she asked, her voice rasping with a thick mix of emotion and skepticism.

He glared at her in mock irritation. "What am I saying? What do you think I'm saying? Only the same thing I've been telling you for the past ten minutes. I love you. I've always loved you. I want to marry you, and have children with you, and grow old with you."

She shook her head, still not quite sure her ears weren't playing tricks on her. Oh, she wanted to believe, so badly. But the logical side of her brain kept insisting he couldn't have changed his mind about her in such a short time…that if he didn't feel this way when they were in bed together, he couldn't possibly feel this way now.

And yet, he'd gotten on a plane—which she happened to know was not his favorite mode of transportation—and flown across the country to see her, to look her in the eye and confess his love for her.

To ask her to marry him!

"I'm sorry about the baby," he said, apparently taking her silence for indecision. "I'm sorry about how I acted after the first time we made love. I couldn't have been a bigger cad if I'd tried. And I'm sorry—so much sorrier than you'll ever know—for not being there when you lost the baby. I would have loved to raise a child with you. Even if I'd been afraid your father would come after me with a shotgun for taking advantage of his little girl, I still would have done the right thing. I still would have wanted to be with you."

Raising his warm, callused hands to her face, he brushed her cheeks, then ran his fingers through the curls on either side of her head. "I want to make more babies with you, if you're agreeable."

His fingers tightened in her hair, but he didn't let go. "I'll understand if you don't want to leave L.A. Your life is here now. I don't expect you to just up and abandon your job and partner." He drew a deep breath, nostrils flaring. "I had a lot of time to figure this out on the plane, and I think I can sell my share of the company to Nick. We're making enough now that he can buy me out, then I can move out here with you. I don't know what I'll do for work, but I'll come up with something. I can always get a construction job, or—"

She covered his mouth with her hand, a smile tugging at the corners of her lips. "Connor, stop."

The smile broke into a full-fledged grin, and she couldn't hold back the laughter bubbling up from her belly. Was it any wonder she loved this man? Beyond his kindness and compassion and his adorable rear end, he was selfless. Once he made up his mind to love someone, there wasn't anything he wouldn't do for them. And she counted herself oh-so-lucky to be on the short list of people he cared that much about.

"There's something I forgot to tell *you* back at the airport, too."

She felt his chest hitch in nervous anticipation.

"What's that?" he asked warily.

"I love you." The tension drained from his body in a rush, and she rose on her toes to press her mouth to his. "I always have, you know that. I wasn't nearly as good at hiding it as you were," she added with a grin.

"I don't blame you for anything that happened seven years ago, not anymore. There's nothing more in the world I want than to be your wife and have another baby…or two, or three…with you. But I don't want you to quit working with Nick. I want to go back to Crystal Springs—with you, with my family. I want to go *home,* Connor."

"Are you sure?"

She didn't even have to think about it. With a nod, she said, "It might take some time. I might have to stay out here a while or fly back and forth until all the arrangements can be settled, but I think Danny will understand. He shouldn't have any problem finding a new partner to take my place in the firm."

Happiness blazed in his eyes, and she knew the same emotion had to be reflected on her own face.

"You know," he said in a low voice, shuffling forward so that she was forced to shuffle back, "we have a lot of lost time to make up for. Months. Years. A decade."

Her hip bumped the edge of her desk and she gave a startled yip when he lifted her onto the flat surface, moving between her legs. He nuzzled her neck, the sensitive spot behind her ear.

"As much as I'd like to, I do have a lunch appointment."

"Buzz your receptionist. Tell her to call and cancel."

His tongue darted out to lick a path of sensual fire from her collarbone to her cleavage and she moaned, letting her head fall back to grant him better access.

"I can't," she all but whimpered. "It's not even my client. I'm covering for Danny."

Bumping her knees farther apart, he pressed his arousal into the apex of her thighs. His busy fingers loosened the tail of her shirt from the waistband of her skirt.

"Then hold on to your law degree, sweetheart. You're about to be fashionably late."

So she did.

And she was.

* * * * *

Don't miss Mr and Mistress *from Heidi Betts in May 2007.*

THEIR
MILLION-DOLLAR
NIGHT

by
Katherine Garbera

KATHERINE GARBERA

is the award-winning, bestselling author of more than twenty books and has been nominated for *Romantic Times BOOKclub*'s career achievement awards in Series Fantasy and Series Adventure. Katherine recently moved to the Dallas area, where she lives with her husband and their two children. Visit Katherine on the web at www.katherinegarbera.com.

This book is dedicated to two of my cousins –
Annette Queck, who is like my mum's twin!
And Michelle Griffin, who is like my sister.
Thanks for making my summer trips to New
Jersey so memorable. First as a teenager when we
spent tons of money on the midway rides in Point
Pleasant. Then as an adult when we went gambling
in Atlantic City and certain ones of us had to lie
about our ages. Finally as a parent when we sat on
the beach huddled in sweatshirts (us Floridians
aren't used to a cold breeze at the beach!)
watching our kids play together in the surf.

One

Roxy O'Malley stared critically at the body in the mirror. For the first time in her life she was embarrassed by how she looked. She skimmed her gaze and her hands down the tight Spandex running bra that ended just below her 36DD breasts. That part wasn't bad.

Always when she got this far, she wanted to stop. She wanted to pretend that the last three months had never happened. Pretend that when she glanced lower all she'd see was the smooth skin of her midriff and stomach. Pretend that her life and what she knew about herself were still true.

She closed her eyes for a brief second, her hand going to her stomach. The ridges of the scars weren't rough against her fingers, but she thought they should be. The texture was different—foreign—and Roxy O'Malley, who'd once been called the most gorgeous bod on the Vegas strip, glanced down at the three scars. Three of them. One would have been bad enough, but three?

"Hey, sexy lady! Admiring the view?"

Roxy glanced over her shoulder at her boss and friend Hayden MacKenzie. She forced a cheerful note into her voice. "Hi, Hay! What's up?"

Hayden was a tall, good-looking man with dark hair and piercing blue eyes that always made Roxy feel like he could see straight to the heart of her vulnerabilities.

Quickly she dropped her hand and picked up the T-shirt she'd left draped on the back of the weight machine. She couldn't look him in the eye until she covered up. She would have turned away from him for privacy, but her back was worse than her stomach. Alan Technety had made sure of that. Because she'd broken up with him, he'd decided to make sure no other man would want her.

He'd also ensured she'd never dance again by cutting her so deeply on her left leg that he'd damaged the muscles and tendons. She couldn't even walk without a limp, which was worse than having the scars. Her body, which she'd always counted on, the one thing in her life that she'd always been able to control, was now out of her control.

Alan had done better than he could have expected. He'd made it so she didn't even want herself anymore. And her face had never been her vanity—Alan had known that and had focused instead on the lean dancer's body that she'd kept honed and in top form through careful diet and exercise.

"I need a favor, but only if you feel up to it," Hayden said.

"Okay, what do you need?" She walked to the small refrigerator in the employees' gym that held bottles of sports drink and water. It was only five o'clock in the morning. Normally Roxy was completely alone in the gym. She was surprised to see Hayden down here so early. The newlywed was besotted with his new bride and everyone in the casino knew Hayden and Shelby had a ritual breakfast every morning.

"Well, I want you to stop dealing," he said.

She froze. For the last month, since she'd been off on medical leave, Hayden had assigned her to work at the blackjack tables. Dealing wasn't really her thing, but she could do it—and she couldn't go back to headlining the European-style revue in the main theatre of the Chimera Resort and Casino. Being a dealer was a bit of a struggle, because she was on her feet all day and thanks to her leg injury, standing was a pain. Literally. But there was nothing else for her to do at the casino and living off charity—even

Hayden's disguised charity—by taking an extended leave of absence was something she couldn't tolerate.

"I can't dance. You know I can't have another surgery for six months…"

Hayden put a hand on her shoulder and turned her around to face him. "I'm not asking for that, Rox. I want you to be one of my VIP hostesses. Entertain the high rollers, keep them happy and in the hotel."

She glanced up at him, feeling like a fool. She never reacted the right way. It was just like old Ms. Wiggins had said back at the group home. Blood always tells. And Roxy O'Malley's blood, much as her name implied, didn't include a pedigree worth mentioning.

She stepped away from Hayden, walking carefully so that the limp wouldn't be obvious. He was always treating her like she was his kid sister, and there was a part of her that *wanted* to be his kid sister.

"When would I start?" she asked, grabbing a towel from the floor and draping it over her neck.

"Tonight."

"Who will I be accompanying?"

"Max Williams. He's a good friend of mine and I think you'll enjoy his company."

"That doesn't really matter, Hay. I'm going to be working with him, right?"

Hayden shrugged.

"Please tell me you're not setting me up with him."

"I'm not. This is a legit job. But if you like him…"

"Hayden MacKenzie, matchmaker. There's something very wrong with this picture," she said. But deep inside, she was touched. "I think I'll stick to the job."

"Okay. I'll have Kathy send you his information. I'll need to see you in my office at three. We'll meet Max in the lobby when he arrives."

She nodded and Hayden started for the door. "Does he know about me?"

Hayden paused. "What do you mean?"

She wanted to chose her next words carefully but the only ones in her head were blunt and honest. "That I was a topless dancer who was attacked by a crazy man."

She knew her words came from old criticisms that she'd thought she was past. But her new scarred body had left her vulnerable in a way she hadn't realized she could be.

Hayden came back to her, put his hand on her shoulder again and didn't speak until she looked up and met his clear steady gaze. "Roxy, you were the headliner in a highly regarded show. I don't gossip about my employees."

She saw something more than the truth in his eyes and it warmed her in a way that she couldn't explain. But no man had ever really offered help to her and she didn't trust it. "I know. But I also know Max is your friend."

"Even to my friends."

She nodded and he left. She slowly made her way out of the gym and into the employee locker room. She couldn't shower here. Couldn't take the chance that another woman would come in and see her scars. She always went back to her condo on the other side of town to clean up. When she'd been the star of the revue, she'd had a private dressing room with her own shower. But not anymore.

She thought about what Hayden was offering her. It was a good job. One that would require her to be charming, funny, entertaining—all the things she used to be, but wasn't sure she was anymore.

Max Williams was tired and frustrated with the businessmen he was dealing with. Each time he negotiated with them and came close to sealing the deal, they came up with another item that had to be settled before they would sell to him. The latest hiccup appeared to be the fact that he was a bachelor and married to his job.

Duke, his right-hand man, had suggested that Max take a break, leave Vancouver and go to Vegas for a few days and let him handle this latest setback.

Max had agreed, even though Vegas didn't hold the same charm for him that it always had. With two of his closest friends recently married, Vegas was no longer the bachelor playground that it used to be. At least not for him, the only single guy in a group of besotted fools.

Every time he turned around lately it seemed that marriage surrounded him. It was the reason Harron was stalling on closing the merger deal, and it was the reason his friends were no longer available for all-nighters.

His father, the five-times-married Harrison Williams, IV, had said marriage was the ultimate match in the man-versus-woman game. And only the player with the most cunning survived. Max wasn't interested in negotiating as hard in his relationships as he did in his work, so he'd always steered clear of those types of entanglements.

The limo pulled to a stop in front of the elegant facade of the Chimera's hotel. Max made no move to leave the vehicle. He scowled and cursed under his breath, then forced the social mask he always wore into place, that mix between interest and confidence that his mother said every successful person should always portray in their smile. He forced that look onto his face just as the chauffeur opened the door. Max stepped out and walked confidently past all the tourists, gamblers and celebrities milling there.

A rock guitarist stood in the middle of a group of fans, minor celebrities and photographers.

As soon as Max entered the air-conditioned comfort of the lobby, Hayden MacKenzie strode over to him. They shook hands and then hugged each other quickly. Max let his smile drop and a bit of his frustration show on his face.

"Glad you're here. Shelby is, too. You're invited for dinner tonight."

"Thanks. I think I have an appointment in the high-stakes gaming room, so I'll have to pass."

"When are you going to have time for anything besides business and gambling?"

Max rubbed the back of his neck. "Not any time soon."

Hayden put his hand on Max's shoulder and Max let the bond of their long friendship ease some of his tension. "So where's Jack?"

"I've got someone new for you this time. She's really great and I think you'll like her."

"Does she have a nice personality? Am I supposed to bring a rose so she'll recognize me?"

"She's your hostess."

"Then why does it sound like you're setting me up?"

"I don't know. Maybe I am. I like both of you, and you're both…"

"Don't go there. I'm here to gamble and that's it."

Hayden nodded. "I thought you'd feel that way. Let me introduce you to Roxy O'Malley."

Hayden turned and gestured to a stunningly gorgeous blonde. She was the embodiment of everything that was feminine and seductive. She took one step toward them, carrying herself with grace. Her second step faltered, and he noticed she had a limp.

He also noticed the frustration that passed briefly over her face.

"Roxy, this is Max Williams. Max, Roxy O'Malley."

Max reached out automatically to take her hand and forced his genial smile back onto his face. He'd been told by his second stepmother, Andrea, that he had the sweetest smile. Duke assured him that was not the case unless one was blind. There were too many teeth in Max's smile to miss the resemblance to a shark. But then, Duke wasn't a woman.

"Pleasure," he said. But the rest of his words stuck in his throat. Her hand was smooth and cold in his. And when he glanced into her eyes, he saw how nervous she was. She was stunningly beautiful and her body was built to make a man think of long nights and slow loving.

He held her hand longer than he knew was polite, rubbing his thumb over the back of her knuckles until a faint blush stole over her cheeks.

"Nice to meet you, Mr. Williams."

"Call me Max."

"Max. I'm Roxy."

"I'll leave you two to it then," Hayden said and then left.

She tugged on her hand and he let her go. "Your luggage is being taken up to your suite. Do you want to stop up there first or head straight to the casino?"

"I want…" *you*, he thought. But knew better than to say it. He didn't understand it, this wild attraction to her. And it *was* wild. He didn't *do* lust at first sight. He had never had any problems controlling his reactions to any woman. Why her?

"Yes?"

"To head to the casino," he said at last. Other than sitting in the boardroom and negotiating a takeover, there was nothing else he liked as much as playing the odds at the poker table.

She smiled at him. "Then let's go play."

"What do you think my game is?"

"Poker. And it was your game long before the current Texas Hold 'Em craze that's sweeping America."

He was surprised she'd guessed it. But then he knew better than to judge a book by its cover. How many times had he been mistaken for a rich brat of a man who never worked a day in his life? Okay, so, not often, but it had happened.

"Don't be impressed. I read your file before you arrived. You won close to $50,000 last time you were at the poker tables."

"What else did you read about me?" he asked, wondering what was in his file. He wasn't concerned.

Hayden kept stats on all the high rollers who came into the casino, even his friends.

She tipped her head to the side and her long hair brushed against her neck. He wondered if it was as soft and silky as it looked. "I can't tell you that. You'd know all my secrets."

He caught her hand and pulled her to a stop. Damn, she had the softest skin he'd ever touched. "All of them? I doubt that. I'd only know the ones about myself. And technically, those aren't yours."

He was flirting, and he hadn't done that in a long time. The fatigue that had dogged him for the last few weeks melted away when she smiled and slipped her arm through his, leading him into the poshest section of the casino. The dinging bells and whistles of the main casino floor faded as they stepped into the high-stakes room.

She paused in the doorway, and Max realized that she must be new to the VIP hostess thing, because she pulled them into a quiet corner instead of urging him to the table.

"Do you really want to know my secrets?" she asked, her voice dipping low and sounding sensual, husky.

Yes, he thought. But didn't say it out loud. He didn't know why he was reacting so strongly to her but knew that he wasn't himself and he needed to get back on track. He wasn't looking for another affair.

In fact, he was damned tired of them. And right now he needed just to play.

When he said nothing, she flushed and moved away from him. "Sorry if that was too personal. Let's get you to a table and I'll get you your favorite drink."

She started to walk away with her limping gait and he almost let her but didn't. He stopped her with his fingers on her shoulder. She glanced back at him, and he saw that damned vulnerability in her eyes again. "I do want to know your secrets, Roxy."

He walked past her and seated himself at a table with a few familiar faces. But instead of concentrating on the cards and the game, he saw only the surprise in Roxy's blue eyes in his mind.

Roxy tried to remember everything that Hayden had said, especially the part about being friendly but never forgetting that business was the focus of her assignment. Keep the gambler happy and at the tables.

Max made that hard. Every time she dropped off another drink for him, or inquired about his needs, he flirted. And for the first time since she'd wakened in a hospital bed, scarred for life, she felt like flirting back.

He played and won for almost four hours before pushing back from the table. Since this was her first hostessing assignment she had no idea if she should try to make him stay longer.

"Are you sure you want to stop now? You're on a winning streak."

"I'm sure. I want to take my hostess to dinner and see if my luck stays."

"I don't know if I'm allowed to do that," she said, knowing she wasn't lucky but not wanting him to know it. Every time she got close to grasping the brass ring of what she wanted from life, it slipped away. So she knew luck wasn't with her.

"You're supposed to keep me happy."

She wanted to laugh at the way he said it. But didn't. "Then I guess I'm going to dinner with you. Where do you want to go?"

"I'll take care of the arrangements," Max said. He pulled her out of the flow of traffic and reached for his Blackberry.

Immediately she knew she had to keep her head in the game with this man. This was a job. She couldn't forget it, no matter how tempting it might be to do so. This new assignment was much better than dealing and she didn't want to mess it up. "No, you won't. That's my job."

"And you take your work seriously?" he asked, arching one eyebrow at her.

She sensed he was teasing, but she couldn't joke about work. Anyone who'd ever lived off the charity of others learned pride at a heavy cost. "Of course I do."

"I thought you were new here."

"New to hostessing. But I've worked at the Chimera for almost ten years now."

"What did you do before?" he asked.

"Danced," she said. She heard the longing in her own voice and cursed herself for it. She should have been prepared for the question. But most people she encountered either knew her story or didn't care about her personal life. Max was the first stranger to ask about her since…

"Why'd you stop?" he asked.

A simple little question. She closed her eyes for a moment. Years of practice and discipline gone in a few short minutes. Gone because she'd judged a man and his intentions badly. *Don't do it again,* she warned herself.

"Injury," she said. The lie fell easily from her lips and she hated herself for it. She'd grown up in a world where lies were traded and accepted for the truth. She was becoming her own mother. Something she'd promised herself she'd never do. "But that's old news. Give me a minute and I'll get us a table for dinner."

She turned away from Max and took out her cell phone to call the VIP office. Thirty seconds later everything was set up, and she and Max were on their way to the exclusive five-star restaurant on the fifth floor of the casino.

"Have you eaten here before?" she asked, hoping

he'd say no so she could slip easily into her role of tour guide. She led Max past the crowd at the front of the restaurant to the maître d', very aware of his quiet presence behind her.

"Yes. In fact, the chef/owner is a friend of mine."

She smiled at the maître d', Henry, whom she knew from her years at the hotel. Henry winked at her and she relaxed a little. This new job was not what she expected. Or should she say that Max Williams wasn't what she'd expected. "Mr. Williams and I are ready to be seated."

"Certainly, Ms. O'Malley. Follow me."

Max put his hand on Roxy's back as they moved through the restaurant. She tried to ignore the heat from his large palm, but she couldn't. It made everything feminine in her pulse into awareness. That long-sleeping part of her, the part that had been dormant even before her accident started to awaken. That scared her.

She was grateful when they reached the table and took their seats. Max asked for the wine list and the sommelier came to their table.

"Do you have a preference?" he asked after the sommelier suggested some wines.

"I usually buy my wine by the gallon in the supermarket," she said. Then flushed as she realized how that sounded. "I mean—"

Max chuckled. "I have cousins who own a vineyard in the Napa Valley. They'd be outraged to hear that anyone in the U.S. still drinks cheap wine."

"Sorry," she said.

"Don't be. Have you ever tried South African wine?"

"Does Gallo make one?"

He laughed. "We'll have a bottle of the Thelema Chardonnay 1998, Stellenbosch."

The sommelier left and Max turned his attention to her. She felt uncomfortable under his intense stare, as if she was naked but not in a sexual way. His gaze was probing as if he were trying to fit together all the pieces that made up Roxy O'Malley. She desperately hoped he couldn't, because Roxy O'Malley wasn't sure who she was anymore. Not a dancer, not a hot body, not any of the things she'd always been.

Finally she couldn't stand it anymore. "What?"

"What, what?"

"Why are you looking at me like that?"

"Because you are a beautiful woman."

His words hurt in a way he couldn't understand. Because at one time she'd have tossed her hair and given him a smile that would have brought him to his knees. "Not anymore."

She couldn't believe those words had escaped. "How long will you be in Vegas?"

"Long enough to convince you that you are beautiful."

"That's not why you came," she said, telling herself that he was here for the Vegas allure. The mindless flirting, the hours of gambling. The vacation from reality and real life.

"My plans have changed."

"Well then, you won't be needing my company anymore. I'll let Hayden know."

He took her hand in his, his thumb stroking over the backs of her knuckles as it had when they first met. "I'll still require your company, Roxy."

She tried to tell herself that things hadn't turned personal, that she was still objective and just his hostess. But she knew she wasn't.

There was a promise of something in Max's eyes that she wanted to claim for herself. Something elusive and tempting, and she couldn't quite make herself ignore it.

Two

After dinner, Max excused himself to return several business calls. Sitting in his suite, he was aware of what his life had become. He was forty and successful but alone.

Alone by his own design, granted. But still alone. No mistress—he'd learned the hard way that even couching an affair in business terms didn't mean a clean break when things were over.

Harron had made several comments about the fact that Max was lacking a wife, a family. But Max had his family. They were paid employees and a small core group of lifelong friends.

There was a knock on his door. He hoped it would

be Roxy, but knew it wouldn't be. Instead it was the bellman with a FedEx box containing paperwork from his office.

He took the papers with him to the minibar and poured himself a Scotch. Looking hard at his life made him realize that in his quest to make sure no one thought he was riding his father's coattails, he'd created a vacuum. A place where no one existed except for himself.

Ah, hell, he was getting morose. He signed the papers, dropped them in the return envelope and then swallowed his drink in two long gulps.

He wanted Roxy.

He wanted to spend more time with the beautiful woman who could be charming until she remembered herself. Then she was awkward and shy. And he wanted to know why. He really did want to uncover her secrets, but he sensed she wouldn't share them. Not yet.

He also couldn't compromise her job. He made a quick call to Hayden and asked that Roxy's job be changed, explaining very little to his friend, but then Hayden was a man known for being quick-witted. "I'll be taking her out of the casino tomorrow for the day."

"Don't allow my business to get in the way of your personal plans," Hayden said.

"You are the one who extolled her virtues."

"That's right. I did, but I didn't count on your interest interfering with my business."

"I won't."

Max hung up the phone then dialed the front desk and asked for Roxy, knowing that even though it was almost midnight she'd be available. Everyone was always available to him in Vegas. To be truthful, wherever he traveled he was seldom turned down. He waited while he was connected to her.

"Hello?"

Her voice was soft and sweet, husky with fatigue, and he knew that if he were a nicer man, he'd just hang up and let her get some sleep. But he wasn't feeling particularly nice tonight.

"It's Max."

"Did you decide what time you wanted to start in the morning?" she asked, her tone warming a little.

Gambling was no longer the reason he was in Vegas. But he knew he'd have to keep that to himself a while longer. "No. I'm going back to the high-stakes room tonight. I need you there."

She hesitated and he wondered if she'd tell him no. "Oh, sure, Max. Only, I went home so it'll take me at least a half hour to get back to the casino."

"Why aren't you staying at the hotel?" he asked. He'd assumed she'd get a room while he was there. That was what his usual host, Jack, did.

"Hayden didn't ask me to. Actually, it never occurred to me you'd need me in the middle of the night."

If she only knew how much he needed her.

"Pack a bag when you come back," he said.

"For what?"

"To stay here until I leave."

"I'm not sure my job covers—"

He didn't want to discuss the fact that her job description had changed. "I'll cover it."

"Max, are you okay?" she asked.

Her voice sounded sweet, but he heard the underlying pique. She didn't like to take orders. And for the first time since he'd met her he had a glimpse into the fact that she was more than a pretty, smiling hostess. Her annoyance wasn't unexpected because most people didn't like to be told what to do. But Max had found the easiest way to get what he wanted was to do just that.

"Fine. I'll see you in the lobby in thirty minutes."

"It may take me longer than that."

"Why?"

"I have to shower and then pack an overnight case."

"What were you doing?" he asked. Jealousy pricked the back of his mind. Had she been with a man? *He* was her job.

And he was the one who was thinking this could be something more than gambler and hostess. He hoped he didn't turn out like his father, desperately seeing a relationship where there wasn't one.

He rubbed the back of his neck. It wasn't personal,

he reminded himself. But he knew that the reminder came too late. He felt something for Roxy whether he wanted to or not.

"Working out."

"What about your injury?"

She hesitated and he knew that she wasn't at peace with it yet. Was it recent?

"It's fine."

But something in her voice said it wasn't. "You never said what type of injury it was."

"I'm not going to, either. I'll meet you in the hotel lobby in an hour, okay?"

"Why won't you answer me?"

"Because it's private and personal. Isn't there something in your life you don't talk about?"

There was a lot, but he had always had a knack for getting people to open up. It was one of the reasons he was so good at takeovers. He could find out exactly the qualm the other CEO had and re-assure them that he'd take care of it.

"Max?"

"Yes, I have things I don't discuss. But I'm asking about an injury, not asking you to bare your soul."

"I wish that were true, but my injury changed who I am."

He wished he was with her so he could read her expressive eyes instead of having to rely on the phone line to figure this out. Not being able to dance must be tied to her sense of self. He'd met dancers before. Knew that they'd usually spent their entire life practicing. Living at the dance studio and keeping their bodies in top shape.

"Tell me about it," he invited.

She said nothing. The silence lengthened, but he knew she was still there. She was waiting him out, trying to see if he'd simply give up and hang up. But Max had made patience a priority when he was ten years old and had never forgotten it. His impatience at age ten had cost him time with his father. Something that had been rare in his childhood, and he'd never forgotten that had he waited an extra thirty minutes he could have gone on an extended weekend with his dad instead of spending time at the arcade with his boarding school pals. Nowadays he could wait for days—even weeks— for what he wanted.

"I'm not going to go away."

"Yes, you will, Max. I can't do this right now. I'm just your hostess. I'm not willing to be your vacation fling. That thing you did in Vegas that *has to stay here* because it's a dirty little secret."

He cursed under his breath. "You know nothing about the type of man I am if you think that I'd pursue a woman just to have a tawdry thrill to bandy about in the boardroom."

"You're right. I *don't* know you."

"Come to the casino with me tonight. Let me show you the man I am."

She agreed and hung up the phone. Max left his suite and headed for the busy casino floor, hoping that by surrounding himself with people he could dull his need for Roxy.

It didn't work.

Roxy had three dresses and four approved pantsuits that Hayden had sent to her to wear for this assignment. But they weren't her style and she hated the feeling she got when she put them on—as if she was pretending to be someone she wasn't.

She took the pants from one of the suits and paired them with her favorite silk halter top. She now had to wear flats instead of heels, and she hated that. Grabbing her overnight bag, she left her house without a backward glance.

She drove the same car she'd had since she'd made headliner. It was a sweet BMW Land Shark convertible. And for the first time in a really long time she didn't have that sinking feeling in her stomach that stemmed from things lost. Instead she put the top down and let the cool summer air whip her hair around her head. She pumped up the music on the stereo, slipping in her favorite Dave Matthews CD when she couldn't find a song she liked on the radio.

She sang at the top of her lungs to "Ants Marching" and refused to let her mind dwell on the joy that had come from…a man. It had come from Max.

His phone call. She never slept at night. *No one knew that.* His call had rescued her from tortured hours of trying to force herself to sleep. Trying to close her eyes and not see images of Alan's face. Or worse, images of herself on stage performing the way she used to before the audience gasped in horror seeing her bright red scars.

Her foot slipped off the gas. Why had she let her mind go down this path?

She pulled into the parking lot of the casino and parked, but couldn't make herself get out of the car. Suddenly everything was there. Every emotion and fear that she'd been running from, every damned thing she'd thought she'd left at her small house was in that car with her.

She put her head forward on the steering wheel and tried to recapture the joy, but it was gone. Dave Matthews kept singing, but now she felt that bittersweet emotion that came from hearing something happy when all you felt was sad.

She switched off the radio and forced herself from the car. She put the top up and locked the doors before walking toward the shimmering lights of the Chimera. The ultimate illusion, she reminded herself. She'd learned early on that illusion wasn't bad. And the Chimera offered her an illusion of herself that she easily embraced.

She forced herself into the lobby, a smile firmly in place. She could do this. In fact, she had done this every minute since she'd come awake in the hospital. She'd learned that most people were fooled by a smile and a quick assurance, because most people didn't like to dwell on things like her attack.

"Roxy."

She stopped and looked at Max. He held a cigar loosely in his left hand and watched her with eyes that seemed troubled. He looked sophisticated and urban. The trappings of success fell easily on his shoulders and in the glittering crowds of Vegas she saw him for what he really was.

There was no illusion in Max Williams. There was only a solid core that made her realize he was the real McCoy. He was successful and sophisticated. She crossed to him and stood, unable to think of what to do next.

Then she remembered the old Roxy, the one who'd been so bold in life. What would she have done? She'd have wrapped herself around his arm and said something flirty. No matter what she felt inside.

"Roxy?"

She shook her head to clear it. She needed to get her emotions under control. Hayden was counting on her to make sure that Max stayed in the hotel and

gambled. And she didn't want to let her friend down.
"Sorry, Max. Let's hit the tables."

"Not yet," he said, cupping his hand under her
elbow and leading her out of the hotel and into the
lushly landscaped gardens. There was a box-hedge
maze that was illuminated by the light of the moon
and subtle horticulture lighting.

"Where are we going?" she asked. She hung on
to her illusion of happy Vegas girl by a thread.

"Somewhere quiet."

"Why?" she asked, closing her eyes as she inhaled
the aromatic scent of his cigar mingled with the scent
of jasmine. For a moment she felt as if she were
somewhere else. Someone else. But who?

He stopped and trailed his fingers up her bare arm,
leaving gooseflesh in their path. She shivered, opening her eyes and looking into his clear gray gaze.

He was watching her with an intensity that made
her hyperaware of herself. Of her femininity and his
masculinity. Of the elemental differences between
the two of them. She put her hand on his biceps and
felt the solid strength in him.

This was a man who could handle everything life
threw at him. She wondered if she could learn how
he did it. If she could figure out what made him tick
and use that knowledge to help herself. Yeah, right,
she thought. The main reason she wanted to know
what made him tick was that she wanted to know *him*.

Wanted to lean up and kiss him. To see if the fire in his eyes would be matched in his embrace. To taste his kiss and see if it would be as exciting as she knew it would be. But he was still a stranger, and she was wary of letting any man too close too quickly.

He ran his finger down the line of her cheek and traced it over her lower lip. "We are out here because I want us to be. And you are supposed to cater to my every need."

His every need. "I'm not sure what you're insinuating. But I've never been that type of girl."

"I know that. I'm not insinuating anything. I don't want you to be my hostess, Roxy."

She swallowed. "Okay."

"I want to be free to spend my time with you. To take you out of the hotel and away from the gaming room."

She didn't know what to say. She only knew that this job had lasted only one day, and she had no desire to go back to dealing. She was going to be out on the streets. She'd have to sell her car.

"I want us to get to know each other," Max said.

She shook her head. She'd have to find another job. "I'm not ready to date."

"Yes, you are," he said. His breath brushed against her face and she leaned into his body, wanting to kiss him. Wanting to feel his lips on hers and see if it would be the intense experience she sensed it would be. She realized that she was falling for the Vegas fantasy. Rich man, beautiful woman, whirlwind romance.

She pulled back, turning away from him and walking toward a bench a few feet away. "You're too bossy."

He didn't follow her, just stood in the middle of the path, taking a draw on his cigar and watching her with enigmatic eyes that saw too much. "I'm used to being in charge."

"This isn't your boardroom and I'm not one of your employees."

"No, you're not. But that doesn't mean that I'm not going to take control."

Max was pushing and he knew it so he backed off. He really did want Roxy by his side, and not just here in Vegas. She was the right woman at the right time. He needed a fiancée and, well, she fit the bill.

Even as the words echoed in his mind, he knew he was walking on thin ice. She wasn't just an accessory he could pick up in Vegas and return with to Vancouver.

"Come with me to the casino. You can be my lucky charm, and then I'll take you to breakfast and we can discuss this further."

"I've never been anyone's lucky charm," she said.

"Maybe you just didn't realize it," he said, steering them through the crowded casino floor toward the high-stakes poker area in the back. Now he hardly noticed her slight limp.

"I think I'd know if I was lucky."

"Maybe your luck is with things you take for granted," he said, knowing that his luck came from making things happen. From never sitting and waiting but getting up and taking action.

She stopped walking. "I think you might be right. I mean, I wanted to win the lottery but didn't. I wanted to keep on dancing and can't."

"I didn't mean to bring up bad memories."

She shook her head, shaking her honey-colored hair against her shoulders. Her hair looked like silk in the casino lighting, and he knew he should be concentrating on her words but instead just wanted to bury his hands in her hair and hold her head still for a soul-deep kiss.

"I just realized that I am lucky in a million little ways," she said.

He took a deep breath and reached for the concentration that he was known for. Then he took her by the wrist and led her away from the noise and the crowds to an alcove tucked away in the corridor. "What are those things?"

She bit her lower lip and his concentration almost flew out the window. What would her mouth taste like?

"It will sound silly," she said.

"I just called you my lucky charm, I think we're already into silly."

"Did you mean it?" she asked.

"Yes."

She smiled at him then and her expression was so…tender that his heart almost broke. "That wasn't silly, Max. It was very sweet."

"Ah, hell, God save me from being sweet. You're supposed to look at me and think, What a sexy guy. Not a sweet man." But he liked that she thought of him that way. No one had ever seen him in that light before. They'd called him ruthless, determined and successful, but never sweet.

"Can't you be both?"

"I don't know, can I?" he counted.

He wrapped his arm around her waist and pulled her closer to him. Her words—that she wasn't ready to date—echoed in his mind as he held her. Hell, neither was he, but holding her soothed that bit of loneliness that had been echoing through his soul.

"I'm not sure this is on the approved list of acceptable activities between a VIP and his hostess."

"Your boss is one of my best friends, so I think I know how to make this right."

"For you?"

He realized again that he was moving too fast. Her comment still ticked him off because he'd always been the kind of man that others respected. "No,

Roxy, for you and when you know me better I'll expect an apology for that."

"I'm sorry. I'm much better at light social talk, or performing up on the stage where I can't say the wrong things."

"You didn't say the wrong thing."

"Yes, I did. I offended you."

"I get offended daily."

"How?"

"Usually from investors of rival companies. Or the board of directors of a company that I want to take over. Sometimes from my second in command, but he says that's to keep my ego in check."

"He's your friend, then?"

Max thought about Duke and nodded. "Yes. He saved my life once."

"Did you repay him?" she asked, with a shrewdness he wished she didn't have.

"Of course I did. I couldn't let that kind of debt languish."

"Have you ever let any debt languish?"

"No, I haven't. I like to keep things even," he said lightly because he knew that he really preferred to keep the balance tipped toward him. To make sure that he was the one who did just a bit more in a relationship.

"But you're bossy. So I'm guessing that you like to be in charge all the time."

He shrugged his shoulder. "What can I say? I run

an international conglomerate. I have to lean toward the type-A personality."

"Just in business?"

He shook his head, uncomfortable pursuing this topic. "You were going to tell me what you were lucky at."

"I was?"

"Yes, you were."

"Is that an order?"

She was sassing him. And he liked it, but he gave her a quelling stare. One that always made the office staff jump through hoops for him.

"I'm not intimidated," she said. "But I will tell you what I'm lucky at…."

She paused and he waited for her to continue.

"I'm lucky in being alive. Now, if I can just re-member how to live."

Three

Max played for four hours straight, insisting Roxy stay close by. She enjoyed being with him but the combined cigarette and cigar smoke was giving her a headache.

"I need to step outside for a few minutes. Breathe some fresh air."

Max nodded. "I'm going to play one more hand and then we'll go get some breakfast."

Since it was almost six o'clock, it would be an early breakfast but she didn't mind. She doubted that he'd only play one more hand.

Most of the men she'd dated had been gamblers. She'd met them all in a casino, and they never left any table or game after just one more hand or roll.

Six months time had made a huge difference in how she spent her days. Normally she would have been arriving at the casino about now and heading to the rehearsal hall for an intense dance workout and review of the previous night's show.

Instead, she was fetching drinks and keeping a man who didn't need the incentive in the casino. She hadn't felt this lost since she'd turned eighteen and realized that she no longer had a place to stay at the group home in which she'd lived. Two months left until high-school graduation, and she'd been on her own.

"Rox?"

She glanced over her shoulder and saw Tawny and Glenda crossing the casino, heading toward the rehearsal hall. Glad to see her old friends, she tried to smile. This feeling of envy, jealousy and embarrassment was exactly why she'd been avoiding them. They were still doing something she no longer could, and she felt a weird combination of envy, jealousy and some joy every time they visited her.

"Hey, girls. How's the show?" she asked. Both of them were still fit and pretty. Roxy looked at them and didn't feel the same sense of belonging as she used to. She shifted her weight, trying to feel as if she could still fit in if she wanted to.

"Not the same without you," Glenda said. "Roger has been really mean lately. One small slip-up and he reams you a new one."

"Well it's his butt on the carpet if the show isn't good," Roxy said. Roger's temper was legendary, but he usually only exploded if the chorus was loafing. And she couldn't imagine Glenda or Tawny loafing. They took dancing as seriously as she did... had.

"I didn't see you at the blackjack tables earlier. I hoped that meant you'd be backstage," Tawny said.

"Not yet. I still have a few more surgeries before I'll be ready." But that wasn't the truth. She'd never dance again. The combination of the strenuous show moves and the weight of some of the headdresses they wore would be too much for her body. The doctor had told her after her last surgery that dancing in Vegas was out. A showgirl no more.

"Get well soon, girl," Glenda said, giving her a hug before the two women moved on.

Roxy leaned back against the wall for a second. She really wanted to sink into it and become invisible. Then she remembered she was in public and straightened up, forcing herself to head for the exit.

The warm touch of a man's hand on her back startled her. She jumped a little. But she knew that touch. The feel of that palm had been embedded in her memory already. She glanced back at Max.

"You okay?"

"Fine," she said.

He rubbed his hand down her arm, linking their

fingers together, and led her away from the casino floor and out of the hotel. "Who were those women?"

"Friends of mine," she said.

"Dancers?"

She nodded. She wasn't ready to talk about that part of her life. Not that he was probing into it. She knew her reaction had a lot more to do with the fact that she didn't know how to deal with seeing her best friends than any question Max asked. "Where are we going?"

"For breakfast. I think I mentioned we'd eat after I finished that hand."

She flushed a little, remembering she hadn't thought he'd really get up and leave the table after one hand.

"Uh-oh, what's that look?"

"What look?"

"That sheepish one."

"I didn't think you'd actually leave after one hand."

"I'm a man of my word," he said, pulling her to a stop in the middle of the path.

She tipped her head back to stare into his eyes. He patiently let her look at him and she sighed deep inside realizing that she'd never met a man like Max before. She doubted she ever would again. He was solid through and through. He wasn't part of the illusion of Vegas.

"Sorry. Most gamblers can't leave."

"I really just do it for fun and to relax."

His fun had a much higher price tag on it than hers did. She could have bought a new house with some of the jackpots that were won and lost while Max played cards.

"Tell me about your job," she said.

"Later. We have to get moving to make our breakfast."

"Are we leaving the hotel?"

He nodded, steering her down the path that led to Hayden's private garage.

"We have some really nice—"

He held up his hand. "I know. I've already talked to Hayden about moving you to be someone else's hostess."

"You did?" she asked. She couldn't believe his gall. Did he think he owned the world?

"Now don't get mad."

"Too late. Do you think that you own me? I'm not sure that you listened when I said I don't work for you."

"I heard that. That's why I spoke to Hayden. I have other plans for you and I, Roxy."

She shook her head. "Maybe I don't want to be a part of them."

He didn't force her closer, but she felt surrounded by him. "I'm not like this normally, but there is something about you that draws me."

"Lust?"

"Yes," he said with a devilish grin. "But more

than that. If you don't feel the same, then say the word and this ends here."

"What is *this?*" she asked, unwilling to admit that she found him attractive. She knew he was out of her league.

"I have no idea, but I don't want to let you go. I want to spend the next day with you, exploring the attraction between us."

His words combined with the fire in his eyes melted her resistance. She knew that this was going to lead to heartache. They were so different. But she wanted to spend more time with him.

Santa Barbara, California, was perfect for his needs. Roxy was quiet as he drove them to the private airport and his waiting Learjet.

"Okay, where are we going?"

"For breakfast on the beach. I want to watch the day begin with you."

He could tell by her expression that she was overwhelmed and that pleased him. He'd been overwhelmed by a need to be with her ever since they'd met.

"The sun rises in Vegas, too," she said vaguely.

"Trust me, this is one you don't want to miss."

"Is this a normal thing for you?" she asked as they boarded the jet.

"Welcome aboard, Mr. Williams and Ms. O'Malley," Lourdes said.

"Roxy, this is Lourdes, our pilot. She's been working for me for five years now."

"Nice to meet you."

"You, too," Lourdes said. "Buzz me when you're ready to go, Mr. Williams."

He nodded. Lourdes went into the cockpit and left them alone. Max crossed to the bar and poured a glass of California sparkling wine and orange juice for each of them. Roxy stayed just inside the jet, her gaze sweeping over the plush carpet and leather seats. She took a step inside and then stopped completely.

"This is not going to work," she said.

He knew she meant the two of them, but Max had already felt that irresistible pull toward her and knew that for him to walk away was impossible. Even if the only thing between them was this heat, then he'd be happy to explore it. But he sensed there was something more. The restlessness that had become a part of him was gone—at least temporarily.

"Give me this morning and then we can discuss our differences on the way back. I think you'll find we have a lot in common." He set the champagne flutes down and pulled her into his arms. She inhaled and held her body stiff. He rubbed his hands down her back, enjoying the feel of her in his arms.

"That's kind of presumptuous."

"Sometimes my instincts get the better of my manners. Please come to breakfast with me."

She nodded.

"Have a seat and I'll let Lourdes know we're ready to go."

He spoke to the pilot via an intercom and returned to Roxy's side. He handed her a glass of the sparkling wine and O.J., and relaxed deeper into the leather seat as they took off.

"Most people go to the Grand Canyon for quick flights."

"Have you been there?" he asked. He wanted to analyze her as he would a company he was thinking of taking over. He needed to figure out what her strengths and weaknesses were. Then he'd figure out how to make her his completely. That one brief kiss wasn't enough.

If he played it right, she could also give him the edge he needed in his merger with Harron. Roxy would dazzle the businessman and Max could finally close the deal. He knew she'd dazzle Harron, because she'd dazzled him without even trying.

"Yes. I met a gambler one time who came to the show and saw me dance and then won five hundred thousand dollars. He took me on a helicopter flight to the Grand Canyon."

Max was doubly glad he'd chosen the beach. He didn't want to be lumped together with some gambler. "And you said you weren't lucky," Max said, not liking the jealousy he felt at her story.

She gave him a wry smile and took a sip of her sparkling wine. "I'm not, really. When we returned he asked me to accompany him to the craps table and he promptly lost the rest of his money. He definitely didn't think I was lucky anymore."

Max reached over and ran a his finger down the side of her face. He couldn't explain it, but her luck stemmed from things that couldn't be won or lost in a casino. "Maybe you weren't lucky for him."

"But I'm lucky for you?" she asked in a throaty little voice. She tipped her head more fully into his touch and he cupped it, loving the feel of her silky cool hair on his skin.

"Something like that. You were in the show at the Chimera?" he asked, wanting to piece together an understanding of her life. He had never been to any of the shows. When he came to Vegas he played hard, and watching shows had never figured into his plans.

"Yes, I was. At that time I was a lead dancer, but not yet the headliner."

She tensed when she talked about it. He put his glass down and took her hand in his.

"That takes a lot of discipline, I imagine."

"Yes, it does, but then dancing is my life. *Was* my life. Now, hostessing is."

"Really?"

"To be honest, no."

"Tell me about your injury."

"Um…it's not that bad. I'm going to have a few more surgeries and then I'll be good as new."

He didn't think so. There was something in her eyes when she talked about dancing that told him she wasn't sure about that part of herself any more.

"What about you? What's it like to be a CEO?"

"Well, for one thing, when I give an order it's usually obeyed," he said, arching one eyebrow at her.

"You need someone to defy you. You're too used to getting your way."

"Maybe so. It's very challenging. I've been at the helm of Pryce Enterprises for more than ten years."

"Why Pryce and not Max or Williams Enterprises?"

"Pryce is my middle name…my mother's maiden name."

She encouraged him to talk about his company. As he did so he realized that he was glad to hear that she was at a crossroads. It made his plans for her and the future easier to achieve.

They took a limo to the beach and Roxy was overwhelmed by the luxury that Max seemed to take for granted. Someone had set up a low table in the sand, and large cushions were provided for seating. There were hanging candles on the canopy that covered the dining area.

The table itself was topped with a large, cut-glass vase full of light-pink and white roses. There was also a small blue box tied with a white ribbon. She'd never received anything from Tiffany & Co. before.

He was seducing her carefully with romance. And it wasn't the kind of romance that she'd ever imagined existed. This was big-time fantasy romance, and she couldn't ever forget that it *was* a fantasy. Max was used to throwing money around on things. For goodness' sake, he had a Learjet.

This was more than breakfast, whatever he said. He wanted more than just a chance to get to know her on the beach. She might not be the savviest woman when it came to men, but she knew a setup when she saw one. The thing was, this setup was straight from her dreams.

"What is going through your head?" he asked, in that way of his that made her feel as though he could read her mind. As though he could see through all the barriers she'd thought she'd erected.

"We are never going to make this work," she said at last. No way could she ever fit in this world. She was flashy and brassy, not sweet romance. She was… not his kind of woman. Was that what he wanted? Some kind of tawdry affair?

"Why not?"

"We are literally from two different worlds, Max. Why can't you see that?"

"I already do. I want the chance to show you that

we have more in common than you think. I'm not going to pretend that this isn't my way of life."

"Flying somewhere for breakfast?"

"It's a mode of transportation. I bet you've driven places and met people for meals."

He wasn't going to let this be an issue and she wanted it to be one. She wanted to somehow convince him—and, okay, herself—that it was money that made the difference between them, and not her own fears that were holding her back. Her fears were responsible for that block of ice in her stomach. A block of ice that had started to thaw in his embrace.

"That's hardly the same thing," she said.

He arched one eyebrow at her. "We'll talk about this some more after you've changed."

He gestured toward a canvas structure that was the size of a dressing room. She was amazed at how much he'd accomplished in such a short time. She'd seen him on the phone before they'd boarded the plane, so she knew he'd made a few calls. She tipped her head to the side and studied this man who was able to make things happen so quickly.

"I didn't bring anything else."

"I've provided everything you'll need. Go," he said, putting his hands on her shoulders and urging her toward the changing area.

She entered the room and saw two boxes from Saks. She opened them both. One held clothes for her, the other clothing for him. She sank down on the wooden bench that was inside the structure and closed her eyes.

What was she doing? What did this mean? She should be at the casino in the gym working out. She should be trying to claw her way back to where she'd been before Alan had taken her life away from her. She should be more leery of being with Max—but she wasn't.

But she was tired of living with the fear that she'd never be fully alive again. Tired of pretending that nothing had changed when everything had. Tired of being scared because she'd never allowed herself to be before.

She stripped out of her clothing and opened the box. Her new clothes were wrapped in tissue and she pushed it aside, sorting through them. There were a pair of capri pants in signature Burberry plaid that hung low on her hips, bisecting one of her scars. The pants only covered part of it.

She dug deeper and pulled out the shirt, which was a cute T-shirt trimmed to match her pants. She pulled it on, but the T-shirt ended an inch above the pants. Her hands shook as she realized that her scars would be visible to Max.

She couldn't do it. This was just one of many things she didn't want to let Max see about her. He might be able to ignore the differences between them, but she couldn't. He was physically perfect—she didn't have to see his naked body to know it.

"Does everything fit?"

She grabbed her silky halter top and held it up to her stomach, trying to make the shirt cover her. But it didn't.

The flap opened. Max stood there on the sand, his shoes removed, his shirt collar open and the sea breeze blowing in his hair. There was a slight chill to the morning and she shivered.

"I can't wear this."

"Okay."

"I mean, it's not that I don't appreciate the gesture but it's—"

He put his fingers over her lips again. Rubbed his thumb carefully against them and she closed her eyes, wanting to lean more fully into him. Wanting to pretend that all the things she didn't like about herself wouldn't matter to him.

But she knew they would. Because her scars mattered deeply to her.

"There should be a sweater in there."

She hadn't looked deeper. She sat on the bench and looked up at Max.

He came and sat down next to her, wrapping his arm around her and pulling her into the side of his body. She was tempted to rest against him. But didn't.

She froze when she felt one finger trace the edge

of her shirt to where the fabric ended and her skin was bare. She knew the moment he encountered the first scar. He didn't pull back or flinch away, just let his fingers continue caressing her, but she couldn't go on.

She pulled back, wanting to run away. To find some place to escape to.

Max lifted his head. "Let me change and then we'll have breakfast."

He wasn't going to say anything.

Grateful for the chance to escape, she stood and left. He knew her secret now—and she wasn't sure she wanted him to.

Four

Max watched the canvas door drop back into place and clenched his fists. Now he knew more about her *injury* than she'd wanted him to. What the hell had happened?

He could call Hayden and get all the details. Hayden treated the staff at the Chimera like family, and Max knew that his friend would have the facts. But he would rather have Roxy tell him.

He changed quickly, barely noticing the clothing, and exited the dressing room. Roxy wasn't waiting at the table but instead was standing close to the water, watching the waves cycle.

She turned as he approached, her face still, as if

she were afraid of what he'd say or do. And his heart ached for her. He realized in a flash that she needed something…someone who could make her forget her scars and the life she'd once had. She needed him—or maybe he could convince her that she did.

No one should ever feel the way she did. And he knew that she felt alone and in a kind of emotional pain that couldn't be expressed. Knew it because he'd felt it himself. Of course, that had been long ago before he'd started taking steps to make sure he'd never be dependent on anyone again.

"Isn't this better than the Grand Canyon?" he asked, striving for a lightness he wished he felt.

"It's definitely one of a kind."

"Well, I try. Want to take a walk? There's a big surf point at the end of the beach. I don't know if the waves will be breaking but if they are, well, it's awesome to watch."

"I'd like that. Do you surf?"

"Not big waves, but some in Waimae. You?"

"No. I can't chance—couldn't chance an injury."

Dancing. He finally started to understand the impact of not being able to perform anymore. "Were you always going to be a dancer?"

"Yes. My mom wanted me to be one."

"Was she living through you? My dad wanted me to row because he'd been on a champion team."

"No, it wasn't like that. She died when I was

four, and it's one of the few things I really remember about her.

"She'd sit in the front room at the dance studio and watch me."

Max slipped his hand into hers as they walked down the beach. He was aware of each step she took and made sure that he kept the pace slow so she wouldn't stumble.

She told him more about her life and he realized that until recently dancing really had been her everything. Listening was the key to his success in business, and when he'd been in his early twenties he'd realized that he could apply those same techniques to personal relationships.

But it was hard to focus on social skills when he wanted to pull Roxy back into his arms. He wanted to have her in his bed where he could remove her clothing and see her scars for himself. He wanted to lave them with his tongue and sooth away the lingering hurt they'd left deep inside her.

"What?"

He realized he'd stopped walking and was staring at her. Staring at her waist. "Nothing. Are you ready to head back?"

She took a deep breath. "I know you felt my scars."

"Yes, I did."

She said nothing else and he wasn't sure how to proceed.

"I just want a chance to get to know you, Roxy. You don't need to tell me anything, any of your secrets. Keep them for now."

They arrived back at their picnic spot. Max seated Roxy and then himself.

"How did you arrange this so quickly?"

"I have a well-paid staff that knows how to make things happen."

He signaled to the caterers, who were waiting patiently nearby to start serving breakfast.

He picked up the Tiffany box and handed it to her. When the caterers had left and they were alone again, he said, "Just a little memento for you."

"You didn't have to."

She held the box loosely in her hands as if it were a time bomb.

"Open it."

"Stop bossing me around," she said, but a smile flirted at her lips.

"No."

She stuck her tongue out at him but slid the ribbon off the box and then carefully opened it. She pulled the necklace from the box, and held it up. He stood and walked to her side of the table. Dropping to his knees behind her, he took the platinum chain from her and fastened it around her neck. The pendant was a diamond-encrusted sea branch.

Unable to resist the smooth length of her neck, he

dropped a kiss there. Her skin tasted so good that he wanted to nibble on her. But she shifted to her side, her hands coming up to frame his face. She turned until they faced each other.

Their breath mingled, their eyes met and Max felt something shift in his soul. Something he hadn't been aware he'd been missing or searching for until this very moment came into focus. And he realized that he wasn't going to let Roxy go.

"Thank you."

She kissed him then, nothing tentative in her embrace, but like a woman who knew what she wanted. Her tongue traced over his lips before sliding into his mouth, tangling with his own tongue. Tasting him with leisurely strokes of her tongue. Strokes that set flame to his entire body.

He angled his head, forcing hers back until he was in control. Control of the kiss and the woman in his arms. She made soft mewling noises in the back of her throat and he swallowed them.

Roxy forgot about the fact that she didn't know who she was. Forgot about the strangeness of this experience that was unlike anything she'd ever known. Forgot that she had a body she no longer liked.

Instead she let herself live in the moment. She felt the crisp linen of Max's shirt under her fingers and how that contrasted with the muscled body underneath. She felt the passion in his mouth as it dominated hers.

She felt the swarm of lust rising in the pit of her belly and overcoming her. She moaned deep in her throat and felt him move.

He stood up and walked back around the table. She touched her lips as he settled onto his cushion.

Every other man she'd ever dated would have pushed her for more. Would have taken the invitation she hadn't meant to issue with her kiss. She wasn't sure if it was Max who attracted her or the fact that he was looking beyond her scars to the woman beneath. Making her feel once again like a sexy, vibrant woman and not handicapped.

If he'd taken advantage she would have known how to handle him. She would have frozen him out because she could barely stand her naked form, how could she let anyone else see it? Even Max.

"It looks lovely on you," he said.

"The flush from your kiss?"

"That, too."

She tried not to be charmed but she already had been. Her cell phone started to ring and she pulled her purse into her lap, trying to mute the sound of the song she'd downloaded as her ring tone.

"Is that 'Dancing Queen'?"

She groaned. Every time she heard it she wanted

to pretend her life hadn't changed even though she knew it had. "Yes, please don't tease me about it."

Now that the cat was out of the bag she might as well answer her call. "Hello?"

"Hey, Foxy Roxy, it's Hayden. Wanted to let you know I've got you scheduled to start working tomorrow morning with the spouse of one of our high rollers. Basically you'll entertain her and keep her busy in the casino."

Hayden was all business and she wondered if Max had ruined her relationship with her boss with his high-handed manner. She needed to make sure that Max knew dating was one thing—were they even dating? Did she want to?

She took a deep breath and turned away from Max. "Is that okay, Hay? I know that Max asked you—"

"Everything's fine. I'm glad to see you and Max enjoying each other."

"It's not like that," she said, wanting to explain but not sure where to begin. There was no other man she'd have gotten on a plane with and flown out of Vegas just for breakfast.

"Whatever you say. I'll see you tomorrow."

Hayden disconnected the call and she turned to face Max. He watched her with that intense gaze of his that made her wish she could read his mind.

"Everything okay?" he asked.

She thought she heard genuine concern in his

voice but that could just be wishful thinking. He'd said he wasn't after a vacation fling and the necklace he'd given her—her memento of the day—cost more than her mortgage payment. So what was he expecting from her?

"Yes. Just Hayden telling me about my new assignment."

"Is it to your liking? I can have him change it to something else."

"You have to back off that. I'm used to being in charge of my own life."

He shrugged. She noticed he was more relaxed than she'd seen him since they met. In the casino there'd been an intensity to his face as he'd gambled. But not here.

"I'm not trying to take over, I promise. I'm only making the way smoother so that we can do things like this."

"I can't do breakfast tomorrow."

"Lunch?"

"I don't know. But my job is important to me."

"I can appreciate that. But I'm only in town for a short time."

"I mean it, Max. I grew up on charity and I have to work. This is important to me. Don't do something like this again."

He nodded. "I'm sorry. I'm used to making things happen."

"You're used to getting your way. But I'm a working girl and I'm not easily managed. You have to ask me before you rearrange my life."

"I can do that," he said.

"You seem different here," she said, before he could comment on the fact that she'd been staring.

"How?" he asked.

She felt silly; she'd never intended to bring the subject up. "I don't know exactly—more relaxed."

"I am in the company of a beautiful, charming lady and we're alone on the beach. What more could anyone ask for?"

"I'm thinking, fewer of those clichéd lines."

"Hey, that wasn't a cliché."

"Beautiful and charming…I know I'm not either of those things."

"How do you know that? Maybe you've never been told before."

She leaned forward, hearing the words of Madame Tremaine in the back of her mind. Her level-three ballet teacher had made sure that Roxy knew her limits. *You're too homely to be the lead without having the skill to keep the audience's eyes from straying to your face.*

The words echoed in her head, and for a minute she was that twelve-year-old at that awkward stage between girl and woman. "I was told by an expert that I shouldn't rely on my looks."

"No you shouldn't, but that doesn't mean you should dismiss them, either."

She didn't know what else he wanted from her. But he didn't stop watching her. "What?"

"I'm trying to figure out what you see when you look in the mirror."

Those words struck fear into her heart and she wrapped her arms around her waist.

Max had no idea how to deal with Roxy. Usually his words had a golden quality to them and people took them to mean more than he ever intended. But he'd never had someone look at him the way Roxy was. And he felt like a jerk.

She was hyper-sensitive about her body and he struggled to understand that. To him she was a woman who worked out and took care of herself. He could tell that she spent time on hair and makeup, yet she didn't have the confidence he would have expected.

He hadn't meant to hurt her but somehow he had. Maybe he should buy her something. Except he knew that money wasn't the solution. He'd learned that at a young age when he'd watched his mother wither from expensive gifts but a lonely life.

Roxy definitely liked the beach.

"Do you want to go to Hawaii for a few days?" he asked. He had a place on the Big Island of Hawaii, which would probably be crowded since it was summer and the height of family-vacation season. "We can get away from Vegas and really have a chance to get to know one another."

She shook her head but the sadness had left her eyes and he felt better. He wasn't even sure what he'd done to make that happen. "I have to start a new job tomorrow, remember?"

She was pretty cagey about that job that she wasn't even sure she liked. But he could respect her need to work and pay her own way. Those were the very two things that had driven him to start his own company, Pryce Enterprises, and not go to work for his family.

"Hayden won't mind waiting a few extra days for you," Max assured her. He was confident that he could pay the wage of a temporary employee so that Roxy's job would be waiting for her when she got back.

"I can't. Why would you even offer such a thing?"

"You seem to like the beach."

She tipped her head to the side, studying him, and he hoped she found whatever it was she was searching for in his gaze. Hoped that whatever was there wouldn't scare her off. He tried not to think about how her breasts had felt pressed against him when they'd kissed. Or the fact that he'd been able to feel her nipples harden. He wanted to touch and taste them.

"I do. But why a sudden trip?" she asked.

He couldn't remember what they were talking

about. He was imagining them both naked in his tropical paradise retreat.

"Max?"

Something about why he'd offered to take her to the beach…he remembered suddenly that it hadn't started out as a sexual thing but more of an emotional one. He'd wanted to stop her from hurting.

"Blondie, you had a look on your face…" How could he say it without upsetting her again. Damn, this was exactly what he wasn't good at.

"What look?" she asked, shifting her legs under the table.

"Never mind, I thought you needed a distraction and it was either offering a trip or kissing you."

"So you opted for the trip?"

"If I kiss you again I don't think I'll be able to stop until I'm buried in that sexy body of yours. And I have the feeling public displays of affection don't rank too highly with you."

"They used to."

"Really? Well, don't let me be the reason you stop."

She laughed. "God, you are so sophisticated I forgot you were a guy."

"What does that mean?" he asked. No one had ever said anything like that to him before. But to be honest, that was true of just about everything that Roxy said. She was a breath of fresh air in his world, which was filled with the jaded and cynical.

She winked at him. "Just that I thought you were too cool for lust."

"Think again." Obviously he'd been a little too gentlemanly in stopping earlier. He should have followed his primitive instincts and made love to her on the cushions.

"I am," she said, with a blush that revealed more than she probably realized.

"So what's your hang-up with public nudity? I think together we can get you past that."

"I don't think so," she said, the humor dying in her as she scooted back away from the table and stood up.

He pushed to his feet and went around to her. Signaling the caterers to start cleaning up their picnic, he put his arm around her shoulders and led her down the beach to a rocky outcropping.

"I did it again. I said something that made you close up. What is it?"

"You're moving too fast, Max. I'm still getting used to the new me. I'm not ready for a man to notice me yet." She moved so gracefully, he could see years of dance training in her posture and in her body. There was no hesitation to her movements today. Her injury, whatever it was, didn't seem to be bothering her.

"How were you injured?"

She looked out at the sea. Suddenly he realized that she must have done something to her body that would require cosmetic surgery. That the surgeries she was referring to were aesthetic.

"Look at me."

She glanced over her shoulder at him and he saw the tears in her eyes. Saw the way she clenched her jaw from saying too much. He stepped up on the rock next to her, easily finding his balance and pulling her into his arms.

He slipped his hand under her shirt at the small of her back, remembering the way she'd frozen earlier when he'd touched her there.

Carefully he brushed his fingertips over her back and felt the ridges left by scar tissue. He lifted her shirt to her midriff and leaned down for a closer look. The scars were still red, still healing, and they were vicious. He heard her gulp in a huge lungful of air and then felt her shaking in his arms. He dropped the edge of her shirt and pulled her into his arms, wishing he knew how to make this right.

Five

Roxy was glad to be back on the jet and headed toward Vegas. She wanted to go to her small house and hide. No matter how attracted she was to Max, they were from two different worlds, and she didn't want to fall for a man who'd be leaving in a few days time.

She especially didn't want to bare her soul to someone who might only be interested in her while he was here. Max hadn't said anything else or asked any more questions, but she saw in his eyes that he wanted to. That he needed to know what had happened.

Lourdes smiled warmly when they stepped back on the plane. Roxy took a seat close to the cockpit and questioned the pilot about her job while Max sat in the back returning phone calls and receiving faxes. Finally it was time for takeoff and Lourdes shut the door, leaving Roxy with no choice but to turn and face the man who saw too much.

She'd found the sweater he'd left in the box of clothing for her and donned it. She didn't think she'd take it off around him again. Not that it would matter if she stripped naked. Now that he'd seen the ugliness she carried around with her he wouldn't want her to.

"Stop looking at me like I'm the Marquis de Sade." He didn't even glance up from his paperwork. She knew he was busy, had heard his phone ring several times when they were on the beach, but he hadn't even glanced at it until they'd boarded the plane.

"I'm not. I wasn't thinking you wanted to have kinky sex with me."

He looked up then, arching on eyebrow at her. "But I do."

His words made her mind jump to images of the two of them in bed, maybe with her hands tied above her head. Max was so dominant outside the bedroom she couldn't imagine him being any other way in it. "Stop teasing me. We both know I'm not the woman you thought I was."

"You say that as though I just discovered you were a transvestite."

"Please stop trying to make light of this," she said around the lump in her throat. She couldn't joke about her body. Not yet. Maybe never.

He caught a strand of her hair in his hand, rubbing it between his fingers. "I don't know how else to deal with this, Blondie. It's either joke with you or give in to the anger that someone would hurt you."

"I used to love my body," she said, because Max was the first person she'd met whom she didn't know from before the accident. "I was more than a little vain about it, and I was mean about people who didn't take care of themselves. I've been struggling with the fact that maybe this is some kind of cosmic payback for that attitude."

He shifted the papers on his desk. "I don't believe in things like karma. I think we make our own. No matter where we start or what kind of baggage we are dragging with us, it's how we handle the present that defines us."

"I hope you're right. But I'm struggling, Max. You're the first man to look at me and make me forget that I'm not who I used to be. And that frightens me, because we both know that this isn't ever going to go beyond an affair."

Max left his desk area and joined her on the low couch toward the front of the plane. She didn't have a magazine and thought about pretending to go to sleep but knew Max wouldn't fall for it. She wasn't surprised when they reached their cruising altitude and he unfastened his seat belt and hers.

"Take your sweater off."

"No."

"The only way you're going to get past it is to stop viewing your body as something abhorrent."

"I don't think seeing it in broad daylight is going to help."

"How about seeing it through my eyes?" he asked, stretching his arm behind her and drawing her into the curve of his body. He was big and strong. Solid in a way so few men in her life ever had been.

She stared at Max, afraid for a minute to trust him. Okay, she was afraid to trust herself. She'd been serious when she mentioned the fact that all they had between them was the possibility of an affair. Max wasn't a forever kind of guy…at least not for her.

"Trust me," he said.

Strangely she wanted to. She'd never have left Vegas with any other man she'd known only twenty-four hours. There was something very trustworthy about Max Williams. "I think I do. But the last man I trusted…"

"Did this to you?" He slipped his hand under the layers of her clothing and traced over her scars.

"I'm not sure about this," she said, grasping his wrist and trying to stop him from moving any farther up her body. From discovering the extent of her scarring.

"Tell me what happened."

She took a deep breath. No one knew the whole truth. She'd been too embarrassed ever to utter the words *My ex-boyfriend is stalking me.*

The words appeared in her head—*A guy I dated over a year ago never got over me. And one night when I went into my dressing room, he was waiting. We had a fight and he...he...stabbed me. Several times. He left my face alone because he said it was my body that I loved and worshipped.*

But they made her feel dirty and guilty and she couldn't say them out loud. Especially to Max, who was all that was sophisticated and polished. For God's sake, the man took her to breakfast in another state. How could she say that her own vanity had driven an ex-boyfriend to come after her?

She couldn't. She liked Max. She wanted him to like her, to think that she was worth this trip to the beach on his Learjet.

He framed her head with his hands and leaned down, kissing her with exquisite gentleness and making her doubts fall away. She wrapped her arms around him and laid her head on his shoulder. Then quietly told him the story of the night that had changed her life.

Max knew that it would take more control than he had at the moment to conceal his anger from Roxy. The quiet rage that had grown as she spoke in that soft, hesitant voice. He held her in his arms and made plans. If it was surgeries she wanted, he would see that she had them.

He'd make sure that Technety never saw the light of day again and that the other women in the show were protected. Because she worried about that as well. He didn't question or understand why what he felt seemed magnified. He only knew that it was, and he couldn't tolerate anything other than fixing this problem.

"You're quiet."

"I'm quiet because I'm trying to find a way to speak around my rage. And no, you haven't disappointed me."

She tipped her head back against his shoulder and looked up at him. "That's the sweetest thing anyone has said to me."

"Ever?" he asked, lowering his head so that his lips brushed against hers. He wanted to make the physical part of the relationship all-powerful so that she wouldn't notice the fact that his emotions were kept hidden away. And he was going to keep them locked away because Roxy made him feel things more intensely than any other woman had, and there was danger in that. Whenever he reacted from that raw emotional place everything in his neatly ordered life fell apart.

"Ever," she confirmed.

He hardened and groaned. He wanted this woman.

He wanted to strip her naked and then take her. Make her forget about the imperfections which seemed so large in her mind.

He pulled his mouth free and dropped kisses down the length of her neck, sucking on the sweet spot at the base. She smelled so womanly, all fresh air and sea breeze, but more than that, her scent was the essence of Roxy. Sassy and shy. Tasting her was addictive.

"You are so beautiful," he said, framing her face in his hands and looking into her eyes. They were fathomless and he couldn't read what she felt there. That bothered him, because he'd thought she would be easy to read. What else was he missing about her?

"Don't talk, Max. I don't want to think—just feel, okay?"

But he couldn't after that. He didn't want her to kiss him because she wanted an escape from her life. He wanted her to want him with every part of herself. He rubbed her back and knew that he was going to regret being noble. Not taking what he wanted went against the grain. But Roxy wasn't just an object to be acquired. She…she was getting to him.

She was quietly illuminating parts of his soul that had been dark and dusty for too long. And he knew that he wanted to be more to her than just a means to forgetting her reality.

"I ruined the mood, didn't I?" she asked, slipping off his lap and back into her seat.

"No, you didn't. I was rushing you and I'm sorry."

"Well, I'm not. Rush me some more. That way I don't have to think about how different we are."

He was tempted. But he'd learned early in life that all the good things were worth waiting for. And he didn't want to make love to Roxy for the first time on the jet. He wanted to do it in his bedroom where he could stand her in front of a mirror and make her see the woman she really was.

"When you're ready for me, the differences won't matter."

Roxy had never been so glad to be back in a casino in her life. She felt unkempt, exposed from her time on Max's plane. She just wanted to escape and find a quiet place to regroup. She stood awkwardly in the portico in front of the hotel while Max tipped the valet and gave him the keys to the Jaguar that had been waiting for them at the airport.

"I guess this is goodbye. Thanks for breakfast."

She turned and started walking toward the employee parking area. Max caught her arm. She felt the steel in his grip and knew that he wasn't happy at the way she'd tried to dismiss him.

Well, she wasn't happy, either. She couldn't look at Max right now, because she was still embarrassed that she'd confessed so much to him.

"We're not through yet."

"I'm tired, Max. I need a break. I know that I owe you an apology for what happened on the plane."

"No, you don't. I really don't mind waiting. When we do make love I want to take you in a bed, where I can stretch you out and really worship that luscious body of yours. But I want it to be about more than sex when we're together."

She warmed inside, where the real Roxy had always lived. The shy dancer who just wanted to lose herself in the movements. She knew the image she projected was of an outgoing woman who could come through anything. But deep inside she'd always felt insecure, still the awkward adolescent who'd been dropped off at a group home.

Max, for all his worldliness, had seen past the facade to the woman beneath.

A group of Japanese tourists were headed straight for them and Max used his body to move her out of the flow of traffic. He backed her up against the sun-warmed wall of the casino, his tall muscular body surrounding hers and caging her.

"Have dinner with me tonight," he said, rubbing his lips over hers. His breath was minty and warm.

She opened her mouth, hoping for a deeper kiss, but he only nipped at her lower lip and lifted his head.

"I'm waiting."

"Are you asking me?" She knew he wasn't. He was so used to having his way.

"Only if I have to. I think there's something between us that deserves to be explored."

"Shouldn't you be playing poker? That *is* why
you came to Vegas."

"I think I've hit the jackpot already."

She started to close her eyes against the charm she
saw in his, but then she forced them open. She made
herself look up and down the strip. To see the fake
Eiffel Tower and pyramid. To remind herself that
this was Las Vegas, baby. The place where sinful
behavior was indulged in. Men like Max came to
Vegas for one reason and one reason alone.

But the way he held her didn't feel as though he
was looking for a cheap thrill. And he'd stopped
earlier, on the plane, when she was willing to go
further. "What do you want from me?"

"A chance."

"Why?"

"Because it's been a long time since anyone has
interested me as much as you do. I love the contra-
dictions of you. The mystery of what makes you tick.
And I want to solve it."

She leaned forward, breathing in the scent of his
aftershave mixed with the salt from the sea breezes.
"Max, I'm not worth all this effort."

"You are to me. I'll pick you up. Does eight
sound good?"

"You're not going to listen to me are you?" she asked.

He gave her a half smile. "I always listen. It's just that sometimes you say things you don't mean."

"How can you know that?"

"Because I've held you in my arms and looked deep into your eyes. I'm beginning to know what makes you tick."

"Then maybe I should pass on dinner. If you figure me out then I'll have no place to hide."

"You don't need to hide from me."

"What about you?"

"I'm not hiding from you."

But she knew he was. He was dazzling her with fancy plane trips and expensive trinkets. He was keeping the focus on her and she was letting him. "What about from yourself?"

"I'm forty, the CEO of an international conglomerate and I've lived a full life. There's nothing to hide."

She tipped her head to the side studying him. She knew he had secrets. Real secrets, the same as she did, and she wanted to know them, because she already liked him too much. She was very afraid that before too long, liking would turn to love. And, as he'd said, he was a sophisticated, successful man. The kind that didn't marry a former topless dancer.

Six

Max spent the rest of the afternoon in the casino. Hayden and Deacon showed up during one of his winning hands and then enticed him to play with them. Deacon Prescott was one of Max's oldest friends. A hell-raiser who'd grown up on Vegas's mean streets and worked hard to make himself into the man he was today. The owner of the Golden Dream Casino was every inch the family man and casino owner. Since they were two of his oldest friends, they played a little dirty, deliberately distracting each other. It was fun, and Max relaxed around the men for the first time since Hayden's marriage.

He didn't analyze it too closely and refused to answer any of Deacon's and Hayden's prying questions about Roxy. He took great pleasure in beating them both and walking away from the table with his friends' money in his pockets.

But as he fastened his tie in a classic Windsor knot, staring at himself in the mirror, he realized that he was doing what he always did. Trying to fix Roxy's life.

Since he'd been eight years old he'd always followed that pattern. As an adult he'd realized that part of the problem was his mother's demand for perfection. She wasn't an uncaring woman; she just had very high standards. And Max was very much her son. But he was also his father's. And if he'd learned perfection at his mother's knee, then he'd learned compassion at his father's—and also how to move on.

The course of his life had been set when he'd befriended Hayden at boarding school. When the two boys had met, they hadn't hit it off at all. Hayden, in fact, hadn't gotten on that well with anyone, spending all his time alone until one night Max had overheard a conversation between Hayden and Hayden's father. The conversation reminded Max of the many he'd had with his mother. And he'd seen that the arrogant boy who no one had liked was really a lot like himself.

Max blinked. Damn. He was still trying to fix people. Hayden had called him on it more than once, but Max couldn't change. He knew that much about himself.

But fixing Roxy in this instance could help him with business. There was no doubt that he wanted her, but he was thinking of her in terms of permanency, and he'd never thought of any woman that way before. Was it simply the effect of having his pals settle down? Did he want a wife because it would make his negotiations easier? Or did he want Roxy tied to him because of emotions he'd rather not acknowledge?

When he arrived in the lobby Roxy was waiting with the two friends he'd seen her talking to the day before. As soon as she spotted him, she smiled and held up her hand, telling him she'd be right over.

He didn't wait for her to come to him. It was simply a power thing, but he didn't want to lose control for a minute. He slipped his arm around her waist and pulled her back against him.

"Hello, Blondie."

"Max," she said. "These are my friends, Tawny Patterson and Glenda MacIntosh. Tawny and Glenda, this is Max Williams."

Max shook hands with both women, who eyed him speculatively. "It's a pleasure to meet you both."

"Right back at ya," Tawny said, winking at Roxy. "We've got to be going. We'll talk to you later."

Roxy groaned as her friends walked off. "They are

not going to be happy until they've pumped me for information on you."

"What will you tell them?" he asked, leading her toward the escalator to the shopping and dining level. The resort was crowded. Now that night had fallen the casino was starting to really come alive.

Max breathed in the sights and the sounds. The feel of the woman in his arms and the sound of her soft voice enhanced the night.

"I'll tell them…I'm not sure, Max. I think I want to keep what I'm feeling for you a secret."

Not, he suspected, just from her friends, but also from him. She was such a blend of blatant sexuality and shyness. It turned him on to watch her go from confident woman to reserved, because he knew that when he touched her, he could make her lose her inhibitions.

"What are you feeling?" he asked, keeping his hand at the small of her back. Her sundress had a deep V in both the front and back.

He stroked his finger along the fabric and watched her body react. Her skin flushed a little and then goose bumps spread up over her shoulders.

"Lust," she said.

"How could you be around me and not experience that?" he said without blinking an eye.

"What an ego you have."

She leaned back into his touch as if she couldn't get enough of his hands on her, feeding his ego in a way that no woman had done in a long time. She tipped her head to the side when he spoke, really listening to his words. And she showed him the real woman behind that perfect face and knockout body. The real woman, with all her faults and fears. That was a bigger turn-on than she could ever realize.

"Hey, you're the one who brought up lust. The way I feel around you, it would be impossible to deny our attraction."

"Impossible?" she said, blinking at him.

"Oh, yeah. You're not going to try it, are you?"

"How can I argue with a crazy man?"

He laughed and realized that he was more relaxed here with her than he'd been at the poker table. That the game which had always been his release valve wasn't working the way it was supposed to.

When they reached the dining level, she paused and glanced at the row of restaurants that would impress the most jaded gourmet. Max was glad that the all-you-can-eat lobster buffets of the past were gone. Now, five-star restaurants and celebrity chefs were the norm in Las Vegas.

"Where are we going?" she asked.

"Dinner, remember? Is that lust thing messing with your mind?"

"Yeah, like that'd ever happen. I meant, where are we going for dinner?"

"I promise you, before our night is over I will

make sure you are totally out of your mind with lust," he said, lifting her hand to his mouth and brushing a kiss along the back of it.

Their dinner was a five-course affair at a themed casino restaurant—the Chimera's Applewood Vineyard of Sonoma—the vineyard sponsored the restaurant and they'd sampled a different wine with every course. She felt very mellow and relaxed as Max led her out of the restaurant and up one more level to one of the smaller clubs on the entertainment level.

While they waited outside for the doors to open, she saw the line to get into the main club revue. *Her* show. Not her show anymore. She'd left that behind…at least for now.

"Is that where you used to work?"

"Uh-huh." She felt butterflies in her stomach as she recalled how it felt each night to wait backstage for the house doors to open. She remembered how they'd all tease and laugh to hide their nerves, but even the fact that they went out on stage every night hadn't dulled the magic that dancing and performing had always held for her.

"Roxy?"

She realized he'd spoken, said something. She pulled her gaze from the crowd of people and looked into his gray eyes. He was watching her with that intense look that was half lust and half something she couldn't read.

"I'm sorry. I haven't been up here since the… accident." She flushed as she realized she'd mentioned something relating to her injuries.

"Do you want to go into the show? Would that help?"

"No. I'd rather go into the jazz club."

The doors to their club opened and people slowly filed in. Max and Roxy waited until the crowd had lessened, and then approached the ticket taker. Max handed over their tickets, and they were seated at an intimate table close to the stage.

Her hands were shaking and she didn't understand why. She looked up at Max, a sense of panic closing in on her. "Talk to me, please. I need some kind of distraction."

"About what?"

"Your job. Are you on vacation?"

"No, I'm here to take a break from some tense negotiations."

"For what? I don't even know what you do."

"I run an international company. We're trying to merge a travel agency into our conglomerate. But the owner of the travel agency isn't too sure he wants a man like me at the helm."

"A man like you?"

"A bachelor. They are very family-focused, and

Harron wants to be assured that I won't let that focus slip."

"You don't strike me as a family man," she said, carefully.

"I guess I'm really not. But that doesn't mean I can't see the value in being one."

She tipped her head to the side. "I've never had a family. Just the girls in the show."

"Will you be able to dance again?"

She shook her head. "Not at the same level, and I'm not one of those people who will settle for second best."

He scooted his chair closer to hers and wrapped his arm around her shoulders. Leaning in close, he whispered directly into her ear.

"Are you wearing a bra?"

She glanced up at him, startled. "I'm a 36DD, what do you think?"

He ran his finger down the V at the front of her dress to the cleavage revealed there. He slipped his finger under the material. She shivered from his touch. His finger was big and warm. Gently caressing her. Moving slowly lower, his finger encountered the lace edge of her demi-cup bra before brushing her areola.

"Ah, yes, you are."

Her nipple had hardened at his first touch. They were secluded close to the stage in an alcove where no one could see them. But the fact that they were in a public place heightened her excitement.

He drew the tip of his finger lazily back and forth across her nipple. With his free hand he stroked her neck, urging her to tip her head back onto his shoulder. She did, and he lowered his mouth to hers.

His tongue teased hers before dipping deeper, thrusting into her mouth in time to his finger strokes across her breast. She squeezed her thighs together as she felt an answering pull in her center.

He lifted his mouth from hers. "Are you wearing panties?"

"A thong," she said, feeling dazed by the sensuality he wove so easily around her.

"Take it off."

She'd never done anything like this before. And it made her feel exciting and daring. "I'm not—

"Please."

No other word would have made her react, but that one did. There was a fire in his eyes that answered the one he'd started in her body. She'd expected him to remove his hand, but he kept stroking her breast and nipple as she lowered her hands to her lap.

The table was draped with a cloth that fell to the floor, so there was no way anyone could see her. She attempted to glance around, but Max stopped her with his hand on her chin.

"No one is looking. There's just you and I and the music. No past or present. But it's up to you...do you want to do this?"

She swallowed hard, staring into his eyes. She nodded. Speaking would break the spell he'd cast around her.

"Lift your dress to your waist."

She did as he asked, pulling the fabric up slowly. His eyes were on hers the entire time. And what she saw in them egged her on. Made her want to be the sexy woman he thought she was. The sexy woman she'd known she was before her attack.

"Is your skirt up?"

"Yes."

He glanced down and his hand tightened on her breast. He breathed a little more heavily, lowering his hand to her thigh. She glanced down as his hand moving higher, slowly, toward the apex of her legs.

"May I touch you?" he asked, again directly in her ear."

She nodded again. He slipped his hand into her thong, his blunt fingers caressing her, slipping lower to find her wet and ready for him.

She inhaled sharply as he slipped one finger into her while at the same time scraping his fingernail over her nipple. She had to bite her lower lip to keep from crying out. Just then the house lights dimmed even further and the jazz combo took the stage.

The tempo of the music was mellow and smooth. But the tempo in her body raged out of control—like a Stevie Ray Vaughan guitar riff that went on forever.

His mouth found hers as he teased her body, driving her closer and closer to a climax. A second finger slipped inside her, driving deeper. He continued to play with her nipple and his tongue matched the thrusts of his fingers. She gripped his thigh with one hand then slipped it between his legs, finding him hard. She stroked him in time with his stroking of her body. Her fingers bit into his thigh as he pressed his thumb to the nub at her center and drove her over the precipice to orgasm.

She felt him lower her skirt over her thighs and he pulled his hand from her breast with one last caress. His erection still strained against his zipper, but when she tried to open his pants and bring him some relief, he stopped her.

During the second set, couples left their tables for the small dance floor. Max watched Roxy watching them, a look of envy flitting briefly across her face.

"Let's dance," he said.

She hesitated. "I'm…"

"Scared? I promise not to step on your feet."

"Not of that. You're poetry in motion."

He arched one eyebrow at her. "No one has ever said that before."

"Well, I'm sure they've thought it. You move like a graceful predator."

"A predator?"

"Not that you're looking for the kill. You're just very confident, very sure of yourself and very aware of where everyone else is."

Since he knew that he was always aware of others, he wasn't surprised to hear her description, but he was surprised that she'd noticed. She seemed to see more of him than others did.

"I want to hold you in my arms, Blondie. I want your luscious body against mine, teasing us both. I'll catch you if you stumble. Trust me?"

She licked her lips. "Okay."

Max escorted Roxy to the floor and held her in his arms. Something he'd been craving since...he realized that he had no idea when the urge had begun, only that he *needed* her in his arms.

Her skin was flushed, and the remembered feel of her warmth on his fingers kept him in a state of arousal. But he wasn't ready to end the anticipation and take her back to his suite. He wanted to keep the tension building between them.

"You're a good dancer," she said.

She held on to him as they moved. Roxy's dance training was obvious to him as they swayed together. Her posture, which was always very good, was even more so here. And every beat of the music came alive in the way she danced.

"Thank you."

"Is there anything you don't do well?"

Yes, but he wasn't about to tell her. He was horrible at cooking no matter how many lessons he'd had. "My mom made sure I knew the basic ballroom steps. My dad has to be coerced onto the dance floor."

She rested her head on his shoulder, shifting closer to him as they danced. And he had a flash image of her underneath him. They'd be a perfect fit in bed. He slid his hands down her back to her hips.

Her mouth was at his neck, kissing him as her hands slid up and down his back. She bit him softly and he reacted immediately, hardening further against her lower belly.

One of her hands was at his nape, her fingernails scraping over the skin there. His breathing deepened, his blood flowing heavier in his veins, pooling in his groin. He knew he'd have a problem when it came time to leave the dance floor, but for now, it felt good to have her tease him.

This was the first time she'd taken the lead, and he savored it, knowing he was starting to unlock the real Roxy, the woman who'd been frozen by the cruel attack.

He lowered his head and breathed in the summer scent of her hair. His hands lowered from her hips. Her butt was full and curvy, and he flexed his fingers against her. She shifted her hips, rubbing her mound against his erection.

He heard her breath come in quick and sharp. Her full breasts rubbed against his chest and he wished he'd left his jacket at the table so he could feel her against him. In fact, he wished they were both naked.

She was toned and in shape. Everywhere he touched renewed the lust he felt for her body. But every touch of hers on his body renewed the affection in his heart. He liked this woman. Liked her in a way that he didn't understand or want to analyze.

The tempo of the music changed, but Roxy didn't seem to notice and he didn't want to either. He maneuvered them away from the center of the dance floor to a corner near the stage where the low lighting didn't reach, and they continued to sway together to a beat that could only be heard by the two of them.

"Let's get out of here," she said.

"Give me a minute."

She skimmed her hand between their bodies, running her fingers over his erection. "I think it might take more than a minute."

He grabbed her wrists and pulled her hands behind her back, then lowered his head till his mouth nearly touched hers. "If you keep that up, it will."

She shifted in his arms, undulating against him. "When we're alone, you're going to pay for that."

"Promise?"

"Oh, yes."

He reached between them, adjusted himself as

best he could and led her back to their table. She grabbed her purse while he tossed some bills on the table to cover their tab. He put his hand at the small of her back as they walked from the club.

Outside, he wrapped one arm around her waist, putting the other under her chin, tipping her head back and kissing her until she softened against him. After a long moment, he lifted his head.

"Come back to my suite."

"Yes," she said. And he took her hand, leading her toward the bank of elevators.

<u>Seven</u>

Max's cell phone rang while they were waiting for the elevator. He took one look at the caller ID and cursed savagely under his breath. "I have to take this call."

She nodded and started to move away, but he held her close, unwilling to let her go. She held his hand and stood patiently at his side. Though it was only ten o'clock in Vegas, it was after midnight in Atlanta where Duke, his right-hand man, was calling from. So he knew that this had to be some sort of emergency.

"Williams."

"It's Duke. Sorry to bother you so late, but I just got a call from MacNeil. He has another objection to the merger that only you can satisfy."

Max was sick of Harron MacNeil. The man was making what should have been a beneficial corporate merger a living hell. Max was ready to change his bid on the company and just take it over regardless of what MacNeil wanted. "What the hell is it now?"

"He wants another face-to-face meeting—tomorrow afternoon."

No way. MacNeil was assuming a lot of bargaining power from the fact that Max wanted the man's company. Too much. "I can meet with him on Friday."

Duke chuckled. "I had a feeling you'd say that. So I scheduled a Friday lunch meeting and he's coming to you."

"Thanks, Duke."

"Hey, that's why you pay me the big bucks."

"Then why did you have to call me tonight?" Max asked. The elevator car came, but he held Roxy by his side. The elevators had really poor cell reception.

"MacNeil is bringing his wife. Just a heads-up. Any chance you found a lady in Vegas who will convince Harron you're a family man?"

He glanced at Roxy, but said nothing to Duke. "MacNeil is going to have to take me as I am."

"No? I have the feeling he's going to be on the phone to you here tomorrow morning as soon as the office opens. Which means either I get up early or—"

"You take care of it before you go home to Cami," Max said. Cami also worked for Max. She and Duke had met when Max had assigned them to work together. Cami never hesitated to take him to task for working Duke too hard.

"I'm already home and she's not too happy. I've been on the phone all night."

"Would a bonus make her happier?" Max asked. He knew that the key to a successful company was happy employees.

"Nah, you know Cami. I think a vacation will satisfy her."

"You can have two weeks at my place in Fiji as soon as MacNeil signs on the dotted line."

"I'm out the door before the ink dries," Duke said. "Anything else?"

"His latest offer should arrive by courier tonight."

"Thanks, Duke." Max pocketed his cell phone.

"Everything okay?" Roxy asked.

"Just business."

She wrapped her arms around her waist and stood awkwardly by his side just staring at him. She seemed...unsure.

He realized too much time had passed and she was thinking about her scars again. He knew it only because in the jazz club he had glimpsed her totally relaxed and wallowing in her feminine sexuality. Now she wasn't. "Changed your mind about going up to my suite?"

She shrugged her shoulder, but she'd dropped his

hand and had her arms wrapped around her waist. "I'm not sure."

The elevator cars opened again and Max knew that if he pushed now he would lose whatever advantage he had with her. But he was physically on the edge and waiting was not going to be easy.

Touching her had a pronounced effect on his body. Going dancing was out of the question. They each needed a distraction, Roxy from whatever fears had crept into her mind and him from the ones that hadn't left his.

"What would it take to make you sure?"

"Could we leave the lights off?"

"No."

She bit her lower lip and once again the elevator car left without them. "You didn't even hesitate."

"I know that I want to see you—all of you."

"I don't think I'll ever be ready for that."

He realized then that his usual take-charge style wasn't going to get the job done. Roxy needed understanding. He'd be understanding if it damn well killed him, and he knew he wouldn't die from not having sex.

"Let's get out of this place."

She blinked at him. "Where will we go?"

"I don't know, but we need to do something active, something that requires me to use my brain."

"Thinking is a turn-off for you?" she asked, with just a little bit of the sassiness he'd come to expect from her.

"With you around, I don't think anything will work."

She took a deep breath and let it out slowly, her hand reaching for his. She led him back to the elevator alcove. And shocked him. "Let's go up to your room."

They stepped on the elevator and he felt the trembling in her body and noticed her hand shaking as she clutched her handbag. They were the only ones in the car.

He put his hands on her waist and held her loosely between his body and the wall of the car. She glanced up at him, her blue eyes wide, but not with fear. Instead he saw desire.

"What?"

He bent his head to hers and took her mouth in the gentlest kiss he had in him right now. Then he lifted his head and stared down at her. "Just wanted to make sure you were still with me."

He lifted her into his arms as the elevator arrived on his floor and carried her down the hall to his room.

In Max's arms there was no room for self-consciousness. Roxy forgot everything except the taste of him on her tongue, the feel of his strong shoulders under her hands and the emotions he drew effortlessly from her.

No man had ever tempted her more than he did. In the jazz club, she'd simply forgotten they were in a public place and found that the world had narrowed to just the two of them. She'd asked him to distract her because her own thoughts had been starting to scare her. And Max had given her a refuge that was so totally captivating and exciting that her fears had melted away.

She closed her eyes and tucked her head against his neck. No man had ever treated her the way Max did, with his demanding sexuality that was at times at odds with the concern he showered on her. He really paid attention not just to how she reacted physically around him, but also her emotional reactions. She suspected it was due to his time in the boardroom. He just knew how to read people. Especially her, and that made her more than a little nervous.

He made her feel needy and she was used to standing on her own. For tonight, though, she would put those fears to rest and enjoy her time with him.

He set her on her feet at his door and opened it with the key card. "Still sure?"

She nodded, not voicing any more of her body concerns. He made her want to stop hiding in the shadows of her former self—her former life—and step back into the land of the living.

She took his hand and tugged him behind her into the room. She stumbled over the carpet and reached out blindly to catch her balance. Max slipped his arm around her firmly holding her in place.

"Okay?"

No, no. But she wanted to be and Max was the one man to offer her that chance. As soon as the door shut behind them they were surrounded by the darkness. She knew that if she let Max take the lead, she'd be standing in a fully lit room with all her imperfections on display.

The only way she was going to come through this in one piece would be to take control now. She'd rarely done that in her relationships. She wasn't aggressive outside of dancing. But dancing was gone, and with Max she…she felt different than she ever had before. She wanted her actions to be distinctive to this man and this relationship.

So she pushed him back against the wall and leaned up to catch his mouth with hers, kissing him deeply and with all the passion she'd been waiting to shower on him since he'd brought her to a climax in the middle of the jazz club.

She sucked his tongue into her mouth and when he tunneled his fingers in her hair and tilted her head to a better angle for him, she nipped his tongue.

"Convinced?" she asked.

"I'm not sure. I might need a little more persuasion," he said, turning on the light.

She froze, then pushed her fears down. This was about Max and what he made her feel. She'd ignore the light for now—distract him—until she could turn it off.

She loosened the knot in his tie but left it dangling. Then she tugged his shirttails from his pants and slowly unbuttoned his shirt, taking her time with each button, leaning down and kissing each new piece of skin that was revealed.

His nipples were hard by the time she had the shirt unbuttoned and his erection strained against his zipper. She smiled to herself at how he reacted to her. It made her feel very much like a woman. Very much in control of this man who made sure he was always the one in charge.

She lifted his collar and slid his tie over it to rest against his skin. The differences between them slipped away and there were only Max and Roxy in this moment. It didn't matter that he had more money than Midas and she'd been a showgirl.

She removed the cufflinks at his wrists and put them in his breast pocket before pushing his shirt off his shoulders and onto the floor.

Undoing the knot and holding on to each ends of his tie, she drew the soft, silk material over his nipples. His breath hissed out through his teeth.

She continued to brush one nipple with the tie while she bent and licked delicately at the other one. Then, when his hands clutched at her shoulders, she bit very carefully at his nipple.

He groaned and his hips jerked toward her. She smiled and switched her mouth to his other nipple while continuing to move the silk over his body. She kissed her way down his chest, following the line of hair that disappeared into the waistband of his pants. She let go of his tie and reached for his belt buckle.

He had six-pack abs that had to have come from working out. She traced her finger over the deline-ated muscles and watched them ripple under her touch. "Do you work out?"

"Yes. Another thing we have in common," he said in that husky voice of his.

Maybe the only thing they had in common. Doubts surfaced, but she pushed them aside. She wanted Max, and to be honest there was little she'd wanted in life lately.

"May I?" she asked, stroking her fingers over his belt buckle. The metal was cool in comparison with his hot stomach.

"Yes, you may," he said, in a voice that was little more a rasp.

She unbuckled his belt and pulled it through the loops. Once it was free, she doubled it up in her hand and snapped it. "Have you ever had your hands tied during sex?"

"Why? You think you can dominate me?" he asked.

She waited a heartbeat and then two before looking at him from under her eyelashes. "I know I can, and I don't need this leather belt to do it."

He arched one eyebrow at her and leaned back

against the wall. He looked like a decadent pasha from an exotic land who could have his pick of glamorous women, and for a moment she faltered. Max could have any woman...why her?

But as she looked at this man, she knew that tonight he wanted only her. She dropped the belt and unfastened his pants. Slipped her hand into his loosened waistband and was surprised to encounter nothing but warm male flesh.

"Commando?"

He shrugged. "I don't like to be confined."

She stroked his length, exploring him with her fingers before reaching lower to cup him. He shifted his stance, spreading his legs farther apart. She scored him with her fingernails, scraping carefully against his sensitive flesh.

He cupped her head and brought her lips to his. His tongue thrust deeply into her mouth before he pulled back and stared into her eyes. He pushed lightly on her shoulders and she knew what he wanted. She lowered herself slowly, not kissing her way down his body but keeping her gaze fixed to his as she sank to her knees.

She leaned forward, letting her breath brush over his erection before twirling her tongue over the tip. Before she could go further, he held her head in both his hands and gently guided her back up until their eyes met. She felt a shift deep inside her and knew that she was falling for this man.

* * *

Max lifted Roxy into his arms and carried her into his bedroom. He placed her fully dressed in the center of his bed. He toed off his shoes and socks and then pushed his pants off before he turned on one of the bedside lamps. The room was cast in soft light and shadows. His tie still dangled around his neck but otherwise he was naked.

She rolled to her side to watch him, the skirt of her dress moving up to her thighs, and she shifted on the duvet. When she noticed how much skin she'd exposed, she stiffened and drew the skirt down her legs until they were covered again. Part of his heart was sad at the way she'd covered herself. Roxy was a woman who liked sensual things and that world had been taken from her when Technety attacked her.

He was determined to give her back that world. To reintroduce her to the pleasure of sensual delight and to her own body. He wanted—no, needed—to make her come apart in his arms.

He approached the bed. "I think you convinced me that you want me."

"Did I?" she asked, a candescent light in her eyes as she watched him.

"Yes. Now, it's my turn to convince you," he said, knowing he had to take it slowly for her but unsure of his ability to do so. He wanted to claim her, to thrust inside her body and make her admit that he was her man.

"How are you going to do that?"

"You'll see," he said. Since she was on her side, he sank down next to her and lowered the zipper at the back of her dress. She rolled onto her back, her honey-colored hair spread out on the comforter and he felt that clenching in his gut as he realized that this woman was his. That she was here in his bed.

He lowered himself next to her on the bed and kissed her, caressing her through her clothing. Rubbing his hands down her back, slipping his hand inside her dress to feel the smooth silk of her skin.

He traced her spine down to her buttocks and cupped both cheeks in his hands, drawing her closer to his body. Her legs shifted, one of them draping over his hips so that he could get closer to her. He pulled her more fully against him and felt the warmth of her center through her skimpy thong.

He slipped his hands lower, dragging her panties down her legs. They tangled in her shoes and he sat up, taking them off and then removing her shoes. He took one ankle in either hand and pushed her legs apart. She watched him and he waited to see her reaction.

She pulled her dress up to her waist and then opened her legs wider. "Come to me."

"Not yet." Starting at her feet, he traced the lines of her legs, all the way up the outside, skimming over the tight curls at their apex and then back down the middle. She had two serious scars on her left thigh, and he ached when he touched them and she flinched. One of them was longer and deeper than the other. That was the one that had given her the limp.

She rolled to her side, reaching for the bedside lamp. He caught her around the waist, holding her in place. He ached for her, for this woman who had lost so much of herself. He wanted to assure her that he'd just found her and he would shelter her. Even though those words felt foreign in his mind, he wanted to offer Roxy something he'd given no other woman. Not just in bed, either. In his life.

He bent his head to her thigh and traced those angry-looking scars with his tongue. She quivered under his touch. If she pushed him, he'd let her turn out the light. But he really felt that, tonight, she needed the light on. If he let her hide from him now, she'd never stop hiding. And that wasn't acceptable.

He slipped his fingers between her legs while he kissed her thigh. She moaned as he slipped a finger into her body.

He levered his body up until he lay behind her, her naked back to his naked chest. Her dress still covered her in the areas that he knew she didn't want him to see.

He slid his free hand under her body and rested it over her stomach, then gathered the material of her dress in his hand and tugged until it slid downward, slowly revealing her full breasts encased in pink silk and lace.

As he kept his fingers moving between her legs, her hips picked up his rhythm, rocking in perfect counterpoint. He shifted her in his arms until she lay on her back.

She reached up and held his head, brought her mouth to his as he continued touching her deep inside until he felt her start to tighten around his fingers. He thrust deeper inside her, petting her until the orgasm had rocked through her.

Then he reached into the nightstand and took out a condom, putting it on with the same hand he'd just had in the warmth of her body. Her dress was bunched around her waist and he reached under her to undo the clasp of her bra. He pulled it from her body and tossed it aside.

Her nipples were hard and red, begging for his mouth. He leaned down and suckled her while caressing her entire body and building the fire between them again. He pushed her dress down her body and she kicked it to the floor, her eyes closing as soon as she realized she was naked.

He pushed her thighs apart and settled himself between her legs. The primitive beast deep inside he tried to always ignore roared in his head, demanded that he make Roxy his completely. That she acknowledge she belonged to him.

"Open your eyes, Roxy."

She did, looking up at him and waiting. "Watch me take you this first time. Watch me make you mine and know that there is no one in the world who's more beautiful to me."

He shuddered as her eyes met his, their gazes locked, and then slowly her eyes slid down his body. If possible he hardened even more as he watched his body slowly sink into hers. Felt her legs tighten around his, moving higher so that he could slide all the way home.

He joined his hands with hers, stretched them over her head and started to move between her legs, thrusting into her again and again, making her completely his and giving himself to her. Needing to hear her soft cries. He moved both her hands into one of his and with the other caressed her entire body, pinching her nipple while he thrust even deeper than before. She made a sound in the back of her throat and then he felt her tighten around him as she cried out with her release. He let go of her hands and held her hips, thrusting into her two more times before he joined her over the edge.

He rolled over, wrapping his body around hers, telling himself that nothing had changed. But inside his soul, he knew it had.

Eight

Roxy waited until she was sure that Max was sleeping before slipping from the bed and turning off the light. She hurried into the bathroom, gathering her clothes as she went.

What had she done? She'd let him see her and now he knew. This man in his perfect world with his perfect life. She wasn't a mass of fears during the day, but tonight she felt so vulnerable, so alone. She was supposed to be in charge, dammit. This night had been for her, to reclaim her shattered femininity. Instead she found that she wanted to stay in the shelter of his arms. To find a way to make him stay in hers, and she wasn't one of those dependent women.

He'd touched her. And she'd forgotten about them. Forgotten for a while that she didn't know what she wanted anymore. In his arms it was easy to pretend that nothing had changed and that the changes that had happened didn't matter.

She sank to the marble floor of the bathroom, sitting in the dark with her knees drawn up. The door opened and light from the bedroom spilled into the room. She glanced up at Max.

"Blondie, what are you doing?"

He leaned against the counter—long, lean and perfect in his nudity. She was afraid to glance up at him. Afraid to reassume the role she'd assigned herself when they came into his hotel room. Fiercely sexual and in control…but she wasn't and she couldn't pretend any more.

"You wouldn't understand, Max."

He gave her a really sweet smile and she felt it all the way to her toes.

"Midnight is the time for regrets," he said.

If he only knew. Midnight was only the beginning. She hadn't had a good night's sleep in a long time. And she wished she'd been able to relax and sleep in Max's arms. But her own fears of what her body would look like in the morning, of his revulsion when his lust had passed…

"What do you regret?" she asked. Anything would be better than dwelling on her own insecurities.

He hunkered down on the floor next to her, cupping her face in those big hands of his. "That the woman I just made love to is sitting on the floor in the dark."

She held on to his wrists, looked him straight in the eye and said, "It's not you."

"It's not you, either," he said, kissing her tenderly. Drawing her up off the cold marble floor and into his embrace. In bed he'd been dominating, making sure she reacted to every move he made, but now he was gentle. She kept her eyes open, afraid to close them and find out that this was all a dream.

She realized something important about Max that she'd never noticed before. He really saw past all the things she used to keep most people at bay.

He lifted his head, rubbing his thumb over her bottom lip. She shivered in reaction to his touch, but he pushed to his feet.

He took one of the thick terry robes from the back of the door and wrapped it around her, then pulled her into his arms. She leaned against him, very much afraid that this was becoming a habit and one she'd never want to break. But she couldn't force herself away.

She'd been on her own since she was twelve and it was nice to have another person really care for her. Even if it was just a sexual thing, or temporary. For this night she didn't have to lie alone in her bed with only her thoughts for company.

"Will you stay with me until morning? Or would you like me to take you home?" he asked.

"I don't sleep. I haven't since…"

"No problem. What do you usually do?"

"Exercise. Watch TV. Sometimes I try to read."

"How does a bath sound?"

"Naked."

He arched one eyebrow at her. "Do you bathe with clothing on?"

"I usually bathe alone. I have body issues," she said, knowing that he must have realized it before this moment.

"I noticed."

"Hey, that's the first unchivalrous thing you've said to me. So the real Max isn't as nice as he pretends to be?"

"The real Max…are you sure you're ready for this?"

"Yes." More than he could understand, she needed to see his vulnerabilities.

"The real Max is a little spoiled, mean and determined."

"I'd say a lot determined."

He smiled at her. "I'll give you that."

He pulled her closer in his arms and she settled there. "I have issues with your body, too. You are too sexy. Every time we're out together, other men keep checking you out. It makes me want to do something to stake my claim. To make sure those men know you belong to me."

"Do I belong to you?" she asked. For most of her life she'd belonged only on the stage when she was dancing. Off the stage the competitive nature of her career had prohibited any deep and lasting bonds from forming.

"I don't know," he said, honestly. "I'm not entirely sure how to deal with you. But I want you in my life."

"For how long?" she asked and immediately wished she hadn't.

He rubbed her back, leaning against the counter-top. She liked how well they fitted together physically. If only she'd get over her body issues, they could both relax together skin-to-skin.

"I think if I said forever we'd both be scared," he said at last, watching her reaction carefully.

He was right. Forever did sound scary, since she'd only known him two days. Two days…but it felt like a lifetime. Too much was happening too fast and it was easy to let Max sweep her along in whatever he had planned because it gave her the freedom of not being responsible for the choices she made. *He swept me off my feet.* Even as she said the words in her mind, she felt disconnected.

For the first time in her life another person was

asking her to make a decision that affected them. Asking her…oh, man what was he asking her? Forever? That was something that she'd never believed in. Her earliest memories were of being alone. Forever with another person—she simply didn't buy into that.

"You can't fool me. Nothing scares you," she said, trying to keep the focus off herself.

He hugged her tightly to him and bent his head so that he spoke right into her ear. "I'm afraid that I won't be able to keep you."

"I'm not a Learjet, Max. I'm not a possession."

"But I want to possess you," he said, shoving his hands through his hair. "I know that I sound…well, not exactly rational. But I *am* rational. If you know nothing else about me, Blondie, know that I'm the kind of man who thinks every decision through."

She didn't know how to respond to that. No man had ever wanted her, her father had left before she was born, no boy had asked her out in high school and once she'd started dancing the men who'd asked her out had always left. All except Alan, who'd scared her with his possessiveness.

She wanted to tell him that she'd be his. "I'm not ready for you."

"No? What about physically?"

She shrugged. Every time he touched her she felt the bonds between them strengthening. She tried to tell herself it was just sex but she was beginning to believe it was so much more.

"I bet you are."

He lifted her in his arms and carried her into the bedroom. That lamp on the nightstand was on again and she knew that this time he wasn't going to let her slowly remove her clothing and pretend that he wasn't seeing the scars.

And she didn't want him to have to treat her as though she was fragile, to have to factor in how to get her out of her clothing without her flinching like some frightened virgin. So she took a deep breath, untied the belt of her robe and slowly let it drop to the floor.

Max appreciated the strength it took for her to stand there in the lamp's light and drop her robe. He had to be honest and say that once she was naked he wanted to forget about everything except making love to her again. But he couldn't ignore the sadness in her eyes. This was a woman who had once felt pride in her body, and he wanted her to again.

"I thought I was supposed to be convincing you," he said, moving toward her.

She held her hand up and he stopped when less than a foot of space separated them. "You already did. Now, I want to do something for you."

"I think we've covered that. Why don't we do something that's for each other?"

"That's why I'm standing here naked. But first I want you to look at me. Really look at me."

"I am."

"Not my breasts."

"Well, they *are* gorgeous."

She stared at him for a minute and then smiled, her expression so tempting that he felt his erection twitch in reaction to it.

He took her hand in his and led her to the mirror that stood embedded in the wall in the dressing area. He hit the light switch.

Roxy wrapped her arms around her waist and tried to shrink her body. He stood behind her, pulling her arms from her body and holding them out to her sides.

"Look in the mirror."

She hesitated for a second and then looked up. Their gazes met in the mirror and he bent and kissed her shoulder. Drew his mouth and teeth along the expanse of skin there until she shivered in his arms and tipped her head, offering him the long column of her neck.

He nibbled at her neck, working his way up to her ear. He sucked the lobe of her ear into his mouth and bit it delicately. "Look at your body."

She shook her head. Max wondered if he was pushing too hard. If he should just back off. But he didn't want Roxy in his bed feeling as though she had to hide part of herself. He wanted her free of her inhibitions.

"Then I'll look at you and tell you what I see."

He cupped her shoulders and she lowered her arms to her sides. "Your arms are so feminine yet at the same time muscled and strong. I like the way they look in those sleeveless tops you wear. I can't resist reaching out and touching you."

He ran his hands down both of her arms, slowly taking his time to make sure that he didn't miss a single inch of skin.

"I like my arms, too," she said quietly.

He tipped her head back and kissed her. She opened her mouth for him, angling her head the way he liked her to, and teased his tongue to come deeper into her mouth. When he lifted his head they were both breathing more heavily. Her lips were wet and swollen from his kisses and her eyes were slumberous.

He skimmed his hands over her breasts. He cupped the full weight of them, and felt her nipples tightening under his touch. "You have gorgeous breasts."

Her eyes were on his hands, his tanned skin a contrast against her pale white flesh. Her body, so delicate and pink and feminine, contrasted with the masculine strength of his. She put her hands over his as she undulated against his entire body, her buttocks rubbing over his erection, her shoulder blades rubbing over his chest, her long silky hair brushing his neck and shoulder.

"Can we stop now?" she asked, her voice low and

husky. She turned in his arms, her hands roaming down his chest. Fingernails scraping over him. "I really like your body."

"I know you do," he said, kissing her harder than he intended because he really couldn't resist her. He turned her back in his arms and held her firmly against him. One hand at her waist, the other right beneath her breasts.

"This is the part you don't like," he said, caressing her stomach from her ribs down to her belly button and stopping before he reached the curls between her legs.

"Yes," she said her voice breaking.

He kept touching her there, stroking over her skin until she relaxed against him. He took her hand in his and moved it over her own body. Sensitive to her reaction, he stopped when she lingered over the first scar. There were seven in total, all varying in length, the longest of them no more than three inches.

It was a miracle to him that she was here now in his arms—whole and complete. He had to batten down his own rage at what she'd been through. He vowed she'd never be that vulnerable again.

"I was very vain, Max. I think I hate these scars because they are proof of that vanity. Proof that I liked my body too much."

He hugged her tighter to him. Words were impossible at this moment. He just rubbed their joined hands over her body. "You are a dancer, your body is your work. It's how you express your art."

She turned in his arms again. There was a sheen of tears in her eyes and another emotion he couldn't define. "Make love to me."

He lifted her and carried her back to the bed. He settled her in the center and then slowly lowered his body over hers. He rubbed his torso against her. Felt the humid warmth at the center of her body. He liked the feel of being totally naked with her. He slipped just a little into her body just to tease them both.

"Yes, that's it. Take me and make me yours. Make us one," she said.

He was tempted to do it like this, with no protection, but he'd made a life of being responsible, so he sighed and pulled back. Their hands met at the box on the nightstand and she took the condom from him. She rolled it onto his body and then pulled him back to her. He slid into her body and she held him with her arms and legs. He moved slowly, rocking them from side-to-side and thrusting leisurely into her body until they were both consumed by waves of pleasure.

He rolled to his side, disposed of the condom and then pulled her back into his arms. She reached out and flicked off the light on the nightstand, then turned to him, resting her head over his chest, and went to sleep.

* * *

Roxy woke up to the smell of coffee and the low rumble of Max's voice. She rolled over and glanced at the clock, surprised to see that it was almost ten. She'd slept the entire night in his arms. This morning she was determined to face what she'd put off last night.

She got out of bed and put on her robe, walking into the other room where Max was on the phone at his laptop computer. He smiled when she entered, reached for the carafe of coffee and poured her a cup. She added cream and then sat down on the settee that faced the windows overlooking the city.

This was his world. She'd glimpsed it more than once. He worked all the time, his job was demanding…it was his life.

She'd expected to feel different this morning. Somehow, her outlook should have changed in a significant way. But aside from some aches from having had sex for the first time in a year, she didn't feel unusual.

He finished his call and came over to her. Bending, he kissed her and then sat down next to her.

"Thanks for the coffee," she said, feeling shy and a bit unsure. She had nothing to wear but last night's dress; she'd bared her soul to this man last night. She wasn't sure she wanted him to realize how much of herself he'd seen.

"I would have had breakfast for you, too, but Hayden didn't know what you liked to eat. I'll order that now."

"Why would Hayden know that?" she asked, sensing there was more to this than breakfast. She'd noticed how Max liked every detail to be perfect. Why?

Max put his arm along the back of the couch and drew her closer to his side. "I know my employees' preferences."

"All of them?" she asked, because from what she understood he ran a huge conglomerate.

He squeezed her tight. "No, smarty, not personally, but I have a file and my secretary accesses the information when I need it."

She was amazed at the amount of detail that implied. Why did Max do that? She tipped her head back to study him more carefully. She sensed there was something underlying here. What was she missing? "Why would you keep a file like that?"

"People like it when you remember little things about them."

Details were the things most easy to forget, Roxy thought. She knew that because, in the group home she'd lived in as a teen, she'd been one of three blond girls. No one had bothered to remember any of their names, just called them all "blond-girl." A name was an important detail, and she'd made sure as an adult that everyone remembered hers. But Max was going beyond that. He was remembering things that some-times even spouses and parents didn't know.

"What are the details about you? What are the things that make you happy?" she asked, hoping he'd reach out and show her some part of himself that no one else knew.

"That's not important. What do you like for breakfast?"

She sighed. Max wasn't going to reveal anything intimate to her. She'd bared her body to this man and he wanted to know what she liked for breakfast. When was she going to learn? "I like toast with blackberry jelly and coffee."

"That's not breakfast. That's what you eat when you're in a hurry."

He wasn't going to let this go. There was more to this than breakfast. From growing up in the system, she knew that everyone, no matter how normal they seemed, had some kind of issue to deal with. This need for facts was Max's way of building a relationship.

"Why are you looking at me like that?"

"I'm trying to figure out what makes *you* tick."

"What you see is what you get. Tell me about you and breakfast."

"What's to tell? I've never had a leisurely break-fast. Mornings aren't really a time to hang out for show dancers." When she was younger, she'd spent all of her time at the dance studio before and after school. Food had just never seemed that important, mainly because it had been scarce.

"Now that you have the gory details about my morning eating habits…what about you?"

Max stared down at her, his hands moving slowly over her shoulder, caressing her as they talked. She settled deeper into the curve of his body.

"I'm usually the one who makes the arrangements, so no one needs to know my preferences."

"What if I'm the one ordering?" she asked. She could never tolerate a relationship that was uneven. She wanted to take as good care of him as he did of her. She was going to make this relationship with Max work. She didn't want it to end when he left, and that meant really getting to know him. She'd shown him way more of herself than she'd meant to, something she'd never done before with anyone. So there was more to Max and her than she'd initially thought.

He arched one eyebrow at her. "In that case, I like poached eggs and Canadian bacon."

"Was that so hard? I'm not going to leak the information."

"You might be the first person to ask what I liked," he said, leaning her head back against his shoulder. He kissed her slowly and with great tenderness.

"I'm sure that's because most people already know." The kind of man he was, he'd surround himself with like-minded people. Hayden might not know what she liked to eat, but he treated his staff like family and she knew he was one of Max's closest friends.

"They don't."

"That must be your fault then."

He waited for her to continue, and she felt as if she might have blundered into something that she didn't mean to say. But she'd noticed that Max took care of the people around him, and not vice versa.

"You don't give anyone a chance to know you. You keep the spotlight focused on them."

"Them, or you?"

"Well, me, and it's very flattering but I forget to ask about you. I want to know *your* secrets."

"I thought Hayden gave you a file on me?"

"That only included your gambling habits. I want to know the real secrets. The ones that no one else knows."

"There are no secrets, Roxy. What you see is what you get with me."

He pushed to his feet and went back to his computer. He lifted the phone and made a call to room service, ordering breakfast for both of them. "I have to work after breakfast for a few hours."

She put her coffee cup down and walked slowly toward the bedroom. Then she realized she was running, the way she always did when things got a little sticky emotionally. She had no idea how to treat Max. But she knew that they both had to be able to pry into each other's lives. It was unfair that he'd seen her in all her imperfection and was unwilling to give her even a glimpse at the inner man he carefully hid.

"Did I offend you?" she asked.

"No, you didn't. I'm not a secrets kind of guy. This really is all I am."

There was a sadness in his eyes, and Roxy knew that there were secrets inside Max but sensed they'd been buried too deeply for him to tell her easily what they were. She'd find them out on her own.

Nine

Roxy wiped her sweaty palms on the legs of her pants and walked into the lobby of the Chimera one week later. Suzi Yuki, the high-stakes gambler whom Roxy had started hostessing for after Max, was a lot of fun. And she needed little encouragement to stay in the casino. Her game was craps and she was a phenomenal player. When Roxy had left Suzi a few minutes earlier she'd been up almost fifty thousand dollars.

Of course, she wasn't nervous at all about being a hostess. That job was turning into something she could definitely get used to doing, even though it didn't hold the same luster that dancing always had.

But she'd realized that dancing would never be the center of her life again.

Max was slowly becoming that focal point, which bothered her because she wasn't sure how she fitted into his life. One on one, they meshed, mainly because Max made sure that they did. He really listened to her and understood the things she wanted, as well as things she was afraid to ask for.

And that made her nervous, because she didn't know what to do for him. Of course, when he'd asked her to join him at a business lunch, she'd said yes.

Now she was having second thoughts. She'd never gone to college, hadn't even graduated high school. Her birthday was in March, so she'd become an adult before she was supposed to have graduated. Having no place to stay she'd started working in clubs instead of staying in school.

What if she embarrassed Max? What if she said something that was—

"Hey, Blondie, I've been waiting for you," Max said, slipping his arm around her waist.

She tried to relax against him and couldn't. "Hey, yourself. Where is everyone else?"

"We're meeting them upstairs in a private dining room. I wanted a chance to talk to you first."

She took a deep breath. "You don't have to worry, Max. I won't embarrass you."

He furrowed his brow. "What are you talking about?"

"Just that I know I don't know anything about your business. I'll keep quiet and just smile. I won't say anything—"

He put his finger on her lips, stopping the flow of words that was growing out of control. In her mind she wanted to apologize for everything she'd ever done and she didn't like that. She didn't like feeling discomfited by the life she'd led when she compared it to his.

"What are you talking about?" he asked quietly.

"I know all I need to about business. I need you here to keep me from saying something I shouldn't."

"That doesn't sound like the man I've come to know," she said. She'd observed Max on the phone and he was always unfailingly polite and to the point. The ultimate professional.

"Well, MacNeil is seriously pissing me off," he said, taking her hand and leading her out of the lobby and into the courtyard that led to another tower of the hotel.

"So what am I supposed to do?" she asked as they walked.

"Just be yourself. He's bringing his wife as well. That's his way of calling a truce."

"Are you sure you want me there?" As soon as she asked she wanted to kick herself. What was wrong with her that she had to doubt her own worth? "Forget I said that."

"I will. Don't be nervous. Harron is a nice man when he's not trying to keep me dangling. And his wife, Sheila, is a huge patron of the arts in Vancouver, especially local dance."

She relaxed a little, thinking that maybe this lunch wouldn't be as bad as she feared.

But Max still seemed tense, and she wasn't sure how to help him out. "Are you nervous?"

"No. Why?"

"You seem edgy."

"Edgy?"

"Don't take this the wrong way…but you remind me of a predator on the hunt."

He laughed. "Good. I want MacNeil to understand exactly how I feel about this delay of his."

"Isn't this just part of the way acquisitions work?" she asked. Max had explained that he was in the process of buying out MacNeil's family-owned travel agency, the third largest in North America.

"Sometimes, but I'm on vacation and I'd rather be in my suite making love to you. Yet duty calls."

"If you hadn't invited me to lunch you'd be in your suite by yourself," she said, because she didn't want him to be too confident in his hold over her.

"You think so?" He pulled her off the walkway and behind a hedge.

There was a fountain gurgling in the middle of an oasis. The Chimera prided itself on its romantic ambience, and this particular fountain was a well-known wedding proposal spot. In fact, it was hidden so that a couple could have privacy and still have a photo souvenir. There was a small area behind the garden area where a photographer could be stationed.

"I know so. There's no way I could have asked Hayden for a long lunch to meet you in your room. Why are we here?"

Max led her to the bench in the middle of the garden. "Please have a seat. I have something I need to ask you before we join the MacNeils."

Anxiety slithered down her spine. "Do you want me to pretend I wasn't a topless dancer?"

He cupped her face in his hands, his long fingers sliding over her cheeks to the back of her neck and holding her so that he could stare down into her eyes. He lowered his head and brushed his lips over hers.

"I thought we already covered this. I want you to be yourself. I like the woman that you are, Roxy."

She swallowed, unsure how to respond to that statement. Sometimes he made her feel too much. A swell of emotion that she was unprepared to handle welled up in her throat. His hands dropped to his sides and he gestured toward the bench again. She sat down, crossing her legs and waiting for Max to join her. When he didn't she tipped her head back to look up at him.

* * *

Max straightened his tie and glanced around to make sure the photographer he'd hired was in position. He'd planned every detail of this proposal carefully. It had been a tight timetable to make sure he was ready for the MacNeil meeting and get the ring he wanted flown in before lunch. But he was used to juggling several projects at the same time.

And this thing with Roxy needed to be settled. He wasn't going to be happy until he'd put his mark on her so that every man she encountered knew she was his. Last night when she'd contemplated going home instead of coming up to his suite, he'd realized that he needed something permanent between them. A bond that even Roxy couldn't deny.

He patted his pocket again and rehearsed the words he'd planned to say.

"What are you doing?" she asked.

Great. First she thought he was nervous and now she probably thought…ah, hell he had no idea what she thought. He only knew that he'd been on his own his entire life and finding Roxy was like finding a piece that had been missing.

"Making sure every detail is right," he said, leaning to the left and finally spotting the pedestal ice-bucket and the bottle of champagne in it.

She raised both eyebrows at him. "For what?"

He took a deep breath and sat down next to her on

the bench. He took her small fine-boned hand in his and traced the veins on the back of her hand. She twisted her hand and slid her fingers through his.

"These last few days have been incredible," he said, not really sure where those words came from. Though they were the truth he didn't want her to know how he felt.

"I feel the same. I never thought that I'd meet someone like you." She smiled at him, her expression so tender that he knew he'd made the right choice. Knew there was no way she'd deny him.

"I think Hayden's finally found a way to pay me back for befriending him all those years ago."

"I don't like the sound of that. I told him I wasn't interested in being set up with you."

"You did?"

"Yes."

"Well my considerable charm must have worked on you."

"Not your charm, Max. Your attention to detail."

Max wasn't sure how they'd strayed onto talking about Hayden and knew he didn't want to discuss his friend. He wanted to discuss them. "Hayden has nothing to do with this."

"With what? You're being vague and that's not like you."

No it wasn't like him. His normal mode of operation was just to take what he wanted and keep moving forward. To acquire businesses, homes, cars, friends. He knew how to do that. But a wife…that was infinitely harder. They'd share everything—a home, a bed, their lives—and he'd never in his forty years shared all that.

Even his childhood home had been a series of empty showplaces that his family members had moved between depending on the season. His father always remarried in June, his mother always retreated to Aspen in November. But he wanted more with Roxy. He wanted to have something—someone—who could be with him all the time. He wanted a person to fill the void his career had always filled.

"I've never done this before."

"Done *what?*" she asked, putting her hand on his thigh.

All his thoughts faded. He wanted to move her hand higher. To bend and take her mouth with his and then make love to her. To reinforce the physical bonds that were between them.

"Done what, Max?" she asked again.

"Asked you to marry me," he said, biting out the words in a way he hadn't planned on them sounding. Dammit, he always screwed up the romantic fantasy when left to his own devices.

"What?"

"Marry me, Roxy."

He stood and pulled the velvet box from his

pocket, snapping it open as he dropped to one knee in front of her. He took her hand in his and looked up into her eyes. They were cloudy with doubts and he understood that. Everything had happened so quickly between them…too quickly, it might seem, but Max had learned long ago to trust his instincts and the way he reacted to Roxy was totally instinctive.

He took the platinum marquise-cut aquamarine-and-diamond-encrusted ring from the box and slipped it onto her ring finger. She didn't say anything, but goose bumps spread up her arm.

He heard the sound of the photographer snapping the pictures. The sound of people on the path that lay beyond the hedges. The soft sound of her every inhalation of breath, but he didn't hear the one word he waited for.

"I have a bottle of champagne and some glasses over here. We'll have a toast and then after lunch, I'm taking you away for an afternoon of pampering."

"I can't go."

"Why not?"

She pushed to her feet, wrapping her arms around her waist. She started when the ring scraped the skin of her arm. She looked down on the large ring and pulled it from her hand.

"Thank you for asking me to marry you, but I can't."

She held the ring out to him, but he didn't take it. He knew she'd change her mind. He just had to find the right words to say. The correct argument to use.

"Why can't you marry me?"

"We hardly know each other, Max. We're still practically strangers."

"No, we're not. We know a lot about one another. I know you inside and out, Roxy. Don't deny that."

"Maybe you know my vulnerabilities, but that doesn't mean we can live with each other day in and day out. I'm still adjusting to my new life, and it's hard. I don't know that I'm ready to become your wife and change my life again."

He crossed to her, taking her chin in his hand and leaning her head back. "Those are excuses."

"You might be right, but I can't marry you now."

He let go of her chin and stepped back. No one had ever told him no before. That wasn't true, he thought, his mind racing to accept the fact that she'd really said no. He forced back the momentary anger that had risen when she'd taken his ring from her finger. Roxy just needed to be persuaded, he thought.

He'd studied the details around Roxy. He knew things about her that few others did. What had he missed? Somehow this wasn't about marrying to make Harron get off his back anymore, but about making sure she stayed in his life.

He didn't say anything, just kept looking at her with a mixture of anger and resolve. Roxy didn't know what to do. Only knew that saying no was the hardest thing that she'd ever done. But she was only just figuring out this new life she had, this life away from dancing, and marrying Max after knowing him for such a short time wouldn't be fair to either of them.

She didn't want to face the truth, but in her soul was the fear that the home she'd felt in Max's arms might disappear if they lived together.

She took his hand in hers and pressed the ring into the center of his palm. She knew he wouldn't beg her to reconsider and she admitted to herself that was the problem. It was almost as if Max knew those details of her life and that he'd figured she'd say yes because acceptance had been so rare for her.

She turned on her heel and walked away, struggling not to limp but so agitated she couldn't keep her gait smooth. Her legs trembled. She didn't know if she'd make it back to some private place before she gave in to the tears she felt welling up behind her eyes. Because for a minute there she'd wanted to give herself to him cheaply. To trade her life for a ring. And she'd always believed she'd never do that.

"Roxy?"

She paused but didn't turn to look at him. She couldn't see him again, knowing she was just the right face at the right time, not the love of his life.

Why did that matter?

Her mind didn't know the answer, but her heart

did. She was falling for him. Heck, she'd fallen for him that first morning on the beach. Saying no was the only way she knew to protect her heart from breaking once again.

"Yes?"

"Where are you going?" he asked in a gruff voice that gave her a spark of hope that maybe he wasn't as unemotional as he was pretending to be.

She pivoted on her heel to face him. The midday sun slanted through the canopy of tree branches in the garden, falling over him, leaving him mainly in the shadows next to the fountain.

He looked so alone and determined that her heart ached. He still stood next to the bench. The ring and its box had been tucked away somewhere.

There was no hint of vulnerability in him, and she wondered for a moment if he'd really just asked her to marry him, because he didn't look like a man who'd had his proposal turned down.

"I…I was going back to work. I didn't think you'd still want to have lunch."

"You thought wrong. I misjudged you, but I won't do it again."

She didn't like the way that sounded. He was focusing on her the same way he was his merger. She bit her tongue before she could ask him if he was going to draw up a statement about the pros and cons of her marrying him. "I'm not a business you are trying to acquire."

"I know that. Companies are a lot easier to get a handle on. All I have to do is look at the P and L and then figure out if I can turn a profit."

"What's a P and L?" she asked to distract herself.

"Profit and loss statement."

"Kind of like pros and cons?" she asked.

"Kind of."

"How'd I stack up?"

His expression lightened as he skimmed his gaze down her body. "Better than I did, obviously."

She couldn't help but laugh at him. She slapped him on the arm. "That wasn't very sophisticated."

"Who said I was sophisticated?" he asked.

"No one had to. You exude breeding and culture with every movement you make. Unlike me."

"Is that why you said no?" he asked.

She wished it were something easy like comportment so she could take a class and fix it. But she knew it was more complex than that. She needed more from Max than a proposal after a few days. She needed emotion, and the man she'd come to know wasn't that open with his feelings.

"I'm going to ask you again, and the next time you will say yes."

"Do you have any idea how arrogant that sounds?" she asked, trying to change her mood and get past the emotions that weighed so heavily in her throat.

"Yes."

She had to laugh at the totally unrepentant way he said it. She knew she shouldn't encourage him because marriage wasn't in her plans, but there was something that felt so right about slipping her arm though his as they walked. "We'll see."

He stopped walking and turned to her there on the path, and there was emotion in his eyes this time. Real emotion that made her hope that he might feel more for her than he did for his business merger. "I want you in my life. If you're not ready for marriage then I can wait."

It scared her how important he'd become to her in such a short time. He was making her change and she knew she'd needed that impetus to start changing, but at the same time she was afraid to trust.

"I'm sorry."

"Don't be. I misjudged something. I'll figure it out and ask you again when the time is right."

"Part of the problem is you thinking that you have to figure this out by yourself. A relationship involves two people."

He scratched his chin. "I'll try, but honestly, I'm not sure I can do what you ask. I'm too used to operating on my own."

"What about your family? Don't you compromise on stuff like where you have holiday dinners and vacations?"

"We're not a close family. My schedule is always available to them, but they are busy."

"That's not what family is supposed to be. Is that how you envision marriage to me?"

"I'm not sure what you're asking."

"I'm asking if I'd get a copy of your schedule and then have to decide when I wanted to see you."

"From your tone, I think my answer better be no."

"We still have a ways to go, Max. We're not ready for marriage yet."

"What do I have to do? I'm good at achieving objectives."

She shook her head at him. "Stop acting like I'm a company you're trying to acquire. And you're going to have to compromise."

He arched one eyebrow at her in that arrogant way of his. "I'm sure you can be very persuasive if you put your mind to it."

"Are you talking about sex again?"

"I listen to you when we're not in bed."

He led the way into the tower building, holding the door for her to enter. She thought about how different Max was from every other man she'd ever been involved with. He did listen to her, and he heard things she wasn't even aware she wanted or needed. But he kept his own dreams and desires hidden away, and she really needed to know him to feel safe spending the rest of her life with him.

Ten

The next two weeks were hectic as Max divided his time between Vegas and Roxy and business trips to Vancouver and his corporate headquarters in Atlanta. He was tired, he missed Roxy and he wanted nothing more than just to hold her in his arms.

The second day in Vancouver, he'd invited her to join him for a mini-vacation while he closed the deal with MacNeil, but she'd refused. She had a job to do and she hadn't yet earned vacation time. Max had made a call to Hayden and asked him to free Roxy from her schedule.

Hayden had refused and Roxy had called Max,

livid that he would try such a thing. It had not been the smartest move on his part.

He'd showered her with gifts, but she'd told him to stop trying to buy her. She didn't need anything, and it made her uncomfortable to receive pricey gifts. Max *had* stopped, but it hadn't felt right.

From his mother's knee he'd learned that women wanted trinkets and baubles, and Roxy's disinterest in them was just another thing that set her apart from every other woman he'd ever known. She'd also told him that he better get used to her working, because she'd never be a lady of leisure.

Tonight she was working until nine o'clock, when her gambler was leaving for the airport. So he went to the poker room to play a few hands. Hayden was there talking to two Japanese men whom Max recognized from his own deep play. They were both whales, big-time gamblers who spent weeks at the casino several times a year. Hayden waved him over but Max didn't feel like socializing so he declined with a shake of his head.

He still had Roxy's ring in his pocket, and he wanted it on her hand. He hadn't asked her again, but had made love to her as often as he could. He'd also taken the time to ask about her dreams and where she saw her future. She wanted to open a small dance studio and pass her love for dance on to others.

She had an idea for opening a showgirl college of

sorts in Vegas and Max had already done some research into what that would take. He wanted to talk to Hayden about space for the facility in the hotel.

He'd called her every night, at first hoping to make her realize how much she needed him in her life. In his arrogance, he wanted to remind her of what she'd said no to.

But instead he'd found that he was the one who needed the conversations. And because dependence wasn't something he could tolerate, he'd deliberately stopped talking to her every day, calling her when he knew she wouldn't be there to prove to himself that he didn't need to hear her voice before he went to bed. He'd have her in his arms for the next four nights. That was the longest stretch of time they'd been together.

Arms snaked around his waist and he felt the cool press of Roxy's lips against his neck. "Hey, there!"

He turned in her embrace and kissed her with all the pent-up emotion that had been bottled inside him for the last five days. "Damn, I missed you."

Her lips were wet and swollen from his kiss. "I missed you, too."

"Are you ready to go?"

"Yes. I just got back from the airport."

"You took Suzi to the airport?"

"She asked me to ride with her. She's really nice and she gave me a huge tip. Dinner tonight is on me."

"No way." No woman of his was buying him a meal. He knew it was an archaic attitude, but he wanted to take care of her because no one else ever had. She'd been working and providing a shelter for herself since she'd turned eighteen, and now he wanted to spoil her. "I'd rather you buy something for yourself."

She shook her head. "I want to do this, Max. You're always showering me with gifts and stuff. And you have everything..."

He started to argue but she put her fingers over his lips. "Compromise."

When she put it that way, he understood where she was coming from.

"Great. Do you have a favorite restaurant?"

He had several and he tried to pick one in the moderate price range. He wanted her to feel good about buying him dinner but not stretch her budget. "There's a nice sushi place near the hotel. I'll have my secretary make us a reservation."

Over the last few weeks he'd come to realize that when she'd stopped headlining, her income had been cut in half. And he admired the way she'd been careful to make sure that she was still able to make ends meet by adjusting her lifestyle.

He kept his hand at the small of Roxy's back as they walked to his limo.

* * *

Two nights later Roxy put the finishing touches on her makeup in the luxurious suite that Max used whenever he was at the Chimera. Max was at a meeting, but they were having dinner with Harron MacNeil and his wife, who had flown to Vegas for the weekend.

Ever since she'd turned down his wedding proposal, Max had been going out of his way to learn to compromise. She knew it was a struggle for him.

"Roxy?"

"In here," she said. She blotted her lipstick and turned as he came in, shedding his jacket. He tossed it on the edge of the bed and crossed the room to kiss her. She loved that he did that.

"I'm sorry, Blondie, I thought I'd have you to myself for a few days but sometimes duty calls." He undid his belt and tossed it on the bed and then went to work on his shirt.

"Sometimes? It calls you all the time." She opened the closet and took out a fresh shirt for him while he went into the bathroom and freshened up.

"This is my life," he said, poking his head around the door and holding his hand out for his shirt. She handed it to him and he shrugged into it.

"I know. When I used to dance I was the same way about my career." She understood Max's dedication and didn't resent it. He always made time for her. The reality was, he was the CEO of a huge company, and there was no way he'd be able to step away from that.

He pulled a new tie from the drawer and put it around his neck, leaving the tails dangling while he buttoned his shirt and tucked it in.

"This should be the last dinner with them. I think MacNeil is ready to sign on the dotted line."

"What's been the hold up?"

"The company has been in his family for the last three generations and he wants to make sure that I don't change the essence of what they do."

"And that is?"

"Cater to families. They pride themselves on their wholesomeness."

"You're not exactly virtuous."

He gave her a wicked grin. "Ah, you know you like that about me."

He pulled her into his arms, leaning back against the vanity table. She rested her hand on his bare chest. "MacNeil is finally convinced that I will keep my word. I told him he could have an opportunity to meet the woman I'm planning to marry."

"Max, I haven't said yes."

"I know that. I was upfront with Harron, told him you were dragging your feet."

She shook her head. Sometimes he was outrageous. She honestly thought that the reason Max was so successful in business and in life was that he simply never gave up. "Harron thinks I'm the key to you keeping your word."

"He does. Dinner tonight is just a formality. Thanks for doing this."

"I don't mind. I really liked Sheila when we met them for lunch. I want to talk to her more about the dance studio she and her daughter own." She liked being a part of Max's business life. Since that was a huge part of who he was, it gave her another glimpse into the complex man she cared for. She stepped away from him so he could finish dressing.

"I've done some preliminary research into starting a showgirl dance college, if you're interested," he said, tucking his shirt in and knotting his tie.

She leaned over his shoulder, catching his eye in the mirror to make sure he saw that she was serious. She'd mentioned her dream of opening a school during a late-night conversation. If she didn't put up some stipulations, he'd use his money to make the showgirl college a reality before she had a chance. "Really. I don't want you to buy it for me. Plus I'm not sure I have the right personality to teach."

"Somehow I knew you'd say that. I ran the idea past Hayden, because it makes sense to have a central training area. Even if you decide not to teach, the idea should still go forward and you should be a part of it."

She shook her head. "I'm going to do this research, not you."

"Did you just tell me no?"

She bit the inside of her cheek to keep from smiling. If only he were as arrogant as he thought he was, it would be easier for her to resist him. Easier for her to pretend this was just an affair. Easier to sleep when they were apart.

"Yes, I did. You can't keep buying me things all the time. You make me feel like a kept woman."

He shrugged into his suit jacket, checked himself one more time in the mirror before turning to her. "Not a very well-kept one. You work as many hours as I do."

"And your problem with that would be?"

"Absolutely nothing, Blondie."

He mixed them both a vodka martini, shaking it perfectly, and handed her the glass.

"To us," he said.

"To us." Their eyes met as they clinked their glasses and even though she knew she wasn't really part of this world—his world—for once she felt as if she was exactly where she belonged.

Their dinner was nice but Max wanted to be alone with Roxy.

For the majority of his life, work had been his number-one priority and it was unnerving to find that a woman was now edging business out. It was early and he should suggest something like dancing or drinks, but all he really wanted to do was get back to his suite and make love to Roxy.

He shook hands with Harron and watched as Roxy and Sheila said goodbye. Niceties over, be guided Roxy back to his limo as quickly as possible without seeming to rush.

He wanted to ask her again to marry him. The words had been on the tip of his tongue every time they spoke, but he knew he only had one more shot to get it right. He couldn't keep asking her without making himself look like a desperate ass, an image he never wanted to cultivate.

"You're quiet," he said as the city lights flashed into the back of the limo.

"So are you."

He raised both eyebrows at her tone. "What's up?"

"I've been thinking about our relationship. I don't see how we can go on this way. I miss you a lot when we're apart."

He pulled her into his arms. "Good."

She punched his shoulder lightly but didn't leave his embrace. Instead she settled back against him as he wrapped his arm around her.

"I don't think so, Max. I'm not sure we can keep on the way we have been."

Finally, he was going to be able to have what he wanted. What they both wanted. He couldn't explain the bond between them. It was like nothing he'd ever experienced before. He only knew that his life paled when he was away from her.

"I agree."

"You do?"

"Of course, I do. I'm not any happier with the way things are. I want to sleep with you every night."

She tipped her head back and he lowered his mouth to hers, sipping from her. Tasting her with long sweeps of his tongue. The brief taste he'd had of her passion earlier wasn't enough. He needed more. He needed it now.

He shifted her in his arms until she straddled his lap. Her hands on his face, her breasts resting on his chest.

"I don't see how that's possible unless you move your headquarters to Las Vegas."

He skimmed his hands over her back, tracing her spine and shifted under her until he had them both as close as they could get.

"I'm afraid I can't do that. Too many jobs are at stake. Why don't you quit working for the Chimera and travel with me?"

She shifted off his lap and to the rear-facing seat. She crossed her legs and wrapped her arms around herself. "I can't. I can't stop working to be with you. I wouldn't be able to live with myself if I did that."

"Compromise, isn't that what you're always telling me?" he asked.

"Yes, I am. But—"

"What?"

"I'm not sure what I want to do," she said.

"I'll support you until you figure that out. You can try whatever you like."

She gave him a hard glare. "I promised myself I'd never live on charity again."

"There's a big difference between being charity and living together with a man you can't get enough of." Even now he couldn't make himself talk about emotions. Hers or his. He wanted her, he could vocalize his attraction for her body and late at night he could admit to himself that he needed her in his life. But he couldn't make himself that vulnerable to her.

"That's really not for me."

His anger bubbled over. He couldn't believe they were having this conversation. He felt like a heel for suggesting that she live with him. *He* didn't want a mistress—he'd wanted a wife. "I asked you to marry me and you said no. So tell me what will work."

"When you say it like that—"

Immediately he regretted his outburst. Eye on the prize. He was focused on getting her into his life. Making her his wife. "Sorry, my temper got the best of me. I know you need time to see for yourself what I already know about the two of us."

"What do you know?"

"I know that we fit together."

"Physically, we sure do. But our lives are very different."

"Variety is the spice of life, isn't it?"

"Yes, it is. But what if this is just the newness?"

"I can't make you any promises for what the future holds, I'd be lying and we'd both know it. But I can tell you that I can't imagine a time when I won't want you by my side."

She shifted in his arms, leaning closer to him. Her head on his shoulder. "I'm so tempted. But reality is hard on those kinds of fantasies. And I'm falling for you, Max. Really falling for the man you are in a way that has nothing to do with sex. Relationships are built on more than what we have."

Fear gripped him by the throat. He knew sooner or later this would come up. "I'm giving you all I can."

She swallowed. "I've always wanted a different kind of relationship."

"What kind?" he asked, knowing that this was the key to Roxy. The key to really understanding her.

"The kind I've never had. That perfect dream family I wanted as a child, the kind that I'd look at when I was at a shopping mall and long to be a part of."

"There's no such thing as perfect," he said. He cradled her closer, wanting to undo all the wounds that life had dealt her in the past. He would give her this if that's what she needed to be happy with him. "This isn't a fantasy or a dream. I'm a real man and I want you in my life. I want you to marry me so that everyone who sees us will know that you belong to me."

She took a deep breath as the car pulled to a stop in front of their hotel, then put her hand on his arm as the driver came around to open the door. "I want that, too."

Eleven

Max lifted her into his arms when she stepped out of the car and carried her through the lobby, drawing the attention of everyone they passed. But he didn't linger or say anything except to tell her to push the elevator button when they arrived at the bank.

She did, and then hit the button for their floor. Max lowered her down his body, his mouth finding hers. She wrapped her arms around him and clung to him, a feeling of complete rightness swamping her, making her feel like the choice she'd made was the right one.

The car stopped on their floor and Max lifted her into his arms again. She'd been carried before in a couple of shows and in ballet class, dancing a pas de deux. But this was different. Max's mouth was on hers, his arms tight around her, and even though he hadn't spoken of love or affection, she felt the commitment in his embrace.

"There isn't going to be champagne or photographers. You caught me by surprise," he said, setting her on her feet to open the door.

She remembered how much effort he'd put into his first proposal and knowing him as she did, she knew he liked every detail planned. It said something to her that he'd kept pursuing her even though she'd turned down his orchestrated proposal. "I don't need those things. I just need you."

"Me neither. I need you, too, Blondie."

He carried her over the threshold and kicked the door closed behind them. A lamp from the living area of their suite was lit and the room was cast in its soft glow. The drapes were pulled back and the lights of Vegas were spread out in front of them. And she felt like this time she'd get the emotion she'd been wanting from him.

"I know I should take this slow, give you a romantic evening to remember, but it's been too long since I've had you."

He found the zipper at the back of her dress and lowered it. She caught his hands and waited for him to look at her. No man had ever looked at her with as much passion as Max had in his eyes at that moment. "Every moment I spend with you is one to remember."

He twisted his hands in hers until he held both of her wrists in his grasp. "Me, too. I don't have the words I know you'd want to hear. Let me show you how happy I am that you've finally agreed to become my wife."

A feeling of joy and playfulness filled her. Nothing in her life had prepared her for the depth of her feelings for Max. She wanted to be with him more than she'd ever wanted to dance and be on stage. She wanted him more than she'd craved a family as a child or security as an adult.

He was an all-consuming passion that welled up inside her and spread everywhere. But he was also a soft and gentle breeze that brought peace and acceptance to her, something she'd never had before him. Sure the other girls in the show had accepted her, but they were all struggling the same way she'd been.

Only Max saw her, flaws and all, and accepted her. She hugged him tightly, her emotions bubbling over. She was so afraid to let him see how much she needed him in her life. Afraid to trust him with the depth of her love.

She bit her lip realizing the truth she'd stumbled on. She was marrying Max but letting him believe that she really wanted just this picture-perfect life when what she was afraid to ask for was his love.

He brought his mouth down hard on hers, his hand tangling in the hair at the nape of her neck, forcing her head back as he plundered her mouth in a kiss that left no doubt in her mind that he was staking his claim on her body. But what about her heart?

She stretched her fingers in his grasp and felt the fabric of his shirt. She skimmed her fingers over it until she could slip her fingertip under the button and feel his warm flesh.

He inhaled sharply, his hand leaving her neck and unknotting his tie. She watched him as he brought her hands up to his mouth and kissed each palm. "Take your dress off."

Was this the way to win him? What if this back-fired on her?

She took her dress off and felt so naked with her newly acknowledged emotions flowing through her. She hesitated as she stood in front of him in the lamplight wearing only her panties and strapless bra.

"Turn around," he said, his voice gruff and commanding, sending shivers down her spine. She loved the way he sounded when his civilized demeanor dropped away and left behind just the man.

She pivoted on her heel, glanced over her shoulder at him. And felt a moment of intense pride in the body that she'd thought was flawed. Because the look on his face was a combination of lust and awe. Where was the love? And was she asking for too much to expect that?

He reached out and touched the skin of her back. "Lace your fingers together."

She didn't want to play sex games with him. She wanted him to drop the facade and show her what he really felt. "What are you doing?"

"Making you behave."

She shook her head. "I can't do this, Max."

Immediately he pulled her into his embrace. His hands rubbing down her back as he held her tightly to him. "What's the matter, Blondie?"

"I don't want to be an object to you. I need to know that I'm more than sex."

He framed her face in his hands and looked down at her. "You are."

"It doesn't feel like it."

"You are my life, Roxy."

He kissed her deeply, arousing her to the point where she stopped thinking. He finished undressing her.

He unbuttoned his shirt and tossed it on the floor on top of her dress. He pulled her into his arms, the hair on his chest abrading the tips of her nipples. She tried to shift in his arms, to move her aching breasts against him, but he held her still.

His mouth moved down her neck, suckling at the

pulse point. She shifted her legs, wrapping one around his thigh, trying to get closer. She needed him. She needed to believe that this was an expression of his affection for her.

He reached between them, lowering his zipper and freeing himself. She shifted against him.

He grabbed her waist and lifted her up. "Wrap your legs around my waist."

She did and felt him slide into her body. He cursed and pulled out. "Forgot something."

She held on to his shoulders, nibbled at his neck while she felt him reach into his pocket. He ripped the condom packet open with his teeth and sheathed himself with one hand.

She looked down into his eyes as he positioned himself and slid into her body, taking her deeply and completely. His gaze held hers as he leaned back against the wall and used his hands on her hips to control both of their movements. She rocked harder against him until she felt everything in her body reaching for her climax.

She fought it off as long as she could, waiting for him. He thrust harder and quicker and then leaned down and bit the tip of her breast as they both came together. She clung to him, holding him tightly.

But as their breathing slowed and he carried her to bed, she realized that she might have taken a high-stakes gamble that she wasn't ready to pay out on when she'd agreed to marry Max. Because she knew without a doubt that she loved him—and she had a hard time believing he felt the same.

Max had an early-morning meeting and got out of bed before Roxy. He left her a note telling her to be ready to make wedding plans that afternoon. He wanted to marry her before she had a chance to change her mind.

He glanced down at her sleeping in his bed. Damn, he wanted to see her in his bedroom in Dunwoody, not in a hotel bed. But the ring on her left hand reassured him that she was his. *His.* He knew she'd object to that statement, but it felt right in his soul.

He left their suite a few minutes later, getting on the phone to start making arrangements. His dad was in Napa visiting his family there and his mother was in Beverly Hills, but both would be in Vegas tomorrow for the wedding. Hayden was happy to make all the wedding arrangements. Duke had agreed to be his best man and was flying out with his wife Cami and their two children.

Max felt like all the pieces of his life were falling into place. He had a full day ahead of him and wanted everything cleared from his agenda so he could take the next two weeks off and fly to Hawaii with Roxy. Spend time, just the two of them in the same time zone. For a minute last night he'd felt her slipping through his fingers. He wanted to make sure she didn't.

His phone rang as he was walking through the lobby. "Williams."

"Hey, it's me," Roxy said, her voice soft and deeper than usual. He had no trouble picturing her sexy body in bed.

"Hey, you. What's up?" he asked.

"I'm trying to figure out what part of 'I don't want to sit around and wait for you' you didn't understand. Hayden just called and gave me the next few days off."

He should have guessed she wouldn't like the way he'd handled this morning, but to be honest, he couldn't concentrate while she was around. He needed to be one-hundred-percent at work.

"Blondie, I heard you, but I have to finish a few last-minute things. I thought you could use the time to get ready for our wedding."

"Are we really going to get married tomorrow?" she asked.

He exited the hotel into the sunny Vegas morning. His driver, Carl, pulled the rented limo up to the curb and got out, opening the door for him.

"Yes. I asked Hayden to make sure Tawny and Glenda are off the schedule for tonight and tomorrow. You should pick out dresses that you'd like them to wear. Let my assistant know and I'll make sure they get the sizes they need. Can you hang on a second?"

"Sure."

He pressed the mute button on the phone and turned to Carl. "I'm going to MacNeil's hotel—he's staying at the Golden Dream. While I'm there, I need you to go to the airport and pick up a package for me."

"No problem, boss."

Max slid into the car and opened his briefcase, pulling out his laptop to start downloading the numbers and e-mails that had come in the night before. He un-muted his phone.

"Sorry about that. I'm back now."

"You're doing too much."

He heard the concern in her voice and it warmed him. Even his parents never said anything about his work schedule. But then Roxy noticed things about him that no one else ever did. She noticed the details.

"This is what I get paid to do," he said lightly, not wanting her to realize that she'd touched on one of his weaknesses.

"Then do what you're getting paid for—running Pryce Enterprises. Let me handle the wedding details. You concentrate on finishing whatever you need to at the office."

"I want you to enjoy this wedding," he said, carefully. It was a character flaw of his that he hated to let go of any part of a project. And he knew he could make the wedding a fantasy dream come true for Roxy. It was that important to him. He knew her life had been hard and she'd worked hard for everything she had. He wanted to surprise her with a complete dream wedding. Although, to be honest, he had no idea what a woman dreamed of for her wedding.

"It's your celebration, too. I can take care of this. I want to do this for us."

"Thank you," he said.

"Silly man, we're in this together. This is what I was talking about. Compromise, remember? We're stronger when we both work together."

"I know you're right, but if you are struggling I can't promise not to step in and make things easier for you."

"That's one of the sweetest things anyone has ever said to me, Max."

"I'm glad." They hung up a few minutes later and he got out of the car at MacNeil's hotel with a lingering fear in his gut that he hadn't covered all the bases he needed to with Roxy.

Her wedding day was picture-perfect. Her dress was a lovely white creation that she never would have chosen if she wasn't marrying Max. It was slim-fitting and formal. The neckline plunged low between her breasts, but covered her entire back.

She'd looked at several lovely gowns that had low-cut backs but in the end she still wasn't ready to appear in public with too much skin showing. She was nervous about walking down the aisle and having her limp observed by everyone in attendance. Yet she hadn't found the words to tell Max.

She'd had barely three hours of sleep the night before and hadn't had a minute alone with him. Max's friends had thrown a party in their honor and she'd learned a lot about her soon-to-be husband. Especially that he was the solid one in his group, the man they came to when they needed anything.

It had amazed her, all the different things he was to so many different people. It was clear they all liked him, but just as clear that Max had carefully manipulated the relationships so that they all owed him a favor. He was never in anyone's debt.

She wanted to be his partner in that. She liked the man he was and realized that he had created his own family from his friends. His parents were more concerned with their own worlds than their son's. Roxy had been surprised, because as a child she'd always imagined that having two parents would fix all of her problems.

"Gosh, girl, you look good."

"Thanks, Tawny. Thanks for agreeing to be my maid of honor, too."

"It's my pleasure. I'm just glad to see you smiling again."

Roxy appreciated her friend's comments but they made the doubts plaguing her more real. Gave them more substance, because a part of her wondered if she was simply marrying Max because he'd helped her get past her scars.

But she knew she loved him. The depth of the emotions she held for him scared her sometimes. Last night she'd been unable to sleep, afraid if she closed her eyes she'd wake up and find that Max, and her relationship with him, was only a dream.

She swallowed hard as Tawny moved off to check her makeup one last time. As Roxy sank down on the padded chair in the dressing room, her hands were shaking.

Who would have thought a wedding would be so nerve-racking? She'd seen many pictures of brides and newly wedded couples at the hotel, and they'd seemed so blissful. But then from Roxy's point of view those brides had been living the charmed life she'd never had.

"You okay?" Tawny asked.

She thought about the fact that things in her life never stayed good for the long term. The bubble always burst and she was left standing on the outside looking in. And she really didn't want that to happen with Max. "Yes. No. I don't know. I've only known him a few weeks."

Tawny put her arm around Roxy, and she leaned on her friend, needing the support of someone who really knew what it was like to have come from nothing.

"I've never seen you like this with any other guy," Tawny said.

"Like what?" Roxy asked in a whisper, afraid to confess her own fears out loud.

"Like you're in love. Before, no man could compete with dancing in your life."

"Would I be in love with Max if I was still dancing?" Did Max love *her?* That was the biggest fear she had.

"I don't know, sweetie, but I really don't think that matters. You're not dancing anymore, and Max is your life."

"That totally scares me."

"It would me, too."

Someone knocked on the door.

"Come in."

Hayden walked in, dressed in his tailored tuxedo. He'd agreed to walk her down the aisle and Roxy was glad to see her friend. "Hi, Hay."

"Hey, Rox. You ready to do this thing?"

"Gosh, boss, did you woo your wife with romantic lines like that?" Tawny said.

"She likes it, says it's part of my charm."

"I think she might be prejudiced in your favor."

Hayden laughed and Roxy started to relax. She was getting married to Max.

"Thanks, Hay."

"For what, Rox?"

"Introducing me to him."

"No problem. A little of the good life is what you both needed."

"I don't know how Shelby lives with your ego."

"She has this way of deflating it," he said with a sardonic grin.

She checked her veil one last time, adjusting it before she took Hayden's arm. Tawny led the way out of the dressing room and they entered the chapel at the Chimera. She stumbled on her first step but Hayden just slowed his pace.

Glenda went up the aisle first, followed by Tawny, and Roxy kept her gaze trained on her friend's back until Hayden tightened his arm around hers and they started walking. She glanced up then. All the way to the front of the chapel. Past the rows of her friends and the rows of Max's family and friends.

There he was. Watching her with a look that was a combination of pride, lust and possessiveness. Her footsteps seemed a little lighter as she moved toward him. She knew that there was more to their relationship than sex and commonality. She saw a deep emotion in his eyes that he couldn't hide from her today.

Suddenly she was at his side and Hayden was placing her hand in Max's. His big hand was warm against hers and he brought her chilled fingers up to his chest, rubbing them against his shirt.

He leaned down to kiss her and whispered in her ear. "You take my breath away."

She didn't know how he knew the right thing to say. Or why it mattered that he had. She could only smile at him as the minister started the ceremony. She wasn't aware of the words she said or the other people who witnessed her vows. All she was focused on was Max and the way he watched her.

He put the wedding ring on her finger and leaned down while the minister was blessing his ring.

"Now, you're mine."

Once she slipped his ring on his finger, she said, "And you are mine."

"Forever," Max said.

Twelve

Max stepped out of the bathroom and found their suite empty. Candles still flickered on every surface in the room. Rose petals still littered the floor. The sheets on the bed were still rumpled from their love-making but his bride was gone.

All night he'd fought against the feeling that she wasn't really his. That the whirlwind romance he'd swept her up in wasn't overwhelming her. But there had been that almost panicked look in her eyes, and he'd sensed that she wasn't comfortable.

He cursed under his breath and grabbed his pants from the floor, pulling them on. He'd given Carl the night off, so his driver wasn't available.

That meant no one had been out front to see when or how she left.

He'd have to call Hayden and ask to see the security tapes. To track her down…oh, man, how the hell had he come to this? He was back in the exact same place he'd been when he was twenty-one. Chasing after a woman who didn't want to be caught.

He left the bedroom and walked into the living room. He was halfway across the room when he realized the balcony doors were open. He turned and saw the silhouette of Roxy. His racing heart slowed, and he moved toward her with a measured stride that should have calmed his temper.

But didn't. Why was she out here hiding from him? He stopped on the threshold. "I thought you'd left."

She had both hands braced on the wrought-iron railing. The lights of the strip were bright and color-ful, an illusory background behind this woman who'd become the center of his life in such a short time. And he felt his hold on her was no more secure than a "sure thing" hand at the poker tables.

She glanced over her shoulder at him, an aura of sadness wrapping around her that made him feel as though all of his carefully ordered plans were falling apart. Getting his ring on her finger had been his focus, but now he knew the other details were going to haunt him.

"Did that bother you?"

"No, it pissed me off."

"I didn't think you got pissed, Max."

"I do. I just don't show it."

"Like all of your emotions."

Please don't do this, he thought. Just once in his life he wanted his failings to be overlooked. Rationally he knew they couldn't be. That she was entitled to have everything she wanted.

"This isn't about emotion, Blondie. This is about trying to find my wife of less than—" he glanced down at his watch "—five hours."

She wrapped her arms around herself. "Why would my being out here bother you? We had a quickie courtship, why not a quickie wedding?"

"I thought I made it clear to you how I felt."

"No, you didn't. And lying in bed, I started thinking about how much I needed you—emotionally—and I realized that you didn't have that same need."

He needed to distract her. To find a way to make her realize what he felt without having to say it. Because even though Roxy would never understand or believe it, she was the stronger of the two of them. She allowed him to see her flaws and vulnerabilities.

"You don't need anyone. You're this great tower of strength and you take care of everyone around you. I'm sure you realize that."

"Yes, I do realize it."

"Why? Why do you do that?"

He didn't want to tell her, but maybe an explanation would be enough to appease her. To get her back into his arms. "I'm trying to make sure that they never leave."

"Who left you, Max? I never realized you were vulnerable until tonight."

"Uh…" He didn't want to tell her. Didn't want to share that intimately embarrassing part of his life. The impetuous young man he'd been was a faint memory. Max had buried that part of his soul a long time ago.

"I stood naked in front of you. You forced me to look in the mirror and see this scarred body of mine through your eyes. Tell me, Max. Tell me so I can believe that I didn't just buy into the Vegas illusion."

He took a deep breath and stepped out onto the shadowy balcony with her. He hoped that somehow in the dark the words would be easier to say.

"I was twenty-one when I thought I'd fallen in love. My parents of course said I was too young. My father wanted me to get established in Williams & Co., the family business. But I wanted…it's hard to remember what I wanted and why, but I definitely wanted Jessica."

"Did she want you?"

"She seemed to. We had a quick engagement, and then the night before our wedding she disappeared. I thought…she'd been kidnapped because of my family's money."

Roxy left the railing and came to sit down next to him on the other balcony chair. "Oh, Max. You must have been terrified for her safety."

"I was. We started searching for her and found her back at college in the apartment she shared with two of her friends. Her parents were angry, I was angry."

She tilted her head to the side, studying him and he was afraid that she might see all the way to the truth. He hadn't been angry. He'd been scared that Jessica had finally seen the same thing in him that his parents and everyone else in his life had. That thing that made them want to leave before he got too close.

"We talked, she gave me back my ring and I left. My dad sent me to Japan to oversee a new operation for Williams & Co."

"Is that when you started channeling all your energy into work?"

"I guess. I didn't do much work then. I partied every night and got myself into a dangerous situation. That's how I met Duke—he saved my ass."

She sat down on his lap, pulling him into her arms, so that his head rested against her breasts. "And since then you've found a way to make sure no one can leave you…everyone in your life owes you something."

"Not you," he said between clenched teeth, knowing the truth of his words and the very real fear in his heart.

"Especially me. I love you, Max. I haven't said

those words to anyone since my grandmother died. You gave me a home here," she took her hand and placed it over her heart. "Where I've been longing to find one."

"Thank you for loving me, Blondie."

"You don't thank me, Max. You tell me that you love me, too."

He stared down into her face. "I'll never leave you."

She pushed herself to her feet. "That's not enough, Max. I need to know how you feel."

"That's the one thing I can't give you."

She backed away from him. He knew he couldn't make her stay. She dressed and quietly left their honeymoon suite.

Max woke the next morning feeling more alone than he ever had before. He'd followed Roxy to her home outside the city limits and made sure she was safely inside before he came back.

Maybe he was just one of those guys who couldn't be married. But in his gut he knew that wasn't true. He wanted Roxy—he was just afraid to tell her how much.

Roxy took her time getting dressed and slowly drove back to the Chimera. She shouldn't have left last night without hashing everything out. Max was the one person she wanted to spend the rest of her life with. The only person who'd ever wanted her for herself, not because she was a good dancer but because of who she was inside.

She had to find a way to his emotions. Had to figure out the details he needed to feel secure enough to tell her how he felt.

She called Max and left him a voice mail asking him to meet her in the atrium café for breakfast. She drove to the hotel and went directly to the restaurant to wait for him.

The hostess told Roxy her table would be available in a few minutes. Roxy sat down on the bench to wait. Trying to gather her thoughts. She heard someone approach the table and glanced up expecting to see Hayden.

Instead, she was surprised to see Harron Mac-Neil standing there, a concerned look on his weathered face.

"Good morning, Harron. What can I do for you?"

He stood still, towering over her. Roxy pushed to her feet.

"Where is Williams?" he asked. He held a newspaper clutched in his hand and wouldn't look her in the eye.

"In his room. He'll be down in a few minutes," she said, hoping that was true. "Why don't you have a seat?"

He nodded stiffly. But instead of sitting he paced around her. She caught the hostess's eye. The woman gestured for them to join her and took them to a table at the back of the restaurant.

"Is Sheila okay?"

"What? Yes, she's fine. This is about our merger."

"What's the matter?"

"Nothing I want to discuss with you."

Roxy pulled back from Harron. She was surprised by the way he was behaving, had thought they'd become friends after sharing several meals together.

"Harron, whatever it is, maybe I can help you."

He pulled today's newspaper from his briefcase and tossed it on the table. The picture of herself stopped her.

The paper had been folded to the society pages and the headline would have been visible even half a room away. The Billionaire and the Showgirl.

She picked up the paper, reading quickly.

Billionaire Max Williams got lucky at more than the poker tables in Las Vegas, where rumor has it he walked away a big winner. He also found himself a bride—the former headliner at the Chimera's famed revue, *Chimère*.

"I don't care how much it costs. I'm going to stop the merger now," Harron said. "Our image isn't about gamblers and showgirls. Topless dancers turned trophy wives are not what my family has spent the last three generations building our reputation on."

She gasped out loud, realizing that she was going

to be responsible for Max losing this new piece of business. A piece he'd worked really hard to acquire.

"I'm sorry you had to hear that," Harron said, shaking his head.

"I'm sorry you *said* something like that. Obviously this paper was looking to stir up some trouble and you are playing right into their hands."

"Don't make this about anything other than what it is. You took your clothes off for a living. I thought you were a dancer."

Did he feel duped? Was that what this was about? "I am a dancer. I was the headliner in *Chimère*. I worked long hours to get to that point. As many hours as you and your father and grandfather worked to make the travel agency one of the top three in this part of the world. How does hard work not fit into your ethics?"

He said nothing to her, and she thought maybe she was getting through to him. She wanted Harron to understand that dancing, topless or not, was just as hard as running a business. Maybe even harder. The struggle, the competition was fierce.

"I started training to be a dancer when I was a little girl, Harron. My entire life was dedicated to dance until I was injured. There is nothing sleazy about what I did. Not in my mind. Not in the minds of the people who came to the shows I performed in.

"We've gotten to know each other over the last few

weeks and the man I've come to know isn't going to let the society pages dictate his business decisions.

"Pryce Enterprises is the kind of company you want to trust your business to, because Max cares about his workers. He remembers their birthdays and little things like what they like to eat at catered meals."

"That's about employee retention."

"It's about a lot more than that. Max actually cares for his workers and treats his employees the way he does his friends."

Max was ready to meet with Roxy and give her whatever she needed to stay with him. He exited his suite and got on the elevator, noticing he had missed a call from Duke. He dialed the callback number.

"It's about damned time." Duke greeted him. Max heard the sound of a computer keyboard in the background and knew that Duke was on his laptop.

"Skip to the good part. I left you in charge for less than twenty-four hours and already you're calling me."

"Actually, there's no good part to this. I wouldn't have called unless I thought you needed to handle this. Have you seen today's paper?"

"No. Why?"

"Because instead of running a bridal portrait of Roxy, they have her publicity photo from *Chimère*."

Max cursed succinctly under his breath. "Where is MacNeil?"

Max didn't have time to deal with this. Roxy was his first priority and he couldn't afford the time away from her. He was fighting for his life with her and he needed to make sure she understood how important she was to him. More important than Pryce Enterprises. Without her, nothing else mattered.

He almost dropped the phone as he realized he loved her. It wasn't supposed to happen like this.

"He wants to call off the merger regardless of what it costs him. He said, and I quote…topless dancers turned trophy wives aren't the image we want at MacNeil Travel."

Max couldn't believe Harron had had the gall to say something like that. Max was sick of this merger anyway. They'd wanted a nice profit-maker for their company and to expand into a line of business they hadn't dabbled in before but honestly, at this point, he didn't want to do business with MacNeil. "I can't deal with MacNeil this morning. I have another fire that needs to be put out."

"What fire? I haven't heard any rumblings from anyone. Is it that damned hockey team you bought?"

"No, Duke. This one's personal. I don't need your help with it."

"You always need my help."

"Not with my wife."

"Oh, you have a point there. What do you want me to do with MacNeil?"

"Let him back out of the deal. We'll do it the aggressive way. We're still going to acquire his assets."

"Are you sure about that? We have our reputation to think of, and we don't do hostile takeovers."

Max closed his eyes. He wanted MacNeil's heart for his angry words about Roxy. He didn't care that he'd built Pryce into the kind of company that everyone respected and admired. Right now he wanted revenge. He wanted to take MacNeil's company and break it into pieces while the man watched.

"You're right. I'll deal with MacNeil later. In the meantime make an offer to Trans/Time Travel. They are MacNeil's chief competition, right?"

"I'll pull together the numbers and information we have. But we don't have to move on the travel company acquisition until you're back from your honeymoon."

"Are you managing me, Merchon?" he asked, because though the two men were friends, Duke had never told him what to do in his personal life before.

"Yes, Williams, I am. Enjoy your new wife and forget about business for a while."

"I don't think I'm going to be able to do that until I take care of the newspaper people and MacNeil."

"Pryce Enterprises has already sent a letter and wedding photo from yesterday's event. I personally sent a letter expressing my outrage."

"You were outraged. I'm touched."

"Yeah, well, I don't have many friends, you know that. When they strike at you, they strike at me, too."

Max was a little humbled by Duke's words. "Thanks, man."

"I think I owed you."

"No you didn't. Touch base with MacNeil later, will you?"

"No problem," Duke said, before disconnecting the phone.

Max rubbed the back of his neck, hoping that MacNeil hadn't said anything to Roxy about the photo the paper had run. Harron and Sheila were staying in the Chimera for a few days gambling. She might not want to be reminded of a career she no longer had.

He entered the restaurant—and saw Roxy talking to Harron. Anger began a slow burn in his gut as he crossed to the corner table where they were sitting. Roxy had her back to him, but he could see that she was sincere in her words.

"Max actually cares for his workers and treats his employees the way he does his friends," Roxy said.

He was humbled to hear her defending him. She'd come to his rescue, even though he'd let her down. Taken what she had to offer but been unwilling to give her what she really needed in return. Not gifts or money or a new career, but love. Even though she'd walked out his door last night, here she was defending him.

The press had portrayed her in a bad light, but she wasn't slinking away from Harron in embarrassment or regret. She put her hands on the table and leaned forward.

"You should be happy to merge with Pryce Enterprises because Max is the kind of man who never rests on what he's accomplished. He's going to take your number-three travel company and make it number one. I know the fact that I was a Las Vegas showgirl doesn't sit well with you, Mr. MacNeil, but I'm willing to bet any profits you'd see from Pryce would go a long way to making you feel better."

"There won't be any profits from Pryce," Max said, crossing to Roxy and MacNeil.

"Now see here—"

"No, MacNeil, you see here. No one insults my wife."

"I didn't mean those insults. I've got a quick fuse and this morning I was surprised by what I read in the paper."

"So surprised that you had to track down my wife to confront me?"

"Yes. We spoke at length about the client base that MacNeil Travel draws from. We once lost ten percent of that base when Sheila's dance studio put on a show from Mikhail Baryshnikov's White Oak Dance Project. And that's a legitimate ballet. Can you imagine how this would affect business?"

"Maybe you don't want those people as your clients. Dance is an expression of emotion, Harron. I'm confident Sheila wasn't embarrassed by the ballet they did."

Harron flushed. "No, she wasn't. And she wasn't too happy with me this morning when I got angry over Roxy's picture."

"I'm not happy, either. Duke will be calling you this afternoon and we'll stop the merger."

Harron started to leave but Roxy stopped him with her hand on his arm. "Wait. I think you two can work something out. You've both worked so hard on this."

Max waited to see what Harron would say. Finally the older man nodded. "I'll talk to Duke this afternoon and we'll work the details out. You go enjoy your honeymoon."

Harron left the restaurant. Roxy faced Max, and he didn't know how to thank her for what she'd done. Nor how to tell her how much she meant to him. He wanted to make sure she realized that Pryce Enterprises wasn't the most important thing in his life anymore...she was.

Max pulled her into his arms as soon as she was close enough. "I'm sorry."

"For the picture? Don't worry about it."

"No. I'm sorry I was too stubborn to tell you how I feel."

"How do you feel?"

I love you. The words were in his head but he couldn't force them out. Not now, not here.

"Did seeing it make you regret not dancing? If you decide you want to dance again…I can open an office here."

"That's a sweet offer, but I think my headlining days are over."

"What about your days with me? Are they over?"

He wrapped his arm around her and led her from the restaurant to the private bench in the maze where he'd first proposed to her. "I was surprised when I heard you defending me."

"Why surprised?"

"I'm used to being the one who makes everything right."

"Well, you've got me now."

"Yes, I do," he said, holding her closer. He kissed her, but now there was something more than passion in his embrace. He should have known when she turned him down the first time he asked her to marry him and he'd decided he had to have her that there was something more than comfort in his mind. Something more than sex and things in common.

She put her hand on his jaw and looked into his eyes. "No matter what happens between us, Max, I'm not going to let anyone hurt you."

He squeezed her even tighter. "I love you, Roxy."

Max's words were like magic wrapping around Roxy and clearing out the hurt that had lingered after Harron's callous words. She relaxed against him and remembered how little she'd had to like about her life just a few weeks earlier before he'd swept into her life and changed it.

Finally, she felt like she found the home she'd never had here in his arms.

"They got one thing right in the article," Max said, picking it up and skimming it.

"What?"

"I did get lucky in Vegas."

"At the tables?" she asked, teasing him.

"When I met you."

* * * * *

Don't miss this upcoming emotional and thrilling story by Katherine Garbera!
The Once-a-Mistress Wife, *coming from Desire in October 2007.*

Available wherever Mills & Boon books are sold.

MILLS & BOON®

THE CONVENIENT MARRIAGE by Peggy Moreland

Abandoned by the man who got her pregnant, Adriana Rocci will soon bring a fatherless child into the world, but one man is determined that will not happen…

REUNION OF REVENGE by Kathie DeNosky

(Illegitimate Heirs)

Once run off this ranch, Nick Daniels is now a millionaire and owns it…along with Cheyenne Holbrook, the woman he nearly married thirteen years ago.

TOTALLY TEXAN by Mary Lynn Baxter

Grant Wilcox is used to getting what he wants and what he wants is Kelly Baker, the beautiful stranger passing through…

ONLY SKIN DEEP by Cathleen Galitz

Bookworm Lauren Hewett had transformed into a bombshell, and she suddenly had Travis Banks's *full* attention. But Lauren wasn't interested in an attraction that was only skin deep…

HOUSE OF MIDNIGHT FANTASIES by Kristi Gold

(Rich & Reclusive)

Reading your boss's mind can lead to trouble…*especially* when you're the one he's fantasising about!

A SINGLE DEMAND by Margaret Allison

Cassie Edwards had slept with her sworn enemy! And what made it worse was that it was the most incredible night of her life – and she wanted to do it again…

On sale from 16th March 2007

Available at WHSmith, Tesco, ASDA, and all good bookshops

www.millsandboon.co.uk

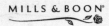

0307/23a

MILLS & BOON

SPECIAL EDITION™

MARRIED IN HASTE by Christine Rimmer

Bravo Family Ties

When it came to grand fiery passions, Angie Dellazola had been there, done that – and got burnt. Marrying steady boy-next-door Brett Bravo seemed like a better idea…until pent-up passions exploded between the unsuspecting newlyweds!

HER BEST-KEPT SECRET
by Brenda Harlen

Family Business

Journalist Jenny Anderson had a great job in Tokyo and a loving adoptive family, but she definitely had trust issues related to her birth. For Jenny, it was a big step to get close to Hanson Media lawyer Richard Warren. But would their fledgling affair run foul of his boss Helen Hanson's secret?

A TEXAS WEDDING VOW
by Cathy Gillen Thacker

The McCabes

When the bride skips town, maid of honour Laurel McCabe has to face the fury of the bridegroom, and finds herself promising to put things right. But never had she imagined that Cade Dunnigan would whisk her up the aisle instead!

Don't miss out!
On sale from 16th March 2007

Available at WHSmith, Tesco, ASDA, and all good bookshops

www.millsandboon.co.uk

MILLS & BOON®

0307/23b

SPECIAL EDITION™

WORTH FIGHTING FOR
by Judy Duarte

Single mother Caitlin Rogers knew exactly what her priority was – her little daughter, Emily. So when that relationship was threatened, Caitlin was lucky to be able to count on Brett Tanner, a man with scars in his past who made a family worth fighting for.

SECOND-TIME LUCKY
by Laurie Paige
Canyon Country

How ironic that family counsellor Caileen Peters was turning to her client Jefferson Aquilon, a foster father, for help with *her* daughter. But Caileen soon found something more in Jeff's arms.

THE PRODIGAL MD RETURNS
by Marie Ferrarella
The Alaskans

Things were really heating up, when Ben Kerrigan came back after leaving Heather Ryan Kendall at the altar seven years ago. Recently-widowed Heather and her six-year-old daughter had a surprise for the prodigal MD.

Don't miss out!
On sale from 16th March 2007

Available at WHSmith, Tesco, ASDA, and all good bookshops
www.millsandboon.co.uk

0307/14

MILLS & BOON®

Blaze™

ROOM SERVICE by Jill Shalvis

Do Not Disturb

TV producer Em Harris has to convince chef Jacob Hill to sign up to her new show. But when she sets foot in Hush, the sex-themed hotel where Jacob works, she develops an insatiable craving for the sinfully delicious chef…

WHY NOT TONIGHT? by Jacquie D'Alessandro

24 Hours: Blackout

When Adam Clayton fills in at his friend's photography studio, he never dreamed he'd be taking *boudoir* photos – of his old flame! Mallory is just recently single, but luckily for Adam, a blackout gives him a chance to make her forget anyone but him…

HER BODY OF WORK by Marie Donovan

Undercover agent Marco Flores had ended up working as a model. A nude model. He'd taken the job to protect his brother, but he soon discovered the perks. Like having his sculptress, sexy Rey Martinson, end up as uncovered as him…

BASIC TRAINING by Julie Miller

Marine captain Travis McCormick can't believe it when Tess Bartlett – his best friend and new physiotherapist – asks for basic training in sex. Tess has been working on her battle plan for years, and its time to put it to work. She'll heal him…if he makes her feel good!

On sale 6th April 2007

Available at WHSmith, Tesco, ASDA, and all good bookshops

www.millsandboon.co.uk

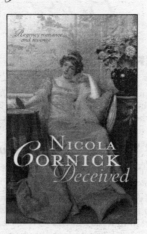

A tale of extraordinary love and passion from *New York Times* bestselling author DIANA PALMER

For anthropologist Phoebe Keller and FBI agent Jeremiah Cortez, the urgent stirrings of mutual attraction are cruelly interrupted when fate – and family loyalties – force them apart.

After three years of anguished separation, the dormant spark of their passion is rekindled when they are reunited by a mysterious phone call about a murder investigation and a robbery of priceless artefacts. But when Phoebe becomes the prime target of a desperate killer, Cortez must race against time to save the only woman he has ever loved.

Available 6th April 2007

FREE!

2 Books
and a surprise gift!

We would like to take this opportunity to thank you for reading this Mills & Boon® book by offering you the chance to take TWO more specially selected titles from the Desire™ series absolutely FREE! We're also making this offer to introduce you to the benefits of the Mills & Boon® Reader Service™—

- ★ **FREE home delivery**
- ★ **FREE gifts and competitions**
- ★ **FREE monthly Newsletter**
- ★ **Exclusive Reader Service offers**
- ★ **Books available before they're in the shops**

Accepting these FREE books and gift places you under no obligation to buy, you may cancel at any time, even after receiving your free shipment. Simply complete your details below and return the entire page to the address below. You don't even need a stamp!

YES! Please send me 2 free Desire books and a surprise gift. I understand that unless you hear from me, I will receive 3 superb new titles every month for just £4.99 each, postage and packing free. I am under no obligation to purchase any books and may cancel my subscription at any time. The free books and gift will be mine to keep in any case.

D7ZEF

Ms/Mrs/Miss/Mr ....Initials ....
BLOCK CAPITALS PLEASE

Surname ....

Address..

....

....Postcode ....

Send this whole page to:
UK: FREEPOST CN81, Croydon, CR9 3WZ